Joanna Johnson lives in a pretty Wiltshire village with her husband and as many books as she can sneak into the house. Being part of the Mills & Boon Historical family is a dream come true. She has always loved writing, starting at five years old with a series about a cat imaginatively named Cat, and she keeps a notebook in every handbag—just in case. In her spare time she likes finding new places to have a cream tea, stroking scruffy dogs and trying to remember where she left her glasses.

Also by Joanna Johnson

The Marriage Rescue
Scandalously Wed to the Captain
His Runaway Lady
A Mistletoe Vow to Lord Lovell
The Return of Her Long-Lost Husband

Discover more at millsandboon.co.uk.

THE OFFICER'S CONVENIENT PROPOSAL

Joanna Johnson

MILLS & BOON

First published in Great Britain 2022
by Mills & Boon, an imprint of HarperCollins*Publishers* Ltd,
1 London Bridge Street, London, SE1 9GF

www.harpercollins.co.uk

HarperCollins*Publishers*
1st Floor, Watermarque Building,
Ringsend Road, Dublin 4, Ireland

MIX
Paper from
responsible sources
FSC® C007454

For the usual suspects

Chapter One

Looking down at the two graves in front of her, one much newer than the other, Frances Nettleford tightened her jaw.

The summer sun beat down on her head with unrelenting strength, bathing Marchfield's churchyard in the same bright glare, but Frances barely felt the sticky heat beneath her gown. At least Uncle Robert was at peace now, even if his passing had left her completely alone in a world that didn't want her.

To see such a strong man growing weaker by the day until he could barely lift a spoon had been a torture she never wanted to endure again and she'd watched helplessly as the one person who loved her, and she loved in return, had been laid out in his shroud. There hadn't been many mourners for a bachelor who'd kept others at arm's length since the death of his sister twenty years before, and fewer still who felt much sympathy for the scandal-ridden niece he'd left behind.

Frances bent to place a bunch of the wildflowers she carried at the base of each headstone. It was some small comfort to see her hand was steady as she straightened the twine-wrapped stems, and she nodded to herself with more resolve than she felt.

Mama and Uncle would want me to be strong. He didn't raise me to turn away from a challenge—although I'm sure even he would think twice about running the farm entirely on his own.

A twinge of anxiety gnawed at her again but Frances braced herself against it. What good would worrying do? Barrow Farm was hers now and she had to step up, as she'd known she must one day ever since she'd been old enough to understand. As the owner of a prosperous farm she would be safe from ever needing a man to provide for her—and safe from the ruinous damage they could inflict on a woman if given half a chance.

Uncle Robert would have moved heaven and earth to spare his niece the fate that had befallen his barely eighteen-year-old sister. Frances knew it had haunted him until his very last hour, and her entire life had been shaped by his determination she would never fall into the same dangerous trap her hopelessly naïve mother had—the arms of an unworthy man.

'Best to bide by yourself, Frances, and rely on no one else.'

She could almost hear Uncle Robert's gruff voice now, repeating the same wisdom he had always imparted, and she closed her hazel eyes to better picture his weathered face.

'No one can hurt you if they can't reach you, nor break your trust if you never give it in the first place. Take heed of your mama's mistakes.'

The memory sent a fresh skewer through Frances's heart and she clenched her hands into tight fists. He'd been so insistent she learn that essential lesson—and just because he was no longer with her didn't mean she would forget it.

The townspeople might think her unfriendly for keeping her distance, but when had they ever shown a moment of kindness that might have softened her guarded heart? All Frances had known since childhood were harsh whispers and disapproving glances, alongside the pain of rejection when none of the other little girls were allowed to play with her, and she'd lost count of the times her uncle had dried her tears before she'd learned to thicken her skin.

Her mere existence was an affront to some and as she'd grown older—and prettier—more than one wife feared her mother's offence might repeat itself, as if Frances would have looked once, let alone twice, at any of their husbands. Trusting anyone was a risk, but to trust a *man* was out of the question entirely. They were fickle beasts, with their wandering hands and eyes that followed her slim figure across the market square, and Frances's face remained stony as she turned away from them all.

It was better to be lonely than to cast her lot with a man who would turn from her the moment she needed him most. If a lifetime of shame and scorn had taught her nothing else, at least she knew *that*, how cruel people could be, something she reminded herself of fiercely whenever her solitary existence grew hardest to bear. It was a hundred times worse now Robert had passed, leaving her without a friend in the world and no hope of ever finding one among Marchfield's narrow-minded inhabitants.

She sighed, a weary breath that came all the way up from her boots.

Confound them all. Every one of those men who couldn't keep their hands to themselves, and every one of those women who forbade their husbands from continuing their employment at the farm once my uncle was no longer there as chaperone.

The fact that she was clearly uninterested in any kind of entanglement apparently counted for nothing. Blessed—or cursed—with a face that was fair even when clouded with wariness, every young man she'd taken on since Robert's death had overstepped the line and been dismissed at once, their caressing fingers and lingering stares sending shivers of revulsion beneath Frances's skin.

Her mother's mistake in being seduced by a married man had put paid to her hopes of employing any of the local labourers who might have been useful. No wife trusted her with their husband, too frightened the inheritance of a scarlet woman might run in her veins. Suspicion bred more suspicion, and neither Frances nor the residents of Marchfield were much inclined to think well of the other…leaving her no choice but to carry on alone or admit defeat.

Which was *not* an option.

With one last long look down at the neat graves, Frances squared her shoulders. Grief still sat inside her like a stone, barely two months on from the funeral only a handful of people had attended, but she had to keep going. Her spine was iron now, tempered over the years by her uncle's insistence on her learning the very independence that would keep her safe and see her through the dark days ahead, with nobody left to hold out a helping hand or tell her they were proud.

Tears gathered behind her eyes as another

fleeting picture of that familiar face flashed before her, but she blinked them away at once, only one managing to trace a burning path down her cheek before she blotted it with a rough hand. She couldn't waste time on crying, not while there was so much for her to do, and with a final tender glance at the stones that bore her mother's and uncle's names Frances turned for where her horse was tethered to the churchyard's fence.

With ease born from years of practice she swung herself up onto Apollo's broad back, settling into the worn old saddle that had belonged to her long-dead grandfather. She always rode astride. It was far more practical than side-saddle, and besides…

I'm already the town scandal. As people will talk whatever I do, I might as well please myself.

Frances shook the reins. 'Come on, boy. Let's go home.'

Barrow Farm stood barely half a mile outside the pretty town of Marchfield, nestled within the serene beauty of the Cotswolds countryside. Most of the families living nearby had been there for generations, few desiring to move away from a place considered as close to paradise on earth as it was possible to get—with one notable exception. Frances's father had fled as soon as her mother's condition became known, packing up his wife and *legitimate* children in the middle of the night and leaving Marina Nettleford to face the town's contempt alone. Rose Cottage had been empty ever since, despite the passing of twenty years, a constant reminder to Frances—as if she needed it—of her disgraceful origins each time she went by the peeling front gate.

Her mind ventured there of its own accord as Apollo trotted towards the street on which the cottage stood, some disloyal part of her always hungry for the answers her uncle would never give.

Was it within those four walls Mama made the error that would cost both her life and good name? Did my father care even the smallest fraction what would happen once nature took its course, laying the taint of bastardy on me I can never wash clean?

Frances gritted her teeth as the same old questions muttered to her, their voices snide and sly. There were enough unfriendly whispers in the town already without her own mind joining in and she pushed them aside, feeling her spirits sink lower as she noticed two older women coming towards her on the opposite side of the street.

Oh, no. Not them. Just when I thought this day couldn't get any worse...

She groaned inwardly as two sets of eyes snapped in her direction, bright and cold as a crow's. Miss Fletcher and her widowed sister

Mrs Campbell delighted in all things not of their concern, scandal and intrigue the only reasons they eased their rheumatic bones out of bed each morning. The sisters lived for malicious half-truths and spreading news—suitably embellished, naturally—and as they bore down upon her Frances raised her guard.

They would never speak to her usually, much preferring to talk *about* her instead, as they had all her life…which must mean they had something to tell so interesting it outweighed their normal scorn, and that could never be good.

'Good morning, Miss Nettleford.'

Even their voices set Frances's teeth on edge, but she kept her face expressionless as she offered a cool nod from high up on Apollo's back. 'Good morning, Miss Fletcher. Mrs Campbell.'

She *felt* their hungry gazes rake over her, taking in every detail and searching out ways she might be lacking.

'I don't suppose you will have heard…?'

'Of course she won't have. We only just saw it ourselves!'

With enormous effort Frances managed to stop herself from rolling her eyes. Doubtless she was supposed to ask *what* she hadn't heard, but she refused to play along. She had too much to do and too little time in which to do it, and refused to waste even a moment on such an unpleasant pair.

'I'm happy to confirm I've no idea what you're referring to. Please excuse me.'

With another coldly polite nod she urged Apollo onwards, a flicker of satisfaction stirring at their visible annoyance. She might even have thought herself victorious if a cloyingly sweet voice hadn't called at her back, the words bringing her up short once again.

'Have you no interest that new tenants have taken your papa's house?'

Frances turned in the saddle. Miss Fletcher and Mrs Campbell watched triumphantly and for a split-second Frances feared the sudden flare of surprise in her stomach had shown in her face.

Somebody has taken Rose Cottage? It isn't empty any more, at long last?

Sensing their prey was caught off-balance, Miss Fletcher pounced. 'We saw them only moments ago, a retired lieutenant and his sister, a Mrs Millard, along with two children. I don't know what he can be thinking, moving into a house in such poor repair... It was always kept so nice when your papa lived there and now it's almost a ruin. The rent must be cheap indeed!'

Mrs Campbell eyed Frances closely, as if looking for a reaction to her sister's spite, and Frances swallowed hard. It was nothing to her if a hundred such families moved into that accursed cottage…and yet some part of her couldn't help but wonder…

She cleared her throat. 'How interesting.' Her voice was carefully flat and she had to clamp down on a humourless smile at the sour purse of Mrs Campbell's lips. 'Thank you for bringing that to my attention. I'm sure you can be relied upon to inform everyone else.'

She turned around, about to tap Apollo into a trot when she hesitated, considered for a moment, and looked back.

'One thing, Miss Fletcher. That man was not my *papa*. He may have been the one who imposed upon my mother, but it was my uncle who fed me, clothed me, raised me to be the woman I am today. If I ever had a papa…' She broke off for a second, determined the emotion threatening to rise within her wouldn't break through. The sisters didn't deserve to know anything of her private pain, her grief nothing to them but more grist to their mill. 'If I ever had a papa it was him and no one else.'

Malicious muttering echoed at Frances's back but this time she didn't look behind. Perhaps goading the two most vicious tongues in Marchfield hadn't been her best idea, but what else could she have done? They'd wanted a reaction and although she'd refused to let them see it Frances couldn't help the unease winding through her as she and Apollo approached the very house about which the whole town would soon be talking.

She saw immediately why the change in occupancy had caught the sisters' all-seeing eyes. The cottage was enveloped in a hive of activity. A horse and cart stood at the leaning fence, stacked with furniture two men were busily unloading, while another hefted chairs and tables up to the open front door. Every window was flung wide and faded curtains fluttered in the warm breeze, the whinnies of the horse and grunts of the men floating likewise through the air. A little girl waded through uncut grass on one side of the cracked path, weeds reaching almost to her shoulder, but she scurried inside at Apollo's approach, disappearing into the shadowy interior that both intrigued and revolted Frances in equal measure.

Pulling to a halt, she watched for a moment in silence, taking in the scene as the sun shone down to burn the back of her neck.

Why would a lieutenant take such a tumbledown house for his family?

Frances allowed her eyes to travel from the thatched roof—in dire need of repair—to the dirty whitewashed walls, a combination of reluctant curiosity and distaste rising within her. It was the longest she'd ever let herself gaze upon the place where her father had lived, although in that moment it was the present that occupied her thoughts more than the past.

I'd have thought an officer could afford something far better than this pitiful cottage. Of all places, why bring his family here?

Marchfield was so pretty it was small wonder someone might choose to move there, but there was no shortage of superior housing the higher ranks could take, houses with gleaming bay windows and pristine fronts, surely well within reach of a man of such generous means. For him to opt instead for an unkempt cottage made no sense at all.

Enough of that.

Mildly irritated with her momentary lapse, Frances frowned. It was none of her business what this person did and that was the end of it. She had more than enough on her own plate without thinking of anyone else, *especially* a strange man, and she shook her head.

Concerning myself with other people's affairs? Perhaps I'm more like Miss Fletcher than I thought.

That was enough to send a shudder through her and she flicked the reins at once, quickly, as if trying to outrun the thought…which was also unfortunately so quick she didn't notice the man walking in front of her until it was too late.

'Steady there!'

Startled by the unexpected obstacle, Apollo lurched to the side, easily spooked as always and the whites of his eyes showing all around. With instinctive speed, Frances grabbed onto the pommel, only *just* stopping herself from flying backwards and instead sliding from the saddle to land clumsily—but far less painfully—on the ground.

A hand shot out immediately to steady her, wrapping around her wrist, and Frances found herself staring up into a pair of brown eyes.

'Are you hurt?'

The voice was deep, with a hint of the north, and for the briefest of moments Frances felt her heart stop. It was a pleasant accent and sat well with those eyes—the colour of strong, sweet cocoa, she noticed vaguely, flecked with chips of gold—but then she snapped back to attention, caution flooding in at once, and she flicked the man's hand away as if it had burned her.

'What were you thinking, walking across my horse? He could have thrown me!'

Frances reached for Apollo's trailing reins, horribly aware blood had rushed to her face as she calmed him with a gentle hand. The stranger watched evenly, evidently not in the least bit cowed by her scowl, and she couldn't help but notice he'd have nothing to fear even if she'd been in a fury. His shoulders were broad and strong-looking beneath an expensive coat, shoulders not *quite* brushed by a thick mane of curling chestnut hair, and the face that sat below the brim of his hat…

Frances stiffened with instant distrust, her cheeks burning hotter. It was a handsome face, if serious and unsmiling, something she'd never thought she'd be vulnerable to noticing, and yet she could hardly deny the evidence of her own eyes. With straight dark brows and a chiselled jaw, he was far more comely than any other man in Marchfield, or indeed any Frances had ever seen before—and that was warning enough to hurry away from him as soon as she could, all Uncle Robert's warnings of the dangers posed by good-looking young men ringing in her ears.

But she didn't move quite fast enough, her attempt to swing back into the saddle cut off by an unexpected question.

'Would you be Miss Nettleford?'

The man's sober expression didn't change, although Frances knew her own must have shown surprise—and then rapid suspicion.

How does he know that?

As if reading her mind, he gestured to Rose Cottage, extending a large hand she saw was scattered with old scars. 'I'm taking this house.

First the landlord and then two of my new neighbours told me the history of it and happened to mention you. I'm not a mystic—they gave me a description.'

Frances's stomach executed an unpleasant flip. So that was it. Mrs Campbell and Miss Fletcher had sunk their claws into the newcomer already, never missing an opportunity to spread their poison. It was fortunate she cared not one iota for what this stranger thought of her, she reassured herself. There was no way he could be in any doubt as to her standing once the town harpies had poured their poison into his ear. But the only thing more vehement than their contempt for her was Frances's own resolve to keep this mysterious newcomer safely at a distance.

'I'm sure they did.'

'Nothing untoward, I assure you.'

Frances's stomach clenched.

A barefaced lie if ever I heard one.

'I don't believe that for a moment,' she replied coolly, hearing the frost in her tone and pleased with it. 'Especially if they told you the nature of my connection to your new home, which I can't imagine they didn't.'

The man shrugged negligently, the movement of his damnably impressive shoulders making Frances swiftly look away as another uncomfortable pinch of *something* worried at her insides.

'Gossip doesn't interest me. I prefer to make my own judgements. All I can say at present is the physical description was accurate.'

Her face must have expressed what she thought of that sentiment, as one stern eyebrow flickered upwards, having a corresponding—and deeply unwanted—effect on Frances's pulse.

'A dark-haired young woman dressed in mourning clothes, most likely with mud on her skirts. That was what they said.'

It was Frances's turn to shrug as she glanced down at her hem, still tightly clutching Apollo's reins as if ready to run at any moment. 'I'll admit that much to be true, at least.'

The man inclined his head and then Frances watched as he made a curious movement of his lips, a stiff stretch that seemed to cause him great discomfort. For a second she simply stared with bemusement, wondering if he was quite well—before realising it was supposed to be a smile, and the hairs instinctively stood up on the nape of her neck.

'Uncommonly pretty too, I was told,' the stranger continued, although so woodenly he might have been a marionette. 'Something *I* see to be true, if you'll allow me to say so.'

Frances took an immediate step back, drawing closer to the comforting presence of her horse.

And there it is. There's the hollow flattery Uncle Robert always warned me about.

Her palms prickled with sudden sweat that had nothing to do with the summer heat. Just like the young men that came to work for her at Barrow Farm who thought they could win her with empty compliments, like the old married ones who tipped her a wink when their wives' backs were turned. Another man looking for a way beneath her armour, her face and the lies told about her mother's easy virtue a siren call for those wanting the same old thing. Probably Mrs Campbell's venom had put the idea into his head already. Abruptly, Frances turned her back on that handsome, waiting face.

Yet another man to avoid. As if there weren't enough already.

'No. I will not.'

In Marchfield less than a day and already added to her list, another to treat with caution and swerve whenever he crossed her path? It was exhausting having to be on her guard all the time, but what else could she do when dangerous men circled like wolves around a lamb? Usually she brushed them off at once…but the strange squeezing of her chest at the first sight of the newcomer's admittedly appealing eyes lingered uncomfortably, something unexplained and unwelcome that made Frances's scowl increase as, without another word, she climbed up onto Apollo's back and turned him about, the man having to step aside quickly to avoid the horse's powerful back end.

Heart racing with aggravation, she tapped Apollo into a trot, leaving the stranger to watch her go. She was almost at the corner when she heard him call after her, the second person to do so that morning and no more welcome than the first.

'Goodbye, Miss Nettleford. And, should it interest you, my name is Lieutenant Jonah Grant.'

Not slowing for so much as a moment, Frances called over one shoulder as coldly as if she were carved from ice. Her pulse still leapt and her cheeks still burned, although whether with temper or something else entirely she couldn't quite tell.

'Let me assure you, it doesn't in the least.'

Jonah watched Frances ride away, making sure she was safely round the corner before allowing the last remnants of the painfully artificial smile to slide from his lips. It had taken every ounce of concentration to appear more agreeable than his usual grave self and an unpleasant taste lingered on his tongue to find he'd apparently misjudged the situation entirely.

Uncommonly pretty? Was that the best you could do?

Jonah grimaced, still standing where Frances had so decisively left him. He'd never spouted such nonsense to a woman in his life and irritation washed over him to think he'd reached thirty years of age without finding it necessary… until now.

Securing Frances Nettleford's good opinion was vital and he had to find a way to win it, whether he wanted to or not.

And he really, truly *did not.*

He pressed his forehead, skin hot beneath the sun as he recalled what his new landlord had told him weeks ago on his first enquiry about the cottage, that one throwaway comment setting gears turning in Jonah's mind. Those two busybodies who'd waylaid him that morning had only confirmed what he'd already been told about the notorious young woman in possession of a valuable farm, trying to run it all by herself and clearly struggling more by the day. The illegitimate daughter of the cottage's former tenant, with a reputation that would make any respectable gentleman shy away from offering marriage…and quite alone in the world, her uncle buried these past two months and her scandalous mother dead after a labour no woman could possibly survive.

If that were the extent of the hurdles in front

of him Jonah was confident he could have overcome them. With his rugged good looks and military bearing, female attention had always come
easily, despite his doing nothing to encourage it,
and Frances was surely as susceptible to a handsome face as any other woman. It was her per-
sonality that it seemed would present the biggest
obstacle to his tentative plans—and what made
Jonah grunt to himself as he retreated into the
welcome shade of the cottage.

*I was led to believe all women liked flattery.
Evidently the other half of the description I received was true after all, sullen and spiky, and
caring for nobody in this entire town. In truth,
she sounds a lot like me.*

'Who was that lady, Uncle Jonah?'

His niece materialised at his elbow, gazing up
at him with the clear blue eyes that marked her
so plainly as his sister's child. Margaret often
reminded him of Jane as she'd been when they
were young, although Margaret would never
know the pain of an empty belly or nurse a
bruise bestowed by a drunken hand—he would
make damn certain of it. He would do whatever
he needed to do to make sure his twin niece and
nephew never experienced the grinding poverty
and neglect he and Jane had endured, and as
he laid an uncharacteristically gentle hand on

Margaret's head he felt his chest tighten at the thought of what lay before him.

'Miss Nettleford. One of our new neighbours, Meg.'

Margaret traced the tip of one boot across the hall's dusty tiles. 'She was very pretty.'

'Was she? I can't say I noticed.'

Jonah's chest tightened further, although this time for a very different reason. He didn't like lying at the best of times, especially not to his niece's face, but the truth was somehow worse.

It was uncomfortable to admit that, despite her terse 'welcome', his first impression of Miss Nettleford was…intriguing. He'd been told she was fair, but that seemed a poor description of the striking planes of her face, cheekbones sitting high and proud above full lips and hazel eyes flashing with unconcealed distrust, and something inside him twisted to recall the heat of her skin as he'd wrapped his fingers around her wrist. She'd knocked his hand away as easily as breathing, clearly possessing wiry strength beneath the deceptively slender lines of her figure, and he couldn't deny the smallest flicker of respect had flared into life at the steely coldness of her gaze…

With the frown that had near permanent residence on his face, Jonah shook his head.

It didn't matter if she was comely. Nothing

could be less important than what this Frances looked like, the idea he'd settled on at first hearing of her remaining the same whether she'd turned out to be milk-faced or beautiful. He still intended to seek her hand, offering himself up as a sacrifice for a far greater cause than his own inclinations, and he had to do it as quickly as he could. The survival of his family depended on it and nothing so trivial as what she looked like—or the small detail that he had never wanted a wife—would make the slightest difference.

Sentiment had never been his strong point, after all.

Trying to ignore his building unease, Jonah smoothed Margaret's untidy hair. 'Where's your mother? And your brother, for that matter.'

At the answering point towards the cottage's open back door, Jonah made his way down the hall, tiny motes of dust dancing in the sunlight streaming through the windows. With a bit of work the house might begin to feel less like a hovel, although as he emerged outside he found himself hoping they wouldn't be there long enough to find out.

'Jane. Should you be doing that in this heat?'

His sister turned around at the sound of his voice, pausing in the act of knocking dirt from a worn rug. Her face was pale as always but two bright spots glowed on her cheeks and, stepping forward, Jonah took the carpet beater from her hand.

'Sit down. You'll wear yourself out, and it's only the first day.'

She tried to grab it back, although the movement was so half-hearted he could tell his warning had come too late. Jane swayed slightly and Jonah's worry increased as he noted the tremor in her fingers, a sure sign she had exerted herself too much.

'It has to be done. If I don't do it, who will?' Her eyes slid away from his, settling on her six-year-old son, Matthew, diligently pulling up weeds from along the fence. 'It's not as though we can afford help…something I know is my fault entirely.'

Jonah felt a muscle harden in his jaw. 'Not true. We have your husband to thank for this.'

'And me to thank for bringing him into our lives in the first place.'

Jane's lips twisted in a grim half smile and Jonah knew he had no retort. What she said was true, after all, even if he wished he could take away the heavy burden of shame and regret that weighed on his sister for her part in their ruin.

'Perhaps you brought him in, but it was me that trusted him with every penny I had,' he muttered, careful not to let his nephew hear but unable to keep the bitterness from his voice. 'I thought myself so clever, leaving my affairs in his keeping in case I didn't return from Waterloo, and see where my conceit left us.'

His moment of failure never grew weary of taunting him, and it came again now to jeer at his regrets.

Ever since childhood he'd known Jane was his responsibility to protect and just because decades had passed didn't mean that had changed. Their drunken, violent parents had barely been able to care for themselves, let alone two children with nobody to turn to but each other, and perhaps it was inevitable that such a brutal existence had slowly turned Jonah to stone. Left filthy and neglected, he'd had no choice but to grow up far too fast, suffering wearing away whatever softness he might once have possessed until he'd realised such feelings were an indulgence he couldn't afford.

Our dear papa never left me in any doubt about that. Jane was always my one weak point—and didn't he know it.

Their father's temper had grown worse with every bottle and Jonah could still remember the look in those bloodshot eyes whenever they fell on the ragged little girl sitting silently in a corner, desperately trying not to be seen. Jane had never put a foot out of line but somehow her meekness seemed to enrage him nonetheless, her defencelessness calling to the bully inside their father that enjoyed hurting those weaker than himself. Almost every day it was the same and without exception Jonah would throw himself in front of Jane to take the beating himself, each lash hammering home the lesson he'd been taught through misery and pain. *He* had to be strong because she couldn't, but his love had painted a target on his back their father never hesitated to exploit.

Allowing somebody into his heart made him vulnerable, prising a gap in his defences through which someone might slide a knife, and at only seven years old Jonah had determined he would never let anybody but his sister expose him to that risk. Life was too harsh to allow any weakness and the fewer people he cared for, the fewer he'd have to defend against a world that was cold and hard and dark, just waiting for a chance to beat him as soundly and undeservedly as his father had with that cracked leather belt. In loving his sister he had tied his fate to hers and now he was bound by it, obliged to stand between her and hurt as best he could, just as he had ever since the day she was born.

She would have died if he hadn't taken care of her, so ill and frail he'd often feared she might die in the early years, and the very first moment he could he had taken her away from the dirt and depravity that had so hardened his heart. Progressing through the ranks from private to lieutenant, he had finally been able to keep her in comfort, life at last growing easier after years of struggle—until she had met that wretch Thomas Millard, and everything Jonah had striven for had been torn from his grasp.

'You weren't to know he would run.' Jane spoke softly, eyes never leaving her son although the pain in them was agonisingly clear. 'Even as his wife, sharing his bed and bearing his children, I had no idea he would betray us all. To leave us with nothing, not even provision for the twins…'

Jonah's throat contracted at the grief in his sister's voice. It was a conversation they'd had many times since Thomas had stolen every scrap of Jonah's savings, taking advantage of his absence fighting overseas to sell every holding and stock and then flee with the profits, although the rage Jonah felt each time they spoke of it never diminished.

'We might take some comfort in imagining his ship sank on the way to the Americas. I know the thought brings a smile to my face when nothing else will.'

Jane tried to smile but managed little more

than a grimace. 'I'm in earnest. How are we going to manage? We were only able to get this cottage because it was so cheap, and apparently there's no question of you joining the regiment, no matter how much I beg.'

She spread her hands in exhausted defeat and Jonah looked away, wishing he was better at offering comfort—and that their situation wasn't every bit as bleak as she said.

How could he go back to the Army when Jane was alone, trying to raise two children when some days it was a struggle for her to even get out of bed? He couldn't abandon her for months on end while he was away fighting and yet they desperately needed money, leaving him only the one stark choice he'd decided on in their landlord's gaudy parlour.

I have to find a way to win over Miss Nettleford. She needs help and I need the income her neighbours seem to envy. Perhaps it isn't the most romantic basis for a proposal but, from what I've heard, she isn't the romantic type—which suits me exactly.

While his fellow officers had talked of the beauties they had waiting for them at home Jonah had barely listened. Pretty women had always flocked to him, his handsome outer shell hiding the decided indifference within. On a handful of occasions he had scratched the physical itch most men felt from time to time—but that was as far as it went. None of them even came close to touching his heart, sealed away behind that impenetrable wall built upon his childhood scars, and that was the way he wanted it. He already had one burden to carry, only enough shreds of compassion left for his sister and the children he had grown to love as an extension of her, and he had no desire for anybody else to attach themselves to him. Another woman would only be another weak point for him to guard, an additional Achilles' heel, and he'd always thought a man must be mad to voluntarily lay himself bare to all the hurt it could bring for what seemed to him so little return.

Jonah glanced at Jane, taking in the new lines worry had etched on her thin face. Her husband's deceit had aged her, unhappiness stealing the lightness from her step and the songs she used to sing without realising. Thomas Millard's dishonesty was a poison that ate away at her more and more each day and, not for the first time, Jonah swore he would never follow his brother-in-law's example of how a man should treat his wife.

I won't pretend to love Miss Nettleford and I've no interest in making her love me. All I can offer is honesty and myself, my hands and willingness to help shoulder the work, something far more valuable than any meagre emotion. If she's as hard-headed as I've been told she might just be willing to accept such an arrangement, given how she's been struggling alone. Or so I hope.

The image of Frances's tight face as she'd pulled away from him surfaced again but he pushed it aside, along with the unexpected gleam of interest at the determination in her eyes that had flared unbidden, confusing and unwanted yet there all the same. Despite the laughable impossibility of her stirring his jaded soul, he couldn't help but admit something about her was intriguing, even if only her singular sharpness and refusal to allow him the slightest liberty…

It was a good thing he never shied away from a challenge. By the look of it, persuading Frances Nettleford to consider him might be the biggest one he'd faced so far.

Chapter Two

Crouching in the gloomy pigsty among blood-stained straw, Frances wished she could take a moment to stretch her aching back. She hadn't stopped all morning and the afternoon would be no different, the prospect of another ten hours' work before she could fall into bed one that made her want to sigh.

'That's it. You're doing well.'

She ran a practised hand over the flank of the pig lying beside her. Seven wriggling new arrivals were already contentedly suckling and Frances checked for another, so familiar with the process of farrowing she could have managed it in her sleep.

Lambing will be difficult alone, though. That was a big enough job when Uncle Robert was here and we had people to help us... I've no idea how I'm to get by with nobody at all.

She watched the piglets' greedy jostling, their

squeaks loud but Frances hardly hearing them. The worry and grief that sat like a constant fist in her chest rose again, anxiety for the future of both herself and the farm gnawing at her insides. What was she going to do? Try as she might, each day felt harder than the last, her body crying out for rest and the sleep she managed to snatch fitful and bringing no solace. Her arms might be stronger now from heavy lifting and never-ending work, but that didn't conjure up more hours in the day…nor did it bring any peace of mind, already disturbed enough by too many concerns and now—as if to add insult to injury—joined by unwelcome recollections of that aggravating Lieutenant Grant.

Frances's lips thinned as she sat back on her heels, irritated by the treacherous direction of her thoughts. They'd darted back to that insufferable man far more regularly than she liked since their meeting three days before, something in those accursed brown eyes lingering to tempt her, and it seemed even the other far more important things she had to occupy her couldn't completely wipe him from her mind.

'Ridiculous.' Leaning against the wall for a moment, Frances addressed the sow, its quiet presence inviting confidence. 'Why on earth would I waste time thinking of a person I met for all of five minutes—who in even that short time managed to make himself as disagreeable as every other man in Marchfield, perhaps even the world?'

It made no sense at all. In only a few moments he had proven himself to be everything she despised—handsome, confident in the strength of his charms and a mutterer of the same sweet, false words a man with bad intentions always spouted. Jonah Grant was precisely the type she'd been schooled to avoid and she clung to that wisdom as one might a life raft, trusting in it to keep her head above water when those around her sought to pull her down.

So why then did the memory of Jonah's deep voice keep echoing—and why had the skin of her wrist burned as she'd ridden away from him, the feel of his fingers against her bare flesh haunting her all the way home?

With a grunt Frances pushed herself away from the wall, the bricks warming from the sun outside. The nape of her neck was damp and she gathered her trailing hair in one fist, twisting it up to allow the air to soothe both temper and temperature alike.

'I was surprised by the sudden manner of his introduction, that's all, and the fact he had taken my father's house. Anybody who'd been almost knocked off their horse by a complete stranger would surely remember the person afterwards and there's nothing more to it than that.'

The sow had more pressing concerns, however. With a ripple of the big pink body another piglet slid out onto the straw and Frances leaned over to pick it up, deftly wiping away the worst of the mess and placing it down beside its mother. The pace of delivery had slowed and from experience Frances guessed that was the final arrival, relief washing over her as she wiped her bloodied hands on her apron.

'Well done. Eight little ones!'

The pig certainly seemed pleased with herself. She snuffled gently at her heap of squirming babies and Frances felt she ought to leave them to get acquainted, something in the sight of a new family always touching her heart. She'd return later to clean out the dirty bedding and check the piglets but for now she crept away, shuffling backwards on her hands and knees until she emerged into the sun.

Out in the yard and finally able to stand upright, she groaned aloud with the bliss of straightening her spine. The sun was achingly bright and she closed her eyes against it, enjoying the warmth on their lids as she turned her face up towards the sky. For the briefest of moments she felt better, the innocent new lives in the pigsty buoying her up if only for a second and she tried to hold onto that feeling, concentrating hard as if she could block out everything else.

'Good morning, Miss Nettleford.'

Frances jumped like a startled rabbit, eyes flying open immediately. The unexpected voice at her back was deep...and pleasing...and could belong to only one man.

The very one she would have given anything not to see.

Slowly, wishing she had the power to make herself invisible, Frances turned around.

'Lieutenant Grant?'

Jonah stood a few paces away, chestnut hair shining in the same sunlight that illuminated those distinctive eyes, and Frances felt herself tense at the realisation they were every bit as fine as she remembered. The question of why he should be standing in her farmyard—*as if he has any right to be here!*—came at once, alongside an unpleasant awareness of the sorry state of her hair and dress, something that wouldn't usually cross her mind for an instant.

There was no trace of the awkward smile he'd worn at their first meeting. Instead Frances reluctantly noted the straight line of his well-shaped lips, his stern natural expression far more appealing than that forced upward curve, although she slammed shut the door on that train of thought as soon as it dared raise its head.

All that should do is put me even further on my guard. If he can fake a smile, what other falsehoods lurk within?

'I don't recall inviting you here.'

Jonah didn't flinch from her rudeness, his unsettlingly attractive voice unaffected by the chill in hers. 'You didn't. I took it upon myself to call regardless.'

Frances's brow furrowed in a hostile frown. Why was he coming to see her? The tiniest flicker of something she couldn't quite name stirred inside her but she poured cold water over it at once at the conceit he imagined himself *welcome* at Barrow Farm. Probably he intended to continue his advances from three days before with another attempt at worthless compliments, and she lifted her chin defensively.

'Coming to call on me? I can't imagine why, when I have neither the time nor inclination to indulge in idle chatter.'

She saw the slight rise of a dark eyebrow, no doubt in reaction to her tone, but his reply wasn't the one she'd expected.

'Eggs.'

'I beg your pardon?'

'One of our new neighbours told my sister your hens laid the best eggs for miles around.

I was duly dispatched to buy some. She'll take half a dozen if you have them.'

Some of the wind left Frances's sails as she squinted up at his expressionless face. *Not* there to pursue her, after all? She felt a glimmer of relief—although she would not be dropping her guard. He might be hoping to lure her into a sense of false security, and warily she threw him a short nod.

'I may have some spare. I'd need to check what I have left in the kitchen.'

'Thank you. I'm sure my sister would be much obliged.'

He stood only a few paces away and Frances couldn't help but catch the pleasing, subtle scent of shaving soap that drifted from him, a clean smell she found she liked. The men hereabouts usually left behind the less delightful combination of horses and sweat on the rare occasion they got close enough for her to notice and she drew back at once, realising Jonah was so near she could have touched his smart red coat.

Her own appearance was far less impressive, she realised with another twinge of that uncharacteristic awareness she was rapidly growing to dislike. With dried blood streaking both her apron and her hands she looked more like a butcher than a farmer, although the straw in her hair would ensure there was no confusion and her hem bore all the signs of traversing muddy fields. She must have seemed like a scarecrow beside Jonah's military neatness and a hot pulse of discomfort made her frown even harder, wondering why on earth she seemed to care what he thought.

'Come then if you must. I don't have all day.'

She strode past him towards the farmhouse, the white walls gleaming bright beneath a slate roof and summer roses climbing round the front door. It was the loveliest house in the whole of Gloucestershire in Frances's opinion, although she couldn't fully appreciate its charms while Jonah followed close behind, apparently taking his lead from her determined silence but his presence at her elbow so deafening he might as well have been shouting in her ear. He cast a shadow over her, standing between her and the sun, and she had the uneasy feeling it wasn't only the sudden shade that made her shiver.

Damn the man. Why couldn't he have gone elsewhere for his blasted eggs?

There was a chance that his insistence that hers were the only ones that would do was another pointless attempt at flattery, and she bristled with sudden irritation. Why did he have to impose upon her, as if she hadn't been clear enough already she wanted none of his attention? Doubtless his interest was the result of the gossips' cruel tongues, and when she pushed open the gate at the side of the house it was with more of a bang than was strictly necessary.

'There's no need for you to come any further. You can wait here.'

She watched Jonah's eyes travel from the house to the pretty cottage garden and then the orchard behind, the tops of waving apple trees just visible above a worn stone wall.

'It wouldn't be easier for me to step into the kitchen, to save you the task of carrying them back?'

'No.'

Frances gave him a warning glare. Loitering on the very edge of the back garden was as far as she was willing to allow a man to get, and especially one like Jonah, whose presence already did things to her stomach that she didn't intend to entertain. She meant to keep him at arm's length, both metaphorically *and* literally, and she made sure to close the low gate behind her as she stepped through it.

'I don't allow men in my house, Lieutenant. You may be new in town but you'll soon find I have no reputation as a hostess.'

Giving him no time to reply, she walked smartly away and in through the back door that opened directly into the kitchen. The eggs she'd collected earlier that morning stood in neatly stacked crates in readiness for market and she snatched up the top one, retracing her steps to practically shove the crate into Jonah's chest.

'There you are. You can go now.'

She stood back, arms folded across her narrow chest as she watched, with the suspicious stare of a circling hawk, as Jonah settled the crate under one arm. Even beneath the cover of his coat she could tell he was sturdily built, that arm clearly well-muscled as if no stranger to hard work, and she nipped the inside of her cheek in a warning not to allow such a thing to occur to her ever again.

'Thank you. My sister will be very pleased.'

He offered a slight bow, a dip of his head that struck Frances as somewhat forced...but he didn't leave.

Standing as stiffly as if he'd been on guard again, Jonah frowned across the yard, apparently absorbed in watching a sparrow pick a stray seed from beneath one of the troughs. He seemed ill at ease and Frances's wariness grew stronger as an uncomfortable pause stretched out between them until at last he cleared his throat.

'Have I done something to offend you, Miss Nettleford?'

Frances's eyes narrowed at once. 'Why would you think that?'

Jonah shrugged, the same gesture as three

days before and no less tempting to watch for the second time. 'An impression I'm forming. I'm wondering why that would be, after such a short acquaintance.'

Taking a cautious step back, Frances tilted her head. She wasn't afraid. He didn't sound angry, as some men did when denied what they wanted, but Uncle Robert's lessons rang in her ears and she knew to take no chances.

'Nothing you should take personally, Lieutenant,' she replied flatly. 'I don't like any young man who sets out to woo me and you are no exception. I find they tend to want one thing, something I have no intention of *ever* supplying, no matter who asks it.'

She saw the corners of Jonah's mouth turn down, more in contemplation than a frown, and he seemed to be seriously considering her words…

Before taking her by surprise.

'I see. What if I were to tell you, then, that *I* have no interest whatsoever in wooing any young woman, and that you are no exception either?'

Picking a fragment of straw off his sleeve, Jonah gave Frances a moment to absorb his response. He'd spoken nothing but the truth but it occurred to him—somewhat belatedly—that he could have softened it slightly, the frank state-

ment perhaps not the best idea when he was trying to recommend himself to the dishevelled
woman in front of him.

There was honesty and then there was blunt-
ness, and for the first time he regretted hardly
knowing the difference. If he was to make Miss
Nettleford an offer he had to thaw some of the
ice between them or risk her slamming the
farmhouse door in his face, destroying his only
chance of pulling his family out of the mud. He
would have to pick his moment carefully, wait
patiently for the right time to take his shot, just
as he would on the battlefield. She didn't have to
like him to consider his proposal, only not *dis*-
like him enough to see the sense of it, although
such a thing seemed far easier said than done
now they stood together in the sunlit yard.

He shifted from one booted foot to the other,
irritated by his atypical fidgeting. Frances hadn't
said a word and he risked a swift glance down
at that tense, admittedly attractive countenance,
immediately wishing that he hadn't when he
caught the look shot back at him in turn.

If one of his subordinates had shown him the
same flagrant disrespect Frances conveyed with
one flash of her greenish-brown eyes, he'd have
had the man court-martialled at the double.

'Is that so? You go about calling every new acquaintance *uncommonly pretty*, do you, without

any intention of flattery at all?' She spread her fingers, eyes so innocently wide he knew he'd made another mistake. 'That must raise some questions among the tradesmen you encounter, Lieutenant. Did the postman enjoy the compliment? And Mr Parkes, the baker?'

Jonah gritted his teeth. Damnation, she was sharp. It had been a colossal mistake to try to win her with sweet nothings, he saw that now all too clearly, and he'd have to think quickly before he lost even more ground than he had already.

How did other men do this? he wondered uncomprehendingly—and, more to the point, seem to enjoy it? His military acquaintances treated chasing women like a sport, something to be practised and mastered, scattering compliments like confetti and honing their approaches until no young lady was safe. If his task had been to bind a wound or fell an enemy with a pistol he could have done it with ease, but this was an entirely different objective.

It felt more like trying to charm a snake than forge an alliance. One false move and Frances's fangs were bared, ready to sink into his unwitting flesh, and his many skirmishes on the battlefield had done nothing to prepare him.

'An unfortunate choice of words I'll have to ask that you forgive,' he hazarded, hoping he'd hit the right note. 'Serving in the Army for years, surrounded by soldiers, did little to teach me how to speak to ladies. It won't happen again.'

Her face didn't soften one bit. 'Is that right?'

'It is. I have no interest in wasting time attempting any kind of romantic connection. Forming an attachment is the very furthest thing from my mind.'

That was something of an understatement, he thought darkly, but it gave him the nudge he needed to continue. 'I can only apologise if I gave any other impression.'

A clear shadow of doubt still lay heavy across her expression and Jonah felt the first stirrings of something uncomfortably close to curiosity move at the back of his mind. Usually women he'd had reason to speak to revelled in his company. His face, he knew, drew them in like wasps to a pot of honey whether he wanted the attention or not. Even as his usual impassive self they laughed at things he said, found excuses to lay a daring hand on his arm… It seemed Frances, however, saw nothing to admire and the irony wasn't lost on him that the only woman he'd ever *intended* to encourage closer was the only one to make such a thing difficult.

'Why are you so sure my aims are otherwise?'

'Because you're a young man.' Arms tightly folded over the worn bodice of her dress, Frances treated him to a glare that might have made a man unused to combat tremble. 'The men around Marchfield hear one whisper about my mother and think history will repeat itself in their favour, even when my farm is the only thing I care a fig about. They don't seem to realise those whispers were never correct in the first place.'

Jonah had the renewed feeling he was on thin ice with no idea of how to skate. 'No?'

'Of course not. Don't tell me Miss Fletcher didn't give you the whole tale—or her version of it, at least?'

The flash of fire in Frances's eyes warned him to tread even more carefully than he had already. The woman *had* been eager to tell him all about the infamous Marina Nettleford, sparing no detail despite receiving no encouragement, and, given what he'd heard, perhaps it was no wonder Frances was so determinedly defensive.

'She mentioned something about the man whose house I took.'

'I'm sure she did. How many seconds more was it before she implied my mother was of loose morals?' Frances's voice was bold, the accusatory edge plain. 'And me too, the apple never falling far from the tree?'

Jonah hesitated.

Hellfire. What now?

What was the right response to a question like that? However he answered would be received

like a lead weight and again he wished he'd bothered to take heed of his fellow officers' talk of
winning their sweethearts' good opinions. It had
never mattered more that he say the right thing
but it was as if she spoke a foreign language, her
words coming from a place of emotion that he
had forbidden inside himself ever since he was
a neglected little boy. He'd had to be strong for
Jane's sake and that meant turning away from
anything that might undermine his resolve, any
finer feelings only standing in the way of turning himself to stone—as he'd had to, his granite
presence the foundations on which three vulnerable people now built their lives.

Warily he shook his head. 'I wouldn't like to
comment on something so delicate as a lady's
reputation.'

'Well, you'd be the only one,' Frances snapped,
shoulders hunched beneath her gown. 'It's the
same old story everybody tells and, let *me* tell
you, it isn't true. She merely entrusted her heart
to *one* man but it was enough to damn both of
us for the rest of our lives. I will never make the
same error with mine.'

She fixed her attention on a cluster of hens
scratching at the straw-strewn cobbles but it
was as though she didn't truly see them. Her
eyes had taken on the faraway glaze of one lost
in their own thoughts, although what she could

be thinking was far beyond Jonah's guess. It could be anything: anger at the gossips' tattle, repeating the same old slander that so spoiled her good name, or perhaps regret for the loss of her mother. All he knew for certain was how suddenly tempting it was to watch her, with her dark hair coming loose from its pins to gleam beneath the sun and her jaw tight with whatever was running through her sharp mind, and to wonder what it would be like to understand its mysterious workings…

He pulled himself up with a start, a sudden jolt bringing him to his senses at once. What kind of thought was *that* when he had a mission to complete, one that depended entirely on him keeping his head at all times?

Brows snapping into a frown, he fought the urge to give himself a shake. He only had one chance to make a better impression before the opportunity slipped through his fingers and, gathering all the sincerity he could muster, he tried one last time.

'As I said when we first met, I like to make up my own mind about people, rather than be told what I should think.' He sensed that she was listening, although she neither turned in his direction nor dropped the stiff set of her thin shoulders. 'Perhaps you'll give me the opportunity to find out for myself what kind of person you are.'

For a moment she said nothing, and Jonah was just beginning to fear he had fumbled his final chance when she slid him a sideways glance. It was no warmer than any other look she'd thrown at him as if it were a javelin, although this time he could have sworn there was the faintest glimmer of curiosity beneath the frost.

'Why would you want to know anything more about me, if not for the same reason as any other man? I think I've made it quite clear any romantic overtures will *not* be accepted.'

Jonah took a wild leap into the unknown. 'And I think *I've* made it clear I don't intend to make any. My family knows nobody in Marchfield. It might be pleasant to have some acquaintance…or perhaps, in time, even a friend.'

A swift gleam of what might have been surprise passed over her face, so quickly it had come and gone in the blink of an eye, but it lasted just long enough to send an uncomfortable twist through him.

Was that *just* surprise, or had there been the merest hint of something else?

Under cover of adjusting the crate, feeling suddenly heavy beneath his arm, Jonah looked away.

She was to be the path towards pulling his family out of the hole his brother-in-law's treachery had thrown them into and nothing more, any accord he managed to broker between them strictly business. So long as he was honest about that he'd have nothing to reproach himself for, and the spectre of Thomas loomed at Jonah's shoulder to remind him not to stray into the darkness of deceit. He wouldn't attempt to make Frances believe he wanted her for anything other than a convenient escape from unfortunate circumstances. Such a thing could never be true, after all. Once Jane and the children had taken their share there was nothing left in him for anyone else, and most definitely not for this hostile woman, who wouldn't want his affection even if he'd offered it. In that regard she reminded him of himself, he realised with a start. The uncanny similarity nagged at him as he forced himself to carry on.

'My sister would welcome a call when we're settled. I know she'd appreciate having someone to show her around the town.'

Out of the corner of his eye he saw Frances reach up to gather her hair into a knot at the nape of her neck, lifting the heavy weight of it as if to cool the skin beneath. Despite the slenderness of her figure, he noticed the definition of her arms, the short sleeves of her dress showcasing more sinew than he'd ever seen on a young lady. It was something he found himself admiring before he could stop the rogue thought. She was far more tanned than was fashionable, a clear indication of how much time she spent outside, but, for the life of him, Jonah couldn't imagine why such a thing was frowned upon when the deeper colour suited her so well, her skin glowing tawny beneath the summer sun like a statue cast in bronze.

Fortunately Frances chose that moment to reply, diverting the unacceptable direction of Jonah's thoughts. 'I thank your sister, but no. I keep myself to myself.' She sounded wry, as if accepting something she couldn't change, and he wondered again at what had passed over her face, to vanish as quickly as it had come. Was it the tiniest glint of wistfulness, the fleeting desire to know what it was to have a friend? From what he'd seen so far, nobody in Marchfield seemed to have bothered to dig below that prickly surface, choosing instead to base their opinions on gossip. No doubt her reluctance to allow anyone close to her stemmed from the rejection she must have borne since she was a child.

Not that it was any of his business, he reminded himself in the next breath. Nothing about Frances interested him apart from her farm, and that would not be changing.

'Your whole family's reputation would suffer from any intimacy with me, and besides… I'm not sure I want to set foot in Rose Cottage, knowing what I do about the former tenant. Too many ghosts.'

At the mention of the cottage Jonah felt himself tense further. She'd ask now, as had everyone else he'd met in Marchfield, why a man of his rank had moved down from Newcastle to take such a poor house for his family when surely he could afford far better, and he tried to remember what bland tale he'd repeated with each new enquiry. Something about the desire for a simple life, wanting a smaller home in which the children could feel secure…

But his explanation wasn't needed.

Frances merely shook out the skirt of her gown, a small cloud of dust rising to float away on the warm breeze, and Jonah found himself appreciating her silence. Either she respected his privacy or she simply didn't care to know the circumstances of his new home. Whichever was most accurate, her refusal to pry was refreshing, a welcome change from the nosiness and whispering he had encountered so far.

She shifted uneasily and Jonah cursed himself, realising he'd been watching her a little too closely.

'If you say so. If you change your mind, however, I know you'd be welcome. My sister feels the same way I do about forming her own opinions.'

Reaching into the pocket of his coat, he drew out a collection of coins. In truth, he had no idea how much eggs cost but he placed the entire lot into her hand, a spark running the length of his spine at the momentary brush of his fingertips against her heated palm.

'Thank you for these.' Jonah nodded at the crate under his arm, uncomfortably aware of the friction at his back. He could only hope Frances didn't notice the sudden hoarseness of his voice—or how he had to struggle not to allow his gaze to linger too long on her rosy, upturned face.

'Good afternoon, Miss Nettleford. I hope we shall meet again soon.'

Chapter Three

With each step he took through Marchfield's market square Jonah's discomfort grew.

A handsome young man arrived in town only a week prior was evidently the most interesting thing that had happened in months, and his stretched reserves of civility were almost at their breaking point already. Eyes turned in his direction wherever he looked, admiring his rigid bearing and the chestnut wave of his hair, and the whispers he'd caught were enough to make a gentler man blush. Tensing his jaw, Jonah touched his hat at another coy nod, irritation rising as a scarlet face disappeared behind yet another coquettish hand. At this rate he'd be tempted to give up on his objective and turn for home, only determination not to lose an opportunity to meet Frances stopping him from doing just that.

Ducking beneath the shelter of an awning,

Jonah took a moment to survey his surround-
ings. The market was teeming, stalls lining the
square and crowds jostling to see what was for
sale. Traders' shouts cut through the warm air,
encouraging customers to come a little closer,
and the smell of roasting meat mingled with the
less pleasant aroma of yesterday's fish. Small
children selling ribbons and other fripperies
nobody wanted flitted about with baskets over
their arms, piping voices pleading for trade, their
faces thin and clothes in such need of a good
wash and mend that the muscles in Jonah's neck
grew tauter.

*I remember when Jane and I looked like that.
All skin and bone and scraping for a penny we
could spend on bread rather than Papa's drink.*

He followed the progress of one little girl with
grim understanding, watching as she darted
among the throng like an eel. Time after time
her entreaties were ignored, the thin arms struggling with the weight of her heavy basket, until
he could stand it no longer.

'Girl. Come here.'

Jonah called the child over with a short jerk
of his head, darkly amused to see her reluctance
to move closer. Perhaps Frances wasn't the only
one who didn't like the look of him after all. His
perpetual frown was off-putting for children as
well as abrupt female farmers, it seemed, even

if his intention towards the former was far less complicated.

'Did…did you want some ribbons, sir?'

The little girl peered up at him timidly, something in her over-large eyes finding a gap in the armour of his indifference. She reminded him of Margaret and he curbed the instinct to grace her with a rare smile as he reached into his pocket.

'No. Keep your trinkets but take this.' He held out a shilling, the girl's eyes growing wider. 'I like to see hard work fairly rewarded.'

Her mouth opened to thank him but Jonah dismissed her with another jerk of his chin. He'd shown more than enough sentiment for one day and if the child lingered for much longer he might be drawn into showing even more—never something to be encouraged.

'Go on. Away with you.'

Without a word the little girl scurried off into the crowd, disappearing quickly as if she feared he might change his mind, and Jonah's stomach twisted as he watched her go.

I shouldn't have done that. I couldn't really spare that coin…and yet…

He remembered what it was to be hungry and poor, he thought bitterly. He'd spent his life ensuring Jane never had to feel that sting again and to think Margaret and Matthew were so close to knowing for themselves how harsh life could be, all thanks to their own selfish father, cut too close to the bone. It was a horrible parallel to his own childhood, betrayed by parents who cared more for themselves than their own son and daughter, and the prospect of history repeating itself made Jonah venture back out again into the sun-drenched square.

Frances was to be their salvation and he would get no closer to securing her if he didn't make an effort, even if their recent interactions had been confusing, to say the least.

Her face flashed before him now as he slipped through the mass of people, no longer even attempting to return the greetings sent his way. Instead the memory of her expression as she'd confronted him held Jonah's full attention, the recollection of that cynical glare fixed in his mind like a brand burned onto leather. Whatever had passed *behind* her face should have gripped him more than anything else, but he found his mind straying more to the stately curve of her cheekbone, as well as the scattering of freckles across her nose like a tiny constellation of stars…

Jonah's frown deepened as he dismissed the wayward thoughts.

So she has no use for pretty words. I can well understand having no patience for them. My task now is to somehow build an acquaintance sturdy

*enough that she might not laugh in my face when
I finally propose.*

Reading between the lines, Frances's existence was a lonely one, her dislike for Marchfield's judgemental residents and distrust of young men holding her back from seeking the companionship most people craved. She'd made it crystal-clear she wanted no wooing—something that suited him down to the ground—but if he could convince her the gossips' cruelty meant nothing to him, that he accepted her based on her own merit rather than being swayed by events that had happened before she was even born, perhaps he might be able to find some way in.

*Because, in truth, it doesn't matter to me what
her pedigree is or what others think of her reputation. The world is unkind whether a person
deserves it or not—and who am I to decide who
is or isn't worthy, born in the gutter to parents
who barely cared if I lived or died?*

With eyes narrowed against both the sun and his own unpleasant memories, Jonah pressed on. There was no doubt Frances would be in the square on market day and he scanned about him once again, seeking through the crowds that stretched out in all directions.

If he hadn't been searching so diligently he might have missed her. Set back in one of the far corners and almost obscured by a shade sewn from rough cloth, Frances stood behind a stall piled with crates of eggs and rosy-green apples, fat potatoes stacked in front while straggling carrots shone orange through a film of earth. She looked as tense as always and Jonah wasn't sure he approved of the stab of relief that lanced through him at finally finding that pretty, glowering countenance, shadowed beneath a wide straw hat but the elegant line of her profile unmistakable even from a distance.

Shaking off the uninvited reaction, he began to weave towards her, trying to recall the plan he'd settled on the night before. He might have more luck this time admiring her wares rather than her person, Jonah thought wryly, although how one went about complimenting a root vegetable he had no idea… But then something in the scene before him brought him up short.

Frances had just finished serving a customer and had turned briefly away when Jonah saw a young man approach her stall. Evidently taking advantage of the lull in trade and Frances's distraction, the stranger slipped unsteadily into the space behind her, stepping so close he was almost touching her and a smirk spreading over his face that Jonah found he didn't like one bit. A hand reached out towards her slim back—and then the man's arm was around Frances's waist and he had pulled her closer, dropping his head to whisper who knew what into her unsuspecting ear, and Jonah's chest tightened as though gripped in a vice.

Who is that? And by what right does he take liberties I know for a fact Frances would never willingly grant?

The stranger obviously had no idea of Frances other than what he must have heard from unkind lips, Jonah realised. Anybody who'd ever had a proper conversation with her would know that attempting to touch her was akin to stroking a wild dog, more likely to come away with a bite than anything else, and his mind spun back to their conversation out in Barrow's yard. She hated the unwanted attention, never intending for anyone to get close to her guarded heart—something he well understood, the strange thread of similarity between them he'd felt that day once again unravelling before him.

Frances was in no way connected to him and he had enough to worry about with Jane and her children to waste his concern… And yet he realised his jaw was set and he was moving forward without having intended to, some incomprehensible force propelling him on. However reluctant he was to consider anyone else, he couldn't turn a blind eye to Frances's discomfort, his role as guardian to those weaker than himself something difficult to shake.

Before he could take even two swift paces, however, Frances had acted for herself.

Still cutting through the crowd, Jonah could only watch as she turned deftly in the man's arms, looked directly up into his leering face and then—to Jonah's surprise—brought both hands up to push him away with all her might, sending him bowling backwards to land on the cobbled ground with such a thud that Jonah thought he heard it above the shouts and clamour of the entire market square.

People turned immediately to see what had happened, mutters rippling out from the central point of Frances standing with her hands on her hips, glaring down at the man sprawled out in the dirt. Somebody helped him to his feet and immediately he lurched in her direction, wrath etched on his red face until Jonah stepped smartly between them, just catching the widening of Frances's eyes before he fixed the other man with a cold, level stare.

'I don't think you have anything more to say to Miss Nettleford.'

'I wasn't—'

'Be on your way, sir. I won't tell you twice.'

At times, Jonah had to admit the harshness of his life had given some benefits. A profession built on the shedding of blood had left him with a particularly hard gaze when he chose and that, coupled with the breadth of shoulder beneath his coat, was enough to send Frances's unwelcome suitor into reluctant retreat.

Not that she really needed my help. I can't say I expected that.

He turned around to meet Frances's narrowed eyes. She'd defended herself with impressive courage and confusion began to circle inside him, new respect taking root where once there'd been nothing but barren ground. It seemed she was more capable than he'd realised and it made him pause, the notion of *not* having to play the protector for once unfamiliar…and not altogether displeasing.

'Lieutenant Grant. Another unexpected visit. Have you come for more eggs or just to frighten away my customers?'

She shot him a searching glance, bright and sharp from beneath the cover of her hat, although Jonah saw the colour in her cheeks was high. The rosy tint suited her and he felt a flicker of a frown cross his face that he'd noticed such a thing, a furrowing of his brows that grew deeper as he heard the onlookers' whispers at his back.

'Neither was my aim when I left home this morning. I suppose I was lucky in regard to the latter.'

Frances exhaled a mirthless laugh, the snakes writhing through Jonah's innards increasing at her composure. She'd almost been assaulted and yet somehow her hands were perfectly steady as she straightened her hat, his unsettling appreciation of her mettle gaining strength at her determined calm.

She cast a dark look over the bystanders evidently discussing her latest scandal and Jonah's pulse flickered at the downward quirk of her pretty mouth.

'Oh, dear. I fear I've disgraced myself again.'

He followed her gaze to a small group standing a short distance from her stall. It was clear from the pursed lips that there were no kind words being exchanged and, despite her defiance, Jonah was sure he caught a shadow pass over Frances's face.

More judgement. More gossip about her for something that wasn't her fault.

There was no justice in it and Jonah found a different novel feeling welling up, a gleam of sympathy, yet another attack on the indifference he had cultivated for so long, but he could no more have stopped it than he could have held back the tide.

A voice in the back of his mind urged caution but he barely heard its alarm. All he could see was Frances's valiantly concealed unhappiness and the strange, fleeting desire to comfort her was not one he could explain. There had been something admirable in her defiance. He couldn't deny that spark of independence was dangerously interesting, completely the opposite of the damsels in distress he'd always tried so hard to avoid, and it whispered seductively into ears he'd been so determined to make deaf.

'The only person disgracing himself was that creature with the wandering hands. Anybody could see what you did was in defence of your own honour and if they can't then they must be lacking even a single grain of good sense.'

Jonah spoke loudly enough for Marchfield's tattletales to hear every word and out of the corner of her eye Frances saw them bridle like a flock of offended hens, feathers fluffed out at his insolence. Nobody had ever defended her so publicly, even her uncle preferring to simply pretend he didn't hear the slander, and for Jonah, of all people, to champion her so boldly was a surprise.

One far more pleasant than it should be.

What did he have to gain from speaking on her behalf, as well as standing between her and the man who had looked as if he wanted to strike her for pushing him away? Lieutenant Grant had seemed to appear from nowhere, placing himself in the way of the drunken youth who'd thought he had the right to touch her, and she couldn't deny she hadn't been altogether *displeased* to see him. It might not have been necessary for Jonah to come to her defence but he'd chosen to nonetheless, the cold challenge she'd seen in his eyes as he'd emerged from the crowd enough to send an unnamed thrill down even Frances's unbending spine. She'd never known a young man make himself useful to her instead of a nuisance. In that regard, at least, he'd just managed to set himself apart from every other male in town.

He was still next to her, whatever he was thinking hidden behind the same shuttered mask he'd worn every time she'd seen him. If she hadn't heard what he'd said with her own ears Frances wouldn't have believed him capable of such candour, his mouth a hard line with no trace of a curve to soften his stern, good-looking face. Her own felt as though it was burning as a flush climbed up to cross each cheek, the market around her busy as ever but somehow retreating into the background as her bewilderment grew.

Hoping none of what passed through her mind had shown in her face, Frances tried to set the whirl of thoughts aside. 'You'll find you're the only one who thinks so. A real lady would never behave so unbecomingly—there will be fresh talk all around town by this evening. About both of us now, I'm afraid.'

Jonah gave a rough snort. 'Fortunate for you

then that you needn't care for their opinions. I know I don't.'

Frances peered up at him. He certainly looked as though he was telling the truth. There wasn't so much as a hint he felt any embarrassment to be seen talking with her, seeming for all the world as if the rumours that followed her meant nothing to him. Perhaps he'd meant it when he said he wanted to make up his own mind about her—the first person to ever bother looking beneath the gossip—or perhaps he'd simply never felt something as weak as shame in his whole life. That was something Frances couldn't claim for herself and suddenly she wanted nothing more than to be safely back at Barrow and out of reach of those who only ever looked at her to find fault. It was exhausting, carrying the weight of their scorn as well as everything else, and she didn't answer Jonah as she leaned forward to begin packing up what was left of her goods.

'Are you going back to the farm already?'

'Yes.' With a grunt she hefted a half-full crate of beetroot onto her hip and reached down for a bundle of rhubarb, the pink stems gleaming. 'I've had quite enough of Marchfield's finest for one day and I have a lot more work to do before the sun goes down.'

She moved away towards where Apollo stood, patiently hitched to the cart Uncle Robert had painted her favourite shade of green. Heaving her load up onto the back of it, she turned to make another trip, conscious of Jonah's intense brown gaze following her every move—and trying to ignore how it stirred the short hairs on the back of her neck.

'Do you do everything yourself?'

'Of course. I have nobody since my uncle died.' Frances lifted another crate, feeling the scream of overworked muscles. 'You know the lies about my mother. The young men think I'm cut from the same cloth—as you saw—and the older married men aren't allowed within half a mile of me. I have no interest in taking a husband of my own, as I believe we have discussed, so, in the absence of anyone else, I have no choice but to work my farm alone.'

She shuffled away again, arms already feeling the strain. There were still plenty of boxes to move and they would all need to be unloaded again once she'd reached Barrow. The prospect made her feel like wilting to the dry ground. Dumping the crate onto the back of the cart, Frances thought she *just* caught Jonah's voice, almost drowned out by the thump.

'What was that?'

'I said *I* could help you.'

Frances straightened up at once, still not sure she'd heard correctly. Jonah hadn't moved, standing like a guard beside her stall, and she felt the ready blush only he seemed able to inspire cross her face yet again. 'Did you say *you* could help?'

At his nod her brows knitted into a frown. 'Why would you want to do that?'

He gestured to the heaps of vegetables awaiting her attention. 'I've already said I'd like us to be friends. I understand friends help each other when they need it.'

Frances returned his unwavering stare. First defending her in public, and now this? They barely knew each other and yet Jonah seemed intent on proving his worth, showing more, admittedly agreeable, concern for her in just over a week than most of Marchfield had in more than two decades—but she couldn't allow herself to trust it.

Barrow Farm was her kingdom and no man would encroach on it, she reaffirmed as she tried to sift through the confusing clamour of her thoughts. On the one hand sat Uncle Robert's teachings and her own resolve never to end up like her mother, taken in and then cast out by a cruel heart hidden behind a handsome face. On the other hand, however, it was friendship and help Jonah was offering, not an entanglement, and Frances gritted her teeth to admit *she* had been the one struck by his charms rather than the other way around. He'd made it quite clear he wanted no romantic nonsense and her own alarming weakness for his warm brown eyes seemed more dangerous than anything he might be thinking himself, a realisation that made her bristle.

'If you feel you absolutely must offer assistance, I suppose you might help me pack up my cart.' She frowned up at him sternly from beneath her hat. 'But that's all. Just because I accept your help today doesn't mean I'm bound to you in any form.'

If she hadn't known better Frances might have suspected she caught the most fleeting glitter of amusement in his eyes, although, of course, such a thing was impossible for the serious Lieutenant Grant. 'Perish the thought. Allow me.'

He stepped round her, passing so close in the narrow space that she felt herself stiffen at the accidental brush of his hand against hers. She *had* to get a hold of the unacceptable effect he seemed to have on her, something dangerous and unwanted, and she had to do it fast. Allowing any appreciation for the shape of his jaw or the strength of his arms was sure not to end well, although it was difficult not to notice the latter as he picked up four crates with as much effort as Frances would a sack of feathers.

With Jonah's help the cart was packed swiftly and Frances graced him with a brisk nod as she settled into the driver's seat, gathering Apollo's reins for the short journey back to Barrow. The sun was still beating down and her head was beginning to ache, echoing the pain in her muscles that even an extra pair of hands hadn't managed to avoid. The sooner she got home the better—both for her poor battered body and to get away from the man who now patted Apollo's flank, his gruff tenderness for her horse making her quickly avert her eyes.

'Thank you. I won't pretend that wasn't far easier with your involvement.'

He dismissed her thanks with a lift of one shoulder. 'You'll need to unload again at the other end. I'm happy to assist with that as well if you'd allow it.'

'Oh.'

Caught off-guard, Frances hesitated. Her first instinct was to refuse, stubborn independence combined with the whisper in her ear that she'd spent more than enough time with Jonah Grant already and shouldn't allow him another minute more. With every second she was straying closer to the enemy and she knew better than to forget the caution instilled in her since she'd been a little girl.

But the sun was so hot…and every sinew in her longed for rest she couldn't afford to take…

In the end it seemed exhaustion was a stronger

force even than pride. It wore her down, weariness for once overcoming wariness as the two battled within her mercilessly.

Frances shifted uncomfortably in her seat. 'I can't deny it would be quicker with two, although… I would never ask…'

Without waiting for her to find the end of her rambling sentence, Jonah swung up into the seat beside her, barely a hair's breadth from where she sat, and any possibility of finishing it died in Frances's mouth.

'You don't need to ask. I offered.' His gaze was fixed straight ahead, the pleasing shape of his profile outlined against the sun, and for a second Frances couldn't look away. 'We can leave now if you're ready.'

Throat suddenly too dry to allow any speech, Frances flicked the reins and the cart began to move forward, edging slowly through the crowds. Even without looking, Frances could *feel* the stares of the bystanders as Apollo moved from the market square, her discomfort growing with every turn of the cart's wheels, feeling her passenger sitting so close. Such a sight would do absolutely nothing to diminish the fresh gossip about her, she thought vaguely, although she found herself too damnably conscious of how near Jonah's shoulder was to her own to spare much consideration for anything else.

Neither spoke as they rattled through March-field towards the rough lane back to Barrow Farm. Frances had to concentrate hard to prevent herself from flinching whenever his arm brushed hers, the bare skin there glowing hotter with every touch. It was only the most feather-light contact forced by the narrowness of the seat, but each time Frances's breath caught as if he'd winded her, a sensation inexplicably pleasurable and frightening bound up in one unintended caress.

She pressed her teeth together so hard they almost squeaked.

What am I doing? If Uncle Robert could see me now...

But he couldn't. The only person who might have observed Frances as she steered the cart down the twisting country lane was Jonah, his shoulder bumping against hers as the wheels bounced over ruts in the scorched ground, the friction building until Frances feared he might hear how hard her heart was beating. She'd never been so close to a man before—apart from her uncle, of course, and this state of breathless fascination was *not* the same thing—and the solid shape of Lieutenant Grant beside her drew her in like a magnet, some primitive part of her *wanting* to curve closer, despite all good sense.

They rounded a tight corner, in her confusion

Frances taking the turn a fraction too sharply. The cart tilted, enough for Frances to curse her inattention, but then her breath caught with sudden force as a strong arm shot out instinctively to anchor her to her seat—and she could have bitten her tongue at the gasp that escaped from her parted lips as Jonah's hand came to rest, for the very briefest of moments and clearly not by design, on the secret curve of her waist.

The heat from the sun was nothing compared to the conflagration in her blood as Frances felt his fingers skim her ribs. Jonah pulled away at once but the damage was already done. With one touch her skin was on fire and her face must have been the colour of a summer poppy as he gave a dry cough, even his usual cool wavering a little at the mistake.

'Sorry,' he muttered curtly. 'Force of habit. I didn't intend to…impose.'

Frances said nothing, only praying he wouldn't notice the crimson of her face beneath her hat. That soft trail of fingertips over her waist, gentler than she ever would have believed such scarred hands could be, did something to her insides and she wished she could slow the rapid skip of her pulse, racing away from her like a deer through a field. She couldn't meet Jonah's eye and she certainly couldn't think of any way to break the silence that stretched out between them, growing more awkward with each clip of Apollo's hooves. The best she could do was keep her eyes on the track ahead and make sure she didn't repeat the misstep, and neither looked at the other again until the cart drew into Barrow Farm's yard.

Still with her heart pounding, Frances pulled the horse to a halt, relief washing over her like a wave.

Finally. I thought that journey was never going to end.

Under the pretence of rearranging her skirts, she didn't look up as Jonah vaulted over the side, hearing his boots ring on the cobbles. Her chickens came at once to see if the new arrivals had any food secreted about their persons, followed close behind by Gyp the terrier, his wiry tail wagging so hard it was little more than a white blur.

She stood up, stretching out her leaden arms. The exhaustion that had so undermined her usual caution hadn't abated one bit. If anything, it had increased during the ride, no doubt in part thanks to the effort of controlling her inexcusable reaction to Jonah's proximity, and Frances sagged a little at the prospect of all the hard work waiting for her return.

Jonah waited by Apollo's head. 'Can I hand you down?'

'No. I can manage.'

She made to climb over the cart's ledge and lower herself to the ground, as she had countless times before. Perhaps on all those occasions, however, she hadn't been *quite* so close to crumpling into a tired heap. Whatever the reason, this time Frances misjudged the distance and her stomach gave a sickening lurch as her foot slipped on the thin wooden step. For one horrible beat she felt herself falling, until—for the second time that day and infinitely more welcome than the first—an arm closed around her waist.

Every last trace of air left her lungs as she looked up into Jonah's face, the power of that single arm enough to keep her on her feet. Pressed against the hard contours of his chest, there was no escaping the overwhelming masculinity of his form, one hand splayed behind her back, allowing no place to hide, and Frances couldn't name the complex emotion she saw flit through his captivating eyes. He stared down at her with that unsmiling mouth so close she could have risen on tiptoes to kiss it. The desire to know what it was to feel another's lips on hers was like a sudden flood that crashed over her as if from a broken dam. When the man in the market had touched her she'd felt nothing but revulsion and anger and yet, held in place by both Jonah's arms and gaze, she realised she didn't want to push him away.

But I should.

Uncle Robert's warning cut through Frances's dulled mind like an arrow, spearing her with its sharp edge. Could there be a situation more hazardous than this—standing perilously close to an embrace with a man whose presence put her in grave danger of doing something so rash it could never be undone? In all likelihood her mother's downward spiral had begun with just such an innocent situation. With her throat feeling full of broken glass, Frances found the strength to step back.

'I think I'll unload tomorrow instead,' she managed, painfully aware her voice sounded strangled. 'Your sister must be wondering where you are. Please give her my apologies for having kept you away so long.'

Jonah's habitual frown deepened. 'Are you sure? You don't need my help after all?'

'Quite sure.'

From the minute movement of one eyebrow it was clear he understood he was being dismissed, although Frances fervently hoped he didn't fully comprehend why. It would be more shame than even she could bear if he guessed the truth, that she needed time alone to rebuild the defences it seemed he could threaten with no effort at all, her own rationality and even Uncle Robert's wisdom under attack for the first time in Frances's

short, unhappy life. She wanted no man's inter-
ference, and Jonah had been clear he wanted
no romantic liaisons either, so how was it she'd
found it so difficult to remember that while a
prisoner in his grasp, looking up into that face,
so serious—yet could it be hiding a hint of softness deep within?

Thankfully, Jonah didn't argue. With a short
bow he turned away, pausing only to drop the
swiftest unexpected pat on the top of Gyp's head,
and then Frances watched him cross the yard
until he passed through the gate and disappeared
into the lane—leaving her at the mercy of her
own whirling thoughts, and with the knowledge
that she needed to strengthen her guard.

Chapter Four

⁓⁓⁓⁓⁓⁓

If Frances had thought it impossible to feel any more tired than she already did, another night spent out in the piggeries was enough to teach her otherwise.

Pushing both hands into the small of her back, she arched her stiff spine, too exhausted to even yawn as she emerged from the pigsty into the feeble light of a new dawn. An inexperienced young sow had begun to farrow around midnight and now, four hours later, six fat piglets lay snuffling and squeaking beside their proud mother, an endearing sight Frances might have appreciated more if she hadn't been dead on her feet. Her eyes felt gritty from straining beneath a guttering lantern flame and her back half seized, the low roof not built with anything taller than a pig in mind and Frances's muscles paying the price.

In a sleep-deprived daze she staggered out of the pen, only just remembering to close the gate behind her. Even the cock hadn't crowed yet, the slow creep of the sun barely touching Barrow's cobbles and all around her eerily quiet as she stood, swaying slightly and trying to force her brain to cooperate despite its longing for rest.

There's no time to go back to bed. I need to keep going.

If she lay down there was a very good chance she wouldn't get up again, Frances thought distantly, and then who would tend to everything that needed doing? It wasn't as if she had anybody she could rely on apart from herself, after all; nobody she could call on to lend her a helping hand when she felt herself near the brink...

Or perhaps that wasn't *quite* true.

She closed her eyes for one blissful moment, feeling the instant relief of having them shut—although the picture that leaped at her from the darkness wasn't one she encouraged.

Jonah had offered to help and it was his face that was imprinted on her closed eyelids, the serious expression sending a hopeless shiver through Frances's nerves.

First he'd come to her defence physically and then with cutting words spoken loud enough for everyone to hear taken her side so clearly there could be no mistaking it. He'd said the town gossip meant nothing to him and she had to admit that so far he seemed to be telling the truth, the lies that circulated about her apparently brushed off like the nonsense they were in favour of unfamiliar respect. It was a perilously agreeable novelty to find somebody willing to look deeper than the surface, as if trying to make out what lived beneath the hard exterior she'd been forced to adopt—but that secret pleasure only served to put her on even higher alert.

I will not allow myself to like him.

Her alarming enjoyment of his proximity in the cart had been inexcusable and her reaction to what had come next, as she'd all but swooned in the unshakable circle of his arms, was nothing short of a betrayal of everything Robert had taken such pains to teach her. She needed to be more careful, to reinforce the boundaries that were the only way to be certain she'd never repeat Mama's mistake, and to do that she would have to ensure she saw as little as possible of the dangerously alluring Lieutenant Grant. He might seem different from the rest of Marchfield's men now, more thoughtful and insisting he wanted no attachment of any kind, but that could change in an instant and she knew better than to let her emotions overrule the cold good sense of her level head.

Picking a piece of straw out of her hair, Frances resolved—for perhaps the tenth time since market day—to set all thoughts of Jonah aside.

Letting him come to the farm would be asking for trouble. It could prove a slippery slope, his offer of friendship all too easily turning into something more, and that would never do. No man could be trusted as far as he could be thrown, even if the temptation to finally have a friend after a lifetime of rejection caught Frances beneath the ribs as she wondered what that would possibly be like. Nobody but her uncle had ever cared what became of her and the loneliness that followed his passing was so deep it sometimes felt like a kind of living death, one hard day following the next with nothing to look forward to but more of the same.

The heavy pulse of grief that sat low in her stomach tried to rise but she squared her shoulders at its assault.

Uncle Robert trained me better than to give in to my despair. I won't forget everything he taught me just to dull the pain, and that includes using Jonah to fill the gap he left behind.

The pale light was getting stronger. Before long the sun would burst from behind Barrow's farmhouse, bringing with it all the heat and work of a new day, and Frances fought back a yawn.

Standing around moping won't get anything done.

On achingly tired legs she moved to the yard's pump to wash the worst of the night's farrowing off her hands. They'd be dirty again soon enough but the cool water helped slightly to order her thoughts and her mind turned sluggishly to the small herd of Gloucester cattle kept in Barrow's top field. One of them had caught itself on a broken piece of fence a few days prior and she had to check the wound. Now was as good a time as any to make the rounds, Frances supposed, and with as much determination as she could muster she crossed the cobbles, her dragging steps taking her out of the yard and towards the fields beyond.

The brown-and-white shapes of her cows grew larger as Frances approached, one or two lifting their heads from the dewy grass to watch her unlatch the gate. They knew her too well to be alarmed and she patted each one she passed, running her sore eyes over the field in search of the one she wanted. She could barely think for the exhaustion making every move an effort, any thoughts that managed to swim up from the deep feeling cloudy and indistinct and giving the uncanny impression of being underwater. Usually she'd be able to pick out the cow in question with no trouble at all and irritation began to grow as she scanned about for the second time.

'Where are you?'

Lifting her skirts out of the damp grass, Frances stumbled away from the gate and further into the open. *Still* the heifer she wanted escaped her burning eyes and she struggled onwards, boots feeling heavier than ever as she drifted into the middle of the field. The gate lay far behind her now, with thick briar hedges bordering every side, their thorns awaiting anyone unwary enough to stray too near, although Frances was barely aware of anything other than her own fatigue as she wearily looked around.

'Ah. There you are. At last.'

The cow stood a short distance away and Frances shuffled towards it, her mind still foggy as a November morning as she closed in on her patient. Perhaps after this she could have a welcome cup of tea, she wondered groggily, and maybe—just *maybe*—a five-minute sit down in Uncle Robert's overstuffed old chair, the same one they used to curl up in together when she was a little girl...

A sound behind her made her freeze.

Standing perfectly still, Frances felt her heart shoot into her mouth, followed immediately by the sensation of being doused in icy water. She knew that sound—a low, angry snort—and knew exactly what it meant. In her exhaustion she'd just made the mistake that might cost her life.

I completely forgot I brought him in here last night. How could I be so stupid?

Hardly daring to breathe, Frances turned her

head a fraction. It was just as she'd feared. Directly behind her, displaying himself from the side to showcase his full might, stood Barrow's enormous Gloucester bull. She'd brought him down from his bachelor paddock the evening before, the huge creature placid enough while led by the ring in his nose and no scent of females to enrage him. Now, reunited with his many wives, however, his protective instincts had come roaring back, his menacing pawing of the ground a clear indication he didn't take kindly to Frances's presence among them. Under any other circumstances she would never have put herself in such a dangerous situation, but tiredness had blunted her good sense and now she felt her mouth dry as horror took hold of her chest and squeezed.

She couldn't run, she thought quickly. The bull would charge at once, catching her in seconds to trample her into grass wet with her own blood. If she stayed still he might leave her alone for a while, but how could she get out of the field without drawing the attention of his rolling eye? He stood between her and the gate, cutting off any hope of slipping past, and the cruel thorns of the hedges on all sides made leaping a fence impossible. The only chance of escape was to pray he lost interest and moved away, although another warning snort from behind told Frances that was unlikely. Another wave of fear skittered down her spine.

Standing out in the open, she was overwhelmed by a sudden sense of her own vulnerability, caught with nothing to shield her from the unstoppable power of the bull who would kill her without hesitation if she made one single wrong move. Every heartbeat seemed to last an age, time slowing down as Frances heard the scuff of the bull's hoof through the grass grow more impatient and his grunts resonate deeper than ever. Out of the very corner of her eye she just made out the tossing of a giant head, horns arcing against the brightening sky—and then terror choked her as the head went down and the horns along with it, and the ground seemed to shake with the thunder of hoof beats bearing down on her, with nowhere to run.

A shout tore through the air, as welcome and as unexpected as a voice from the heavens.

'Here! Over here!'

Frances and the bull turned as one to look towards a figure vaulting over the gate. The bull hesitated, turning its head back to Frances, but another shout sent it charging away in the direction of the newcomer running alongside one fence and, seizing her chance, Frances fled.

Her legs carried her more swiftly than she'd known they could, dazed exhaustion forgotten as pure instinct coursed through her to spur her on with barely a thought for where she was placing her feet. Slipping on the dew, she went down like a felled tree, knocking the breath from her body. A sharp pain flared in one knee but she was up again at once, fingers sinking into the soil to haul herself forward. With her heart pounding and her pulse flown up to the sky she reached the gate and leaped over it, landing awkwardly and stumbling a pace before the ground came up to meet her and she found herself sprawled full stretch on the grass.

She lay face down for a moment, feeling dampness against her cheek. Her chest rose and fell as quickly as a bird's and her mind was blank as a piece of parchment as she waited for her senses to return, only aware of a vague feeling of relief unfolding that turned to distant surprise as someone—very gently, as though being careful not to hurt her—placed a hand on her shoulder and turned her onto her back.

At first she couldn't see who it was. Silhouetted against the sun, her rescuer's face was in shadow, a dark shape hovering between her and the azure sky. It was only when he spoke that her pulse started to bound more quickly than even the bull had managed.

'Well, Miss Nettleford. It appears my assistance might have been warranted after all.'

* * *

Crouching by Frances's side, Jonah tried to slow the pace of his breath, made shallow by running. It should have been easy but somehow, being so close to Frances as she lay on the grass, hair fanned out around her like a raven cloak and the bodice of her gown moving so distractingly, made regaining his composure much more difficult.

Her eyes had closed, their sharpness hidden from him by the sweep of long lashes, and for a moment he allowed himself to drink in the uncharacteristically still planes of her face. She was a handsome woman and the unease he had been stubbornly suppressing ever since market day returned with a vengeance to make him curse under his breath.

Not this again. How many times must I rationalise the same blasted thing?

The memory of Frances in his arms haunted him, its spectral hands tightening around him and refusing to let go. She'd looked up at him with such bewilderment, the first glimpse of vulnerability she had ever shown, and the realisation there might be something hidden behind her severity had touched something inside him he'd long since thought dead. Frances's confusion held a mirror up to his own hidden self, the softness he'd made up his mind to crush when he was a neglected child struggling to survive, now a man still resolved never to allow any weakness to prosper. He had more than just Jane depending on him and he had to be strong, and that meant turning his back completely on anything—or anyone—that might thaw his heart.

A rising morning breeze stirred the tendrils around Frances's face and Jonah saw her eyelids flutter, hastily averting his gaze so she wouldn't suspect he'd been watching. There was a curious intimacy in being so near a resting woman, calling to mind an echo of the bedroom before he could stop it. For all the ice in his soul he was as human as any other man and the image of how Frances might look laid back against his pillows rose unbidden, alarming but so seductive for one sharp second he struggled to breathe.

'Lieutenant Grant…' Her voice at his elbow was a welcome distraction from the dangerous turn of his thoughts. 'Where did you come from?'

He leaned back as Frances pushed herself upright. Her breathing was still a little fast and her cheeks flushed but the composure he so grudgingly admired was returning already, the only real clue she'd been frightened a slight tremor of her hand as she reached to gather her hair—an action that quite unintentionally highlighted the length of her neck, a warm curve Jonah's fingers instinctively twitched to reach out and touch…

He gave a gruff cough. 'I often wake at dawn and take a walk before breakfast. It just so happened that this morning I took the lane that passes by Barrow Farm and saw what was unfolding in your field. On any other day I wouldn't have been there at all.'

'I ought to be grateful you chose this particular occasion to roam the lanes then. I dread to think what would have happened otherwise.'

With a shudder Frances leaned forward, bringing her legs up to hug them to her chest. Briefly she rested her forehead on her knees, swiftly sitting up again to reach one hand under her muddy skirt.

Her fingers were stained with blood when she withdrew them and her face crumpled into a grimace. 'I thought I felt something when I fell. It looks like I was right.'

Jonah was about to reply when, with a rustle of muslin, she hitched up her skirts to reveal long shapely legs. The words died in his mouth as, with a complete lack of self-consciousness, she inspected one scarlet-streaked knee. It should have been the fresh blood that drew his soldierly eye but instead the exposed skin captured his attention like an arrow to a target, so much whiter than the tan smoothness of her face but no less beautiful for its pallor. With a valiant effort he tried to tear his gaze away, although the siren call tempted him to take another look, one more glimpse before rationality triumphed over the instinct to stare.

No *respectable* woman would ever do such a thing...but Frances refused to play by the rules of a society that would never accept her, he was learning. His admiration of her for it joined the worrying appreciation for those scandalous calves in setting alarm bells ringing in his head.

He knew he sounded choked but couldn't seem to help it. 'If you're injured, the wound should be washed and dressed immediately,' he ground out through gritted teeth, reverting to the safety of stiff military address in the face of his unease. 'Any delay could lead to infection, or gangrene, or worse.'

Frances's eyes widened. '*Worse* than gangrene? What could be worse than *that*?'

Jonah hesitated, realising he might *just* have veered off course. He was supposed to be winning Frances, not scaring her with tales of things he'd learned in the gory aftermath of wars when the surgeons' tents were crammed to bursting and the iron tang of blood hung heavy in the air...

He groaned internally.

Surely nobody ever secured himself a wife

with tales of amputation? Think, Grant—think before you speak!

Irritated by his foolishness, Jonah shook his head. 'Nothing. I only meant we ought to return to Barrow. I know how to care for a wound, if you'll allow me the liberty of tending to it, and the sooner it's treated the sooner it will begin to mend.'

Frances regarded him narrowly, the brightness of that glance undimmed by the pain in her leg. 'You want to come to the farmhouse? Even after the first time you weren't allowed to cross the threshold?'

'I thought perhaps having saved your life you might be more inclined to trust me.'

Looking down, Frances plucked a dock leaf from the grass, using it to carefully wipe the crimson stain from her fingers. When she finally lifted her head there was still a shadow of her usual caution, although the smallest glint of something else made Jonah wonder what was passing through her busy mind.

'I don't trust you, Lieutenant—but I'm willing to admit, given your service to me this morning, I might not dislike you quite as wholeheartedly as I did at first.'

Coming from Frances that felt almost like a declaration of true love. Jonah certainly had no idea what the correct response was, hoping his face didn't betray him as he got to his feet and brushed the hay from his breeches. A glance over his shoulder at the gate behind showed the bull watching malevolently from a short distance away, something Frances noticed too once standing—a little unsteadily, but with great determination—beside him.

He nodded towards the field. 'A dangerous beast.'

'It was my fault entirely.' Frances shrugged, beginning to lead Jonah away. 'I shouldn't have gone into that field in the first place. Being so tired all the time, I'm beginning to make mistakes.'

She walked with a limp and Jonah felt the urge to offer his arm. A tentative gesture in her direction soon put paid to that intention, however. Frances shied away from his hand like a skittish foal, the rejection setting a curious mixture of relief and disappointment nagging at him that he couldn't quite separate out.

Careful, man, he chided himself sternly as he followed Frances's uneven steps back to the farmhouse. There was a very real chance he'd damaged his chances when he'd caught her falling from the cart, some part of him knowing he should never have kept hold of her for as long as he had. If he didn't rein himself in she might retreat again and his efforts so far would be for nothing, all the progress he'd made with today's heroics lying in tatters at his feet.

The pretty house gleamed white in the morning sun beneath its crown of slate as they neared the gate to Barrow's yard, the wisteria-shrouded walls beckoning him closer, and something strange settled in the pit of Jonah's stomach. Frances was allowing him into her sanctuary, the outer ramparts of her fierce defences possibly starting to give way, and he realised he found her grudging acceptance far more pleasing than he should. If she was lowering her guard it would benefit the business proposition he was planning to make… So why did he feel a sudden flicker through his innards as Frances bent to greet the little white dog that ran out of the open door, before hesitantly waving him inside the very place she'd sworn so vehemently he would never gain entry?

He tried not to consider that question as he ducked through the low doorway to find himself in a clean and comfortable kitchen. The flagged floor looked freshly swept and a jar of white roses on the large, knife-scarred table filled the room with a delicate scent, and he found himself wondering where Frances found enough hours in the day to keep the place so neat on top of everything else. The stove was well blacked and the copper pans which hung from the ceiling gleamed, a clear sign she worked just as hard inside the house as out of it.

She stood leaning against a dresser stacked with blue and white china, arms folded and watching closely as if daring him to make a wrong move. From the air of defensiveness that radiated from her Jonah could tell she was on the brink of regretting letting him cross the threshold and he swiftly pulled out two of the stools set around the table before she could change her mind.

'If you sit here I can see to your wound. Do you have water and some rags?'

With another guarded glance Frances went to fetch what he needed, returning with a bowl and an old sheet. Perching on the stool next to Jonah's, she said nothing as he tore the material into smaller strips, although the look that flitted across her face when he laid a piece over his lap was more expressive than any words.

'Why have you done that?'

'Done what?'

Frances gestured to the ragged scrap of sheet across his thighs. 'I hope you're not implying I put my leg… ?'

Jonah raised one quizzical eyebrow. 'How else did you imagine I'd clean that wound, unless you'd prefer to lie on your bed?'

She bridled at once. 'Certainly not!'

'Then you'll have to allow me to do my work here. The sooner it's done the sooner you can get on with your own.'

Frances's mouth opened as if she had something more to say, but nothing came out, only a spot of pink appearing on each cheek to give away whatever she was feeling. She didn't meet his eye, looking down instead at her little dog as she gathered up her skirt for the second time that morning and then—with the air of one re-evaluating all of her life choices—placed her injured leg into his lap.

It seemed to Jonah the whole atmosphere of the room changed the moment Frances touched him.

Everything else fell away as he felt the heat of her beneath his fingers, the pale stretch of her leg snaking like a burning river across his lap. It was by no means the first time he'd been so close to a woman, but nothing had prepared him for the lurch of his heart at taking the slender calf in his hand and hearing Frances's soft gasp, an involuntary sound that made him look sharply up into her face—and then wish he hadn't.

With her cheeks aflame and full lips slightly parted she was too beautiful by far, threatening the cold restraint he'd built up all his life with one single flash of those hazel eyes. She blinked, dark eyelashes veiling their brilliance for a half-second, and before he had time to wonder what that tiny, *enticing* breath had meant Frances had turned her face away to fix her gaze firmly on the open kitchen door, the sunlight streaming through doing nothing to illuminate whatever she'd felt when his fingertips brushed her skin.

He bent lower over his lap, refusing to acknowledge the clamour rioting through him. 'I'll wash the blood off first. It's important for the wound to be clean before I bind it.'

Out of the corner of his eye he caught Frances's short nod but he didn't look up, instead soaking a strip of cloth in the warm water and laying it over her scarlet-crusted knee. She stiffened but didn't pull away from the sting and he began to carefully wipe away the mess of dried blood and dirt that surrounded the narrow gash, trying to make his movements gentler than he would have been for one of his injured soldiers. In his experience it was the biggest men that could be the most cowardly and he found himself approving of how Frances took the pain, submitting to his attentions without a single murmur.

She was brave and her stoicism, combined with how quickly she'd recovered from her fright, was something he had no choice but to respect. With each meeting she showed more strength than he'd expected, a million miles away from the burdensome prospect he'd always thought another woman would be and instead able to stand on her own two feet, an individual used to fighting her way through life's trials, just as he did himself. Frances didn't need a protector and looked to him for nothing, equally as determined to get by on her own as Jonah knew he was himself—and the novelty of such a thing was intriguing, far more so than Jonah knew he should allow.

The wound wasn't deep enough to need stitching although the water in the basin grew steadily more and more pink with each repeated dip of the cloths until finally he blotted her skin dry and bound it neatly in the last length of sheet.

'There. That should tide you over until tomorrow at least.'

He sat back and Frances withdrew her leg at once, muttering a low word of thanks Jonah barely heard. His thoughts were still far too busy to focus on much else, although from somewhere a gleam of his usual discipline came to take him firmly in hand.

Picking up the bowl of bloodied water, he carried it to the open back door, glad to be away from Frances as she examined his handiwork. Slightly nipping her lower lip only drew more attention to her mouth—the same mouth he'd been close enough to lean over and kiss, if he'd so chosen—and he steeled himself for what would come next as he emptied the basin onto the scorched earth outside.

Still with his back to Frances as he stood at the door, Jonah closed his eyes.

'My sister was wondering if you'd come to dinner tomorrow. She's keen to meet you and the children would like hearing about the farm.'

For a moment there was no answer, only the sound of the weathervane squeaking atop the farmhouse roof and the gentle bickering of Frances's hens as they went about their business. He was just wondering whether he ought to repeat himself when he heard her shift uncomfortably on her stool.

'I don't think I'll have the time.'

He turned from the door. 'Even you must stop to eat occasionally.'

Frances gave him a sideways glance, her cheeks glowing like a summer poppy, and Jonah felt his throat tighten.

The aim was to encourage Frances to think better of him, *not* for the situation to reverse itself. An invitation to dine with his family had indeed been issued by Jane and would present an ideal opportunity to draw Frances closer until she might be more receptive to his proposition, although after today's unsettling—and unexpected—meeting Jonah couldn't help feeling a shadow of reluctance. With Jane and the twins' futures at stake, however, he had to press ahead, although with that pair of pretty eyes upon him he struggled to think how.

'If nothing else, it would mean one less evening eating alone.'

It was a poor choice of words, accidentally referencing Frances's obvious loneliness, and a flicker of regret lanced through him as he saw her blink. He half expected her to refuse—even *wanted* her to, such clumsiness deserving no success—but then she dropped her chin, loose hair hanging forward to cover her face, and he watched as a wistful expression passed fleetingly over her countenance.

'I suppose… I suppose *one* evening away from the farm might be acceptable.'

Jonah managed a tight nod, hoping it might pass as pleased. She'd given the answer he should have wanted, but something inside him couldn't quite find the will to triumph. 'I'll tell Jane at once. I imagine you must have been wanting me to leave for some time anyway.'

Placing the basin on the kitchen dresser, he dipped a short but definitive bow, determined to cut their interview short. He'd achieved what he had set out to do, wearing away a little more of Frances's dislike of him, and he knew he needed to leave before any of the pointless sentiment he feared might be circling managed to sneak in. It was a weak, useless notion he wouldn't indulge, only leading to more unnecessary complications, and he was just about to walk away when Frances got to her feet.

'Lieutenant. Before you go.'

She hesitated before stepping forward, her skirts falling to cover those pale legs that had caused Jonah so much trouble. Her dark hair was swept over one shoulder and she fiddled with the ends of it, her brow slightly furrowed as if unsure of whatever she was about to say.

'Thank you for what you did this morning. It isn't easy for me to find pretty words, but I am truly grateful to you for saving my life.' Frances allowed him one swift look, fleeting as a rabbit running through fallen leaves, and Jonah felt his stomach clench. 'I'm not much used to anyone other than my uncle caring what happens to me, but… Well. I'm very glad you did.'

Jonah was a hard man. Life had not been kind, the scars carved into his soul by suffering and death too deep to ever fully heal, and he had long since determined there was no compassion left in him for anything other than his own flesh and blood. Frances was a means to an end and nothing more, and her words seemed to suggest his plans for the future might finally be starting to bear fruit… But for some reason that was difficult to remember as she stood before him, cheeks blazing but still radiating the independence he had already come to admire, and he found he was only able to touch his hat silently and turn away to leave her alone.

Chapter Five

Frances hovered beside the leaning fence where she'd hitched Apollo, breathing in the warm evening air and gazing up at the house in front of her with growing regret.

What was she doing *here*, of all places? Her distrustful eyes ran over the grimly familiar walls, their white admittedly brighter now and the windows far cleaner, but still the idea of going inside made her shudder. There were so many reasons why she shouldn't be anywhere near this cursed cottage and they taunted her now as she considered whether it was too late to turn back the way she'd come.

My wretch of a father lived here... My mother was probably dishonoured beneath this very roof... And now Jonah is in residence, possibly the very last person in all the world I wish to see.

She was undeniably grateful to him for having saved her from the bull, yet again demonstrating that beguiling concern for her that so set him apart from other men, but *not* for how easily he seemed able to commandeer her thoughts.

In the crackling tension of her kitchen he had taken her by surprise with his invitation, her mind already muddled by the scalding brush of his fingers against her skin. Even a day later she could still feel the ghost of it, the friction of the bandage he'd tied a constant reminder he had touched her where no other man had ever been permitted to stray—and that some dark, shameful part of her had *liked* it. That should be enough to warn her to be more careful. Now, the idea of dining with his family felt more like stepping into a lion's den.

Still working up the courage to enter the front gate, Frances patted Apollo's gleaming flank, unease growing by the second as doubts crowded in like hungry wolves. There was too much to do around the farm to be taking an evening off, and besides, surely there was no way Jonah's sister would enjoy her company. There were bound to be awkward moments where Frances said the wrong thing, her usual frankness taken as an insult or the soil beneath her fingernails noted and judged...

But damn it all. Something in her hadn't been able to refuse, and Frances could only reproach herself for her weakness. Living alone for so long, the temptation to feel some kind of acceptance was too great, even almost managing to outweigh her fear of the effect Jonah had on her wary heart. Spending more time with him was a mistake she couldn't afford to keep making, but the ache of loneliness persisted, no matter how strongly and stubbornly she might deny it. *One* night out of an entire life lived determinedly apart from others couldn't be her downfall, surely…or so Frances hoped, hefting down the crate she'd tied to the horse's saddle and finally walking up the garden path.

The door was answered at her first knock, swollen wood scraping inward to scuff over the hall's tiled floor, although the regrettable lurch of her innards as she saw who stood framed by the stone lintel meant she barely noticed anything else.

'Good evening, Miss Nettleford.'

Jonah had to duck slightly to fit through the opening, stepping to one side to let her pass. 'I'm glad you decided to join us. I wasn't completely sure you would.'

With a deep breath Frances entered the shadowy hall, wishing her heart hadn't begun to bound quite so loudly. Whether it was being inside her father's cottage or the closeness to Jonah she couldn't tell, muttering under her breath as he closed the door behind her and all hope of escape was lost.

'Neither was I.'

He looked at her but when she didn't repeat herself he let it go. 'May I take your hat?'

The crate she held making it slightly difficult, Frances undid the ribbons beneath her chin. She'd taken the precaution of wearing her best bonnet and cleanest gown, sure Jonah's sister must be as handsome as he was, but something other than her toilette occupied her mind as she handed it over.

Why was Jonah playing the part of a maid? Rose Cottage wasn't huge but certainly large enough to house at least a couple of servants, Frances thought as she took in the well-proportioned hall and passageway that led deeper inside, curiosity momentarily overcoming her unease. It was odd indeed for the master to open his own front door, let alone take a guest's hat, a notion Jonah must have realised as he hung her bonnet on a hook fixed to one wall.

'We have no help at present. I'll get round to arranging it but for the time being we can fend for ourselves.'

She nodded, a prickle winding its way down her spine as Jonah came a step closer. 'That's how my uncle and I used to live. He didn't hold with paying someone else for things we might very well do ourselves.'

'I agree with him. It's no hardship for a man to take care of himself—stops him from having too great an idea of his own importance if nothing else. It sounds as though your uncle spoke good sense.'

A small spark of pleasure glowed in Frances's chest at Jonah's compliment to the one person she'd ever loved, although it was rapidly replaced by a flare of panic as he reached out his hand. It was the same hand that had wrenched that accursed gasp from her lips, a tiny breath of scandalised delight at his skin on hers that she'd wanted to bite back as soon as it escaped, almost betraying herself to the very man she knew she had to shy away from like a startled fawn—

'And the crate?'

'Oh. Oh, yes. Of course.' Flushing right up to her ears, Frances let him take it, more thankful than ever Jonah couldn't read her mind.

You need to calm down, she chided herself as he lifted the crate's cloth to see what was inside. *He wasn't trying to touch you. If you carry on being jumpy as a scalded cat he'll suspect something's amiss, and you'll have no one to blame for it but yourself.*

She felt her fingers twine together self-consciously. 'It's only some fruit and flowers from the orchard. I confess I didn't know what kind of gift to bring for your sister after a dinner invitation, never having received one before.'

'Your generosity only underlines how great an injustice that is.' Jonah's voice was tight, although Frances quickly dismissed the notion it could be out of sympathy. 'It wasn't necessary to bring anything but I…rather, my *sister*, will think it very…kind. Thank you.'

Frances gave a vague dip of her chin that she hoped would be taken as a nod.

'It's the least I could do after yesterday's events. My leg is already feeling better, thanks to your…your…'

Mentioning the previous day was not a good idea, she realised at once. Already quickened by standing so close to Jonah, her heart raced faster still as the thought of his hand on her skin pushed its way to the fore and suddenly she couldn't think of anything else to say, allowing her sentence to tail off uncomfortably as she looked down at the ground.

Perhaps aware the situation teetered on the brink of awkwardness, Jonah gestured to the corridor ahead. 'I'm only pleased to have been of some assistance. But come through to the dining room. Jane and the twins are waiting for you.'

He led Frances down the narrow passage, her

nervousness rising as he stopped at a door left carefully ajar.

'Jane. Miss Nettleford has arrived.'

He stepped back to let her enter before him. Frances was just about to move forward when her breath froze.

Jonah's mouth was inches from her ear, his low murmur sending a great wave of heat beneath her skin to warm her from the soles of her boots to the top of her head. She swayed with sudden dizziness, unable to fully comprehend what he was saying as each word stirred the tendrils of her hair.

'One thing I would ask of you. Don't mention my sister's husband, the children's father.'

His quiet breaths teased the sensitive shell of her ear, tempting Frances to curve closer. Only a fraction more and his lips might actually touch her skin, surely the journey then from lobe to neck a short one Jonah could make with barely needing to stoop...

'He was lost to us quite recently and I would spare them the pain of talking of him until the wound has time to heal.'

Aware that all her blood seemed to have roared into her cheeks, Frances managed a feeble nod. So that was why Jonah was living with his family—to support his widowed sister?

Somewhere, in the last vague and distant

corner of her mind not completely overcome by sensation, she wondered at this newfound hint of compassion he had so reluctantly revealed. Stern, unsmiling Jonah had forsaken his career and comfort to take care of his lonely sister, a sacrifice that touched Frances somewhere close to the bone. It was so similar to the devotion Uncle Robert had shown Mama. It was not something Frances had seen for herself but obvious in every story her uncle had ever told of the young girl he'd lost far too soon. The likeness was uncanny, so at odds with everything she'd been taught about the selfishness of men that she wasn't sure what to think. There was only one thing Frances knew for certain.

You need to pull yourself together.

She ought to be ashamed of herself, feeling so flustered when a woman had lost a husband and children their father, and it was with her cheeks still aflame she tottered into the dining room to see a woman and two children seated at one side of a long table set with a clean white cloth.

This time when Jonah spoke it was loud enough for everyone to hear. 'Miss Nettleford. May I introduce my sister Jane and her children, Matthew and Margaret?'

Frances tried not to grimace as Jonah's sister stood up and came towards her, hand outstretched. *Her first impression of me will no doubt be a red beetroot crossed with a goldfish.*

'I'm so glad you came! It's such a pleasure to meet you.'

Frances took the proffered hand, feeling the bones no stronger than a rabbit's as she examined the other woman's face. Jane looked genuinely pleased to see her—more than could be said of most people in Marchfield—and Frances couldn't help the surprised words that came out of her mouth.

'Is it?'

Jane laughed kindly. 'Of course. My brother told me all about you and Barrow Farm—I almost feel I know you already.'

Frances's eyes flitted to Jonah and back again, one quick glance before she got herself under control. He stood beside the open door now, having set the crate down on the sideboard, impassive as always, apart from the smallest movement of a muscle in his jaw. It seemed unlikely he'd had much good to say about her, so tall and grim he looked more like a guard than a brother.

'I fear he must have exaggerated.'

'I wouldn't be so certain.' Jane waved towards a chair, dropping back into her own with barely concealed fatigue. 'Jonah has never been one to waste words on anything he deems undeserving, which more often than not appears to be most of the world.'

Privately agreeing with that sentiment, Frances took her own seat, wishing the two silent children would at least blink while watching her every move. Unease still swirled inside her but reluctant curiosity edged forward, trickling into the gaps left by Jonah's disturbing presence as she tried to curb the urge to look around the unfamiliar room. Her mother might have come to this very place and her father had lived there for years, the spectre of him filling every corner as Frances tried instead to focus her attention on her hostess.

There wasn't much resemblance to Jonah, she noticed as Jane gestured for her brother to seat himself. She had the tired fragility and pallor of one often unwell, the very opposite of his weather-beaten tan, and her china-blue eyes were unlike his warm brown ones, but both were undeniably striking and Frances could well imagine Jane had turned heads before widowhood dimmed some of her spark. She was a far less alarming prospect than her dour brother at least, her smile so inviting Frances felt the novel desire to return it with one of her own—until Jonah took the empty chair beside hers, accidentally brushing her arm as he sat down and for a moment making any movement of her lips quite impossible.

Saying grace saved her from having to speak although even with her eyes closed she was aware of Jonah's shoulder almost touching hers. It was uncomfortably reminiscent of the tense cart journey back from the market square, when the heat of his palm had burned through to her waist, and Frances didn't dare look at him as he ladled a rather thin stew onto her plate.

'I feel I ought to apologise for this in advance,' Jane murmured regretfully. 'I'm afraid I've never been much of a cook.'

She spread her napkin daintily over the lap of her pretty gown, something Frances noticed with a flicker of curiosity. Such a fine dress befitted a well-to-do lady, and yet she kept no kitchen staff and the stew had barely any meat. Clearly the family's circumstances had been drastically reduced, but how a man as high and mighty as the Lieutenant came to stoop so low remained a mystery.

As does the reason he took this house. Of all the places to choose, I wonder why Jonah thought this the best option?

Jonah's voice was deep as ever in the otherwise quiet room. 'I'm sure Miss Nettleford has no complaints, Jane. She isn't the kind of person who expects a great deal of those around her.'

He kept his eyes on his plate and Frances was glad he couldn't see the surprise that flitted over her face at his shrewd observation. It was true— if one kept one's expectations low they could never be disappointed when ultimately things went wrong, as—in her experience—they so often did. She'd had the habit all her life and Jonah spoke as if he understood it, perhaps even appreciating the distrustful side of her others found so unpalatable.

'Of course not. It was kind of you to invite me to share it, Mrs Millard.'

'Do call me Jane.' The other woman leaned forward earnestly, her smile returned full force. 'I should so like us to be friends. Marchfield is such a lovely town but I confess I find the society somewhat…somewhat…'

'Small-minded?' Jonah broke in drily, sparing his sister a brief glance. 'Desperate to know every detail of our lives, to spread like an infectious disease? Both are accurate.'

Jane tutted, although Frances saw she didn't entirely disagree. 'I was *going* to say lacking. I suppose there's no point asking you to moderate your views in front of your niece and nephew, who hang on every word you say and may very well repeat them?'

The children sitting opposite Frances giggled, the first sound she'd heard them make since her entrance to the room had apparently sealed their lips. Clearly they thought much of their gruff uncle. Her heart gave a strange leap to see the wry half-smile he shot their way—more evidence he might not be quite as unfeeling as she'd assumed. His mouth looked so different when set in a genuine curve, softer and so tempting that it was hard to look away.

'I sometimes think it's a good thing my brother has no intention of forming a connection of any kind,' Jane continued archly, thankfully unaware how her guest's thoughts were occupied. 'There's barely a person alive Jonah is able to tolerate for any length of time—indeed, it's almost a relief he's always been so adamant never to marry. I don't know that he has the patience for a wife.'

With her mouth full of watery gravy Frances could make no reply, although her gut contracted with involuntary swiftness.

Oh, no. Don't you dare.

It was a *relief* to have such solid confirmation that Jonah's intentions were pure, she instructed herself firmly as she tried to swallow a piece of beef that suddenly seemed to stick in her throat. A strange kind of friendship was the extent of what he offered and nothing more, and that hint of something approaching disappointment that had just turned in her stomach was to be crushed at once.

She should be grateful for what she had already—or at least the prospect of what might unfold. Despite her misgivings, it felt good to be among company, even if one of their number caused her insides to flutter like a trapped bird. Not since Uncle Robert died had anyone laughed at something she'd said. Jane's easy smile was like a ray of sunlight coming through the cloud of Frances's lonely existence, and she shouldn't do anything to jeopardise her good fortune. If this was having a friend then she liked it, Frances realised with a start—she hadn't known how much she'd wanted it until it had fallen into her lap, hardly able to believe it was possible after a lifetime of cruel whispers and hurt. It seemed at long last that somebody apart from her uncle might be willing to know her, and Jonah's thoughts on marriage ought not enter into things for a moment.

And they do not, the stern voice in her head piped up again, bringing along with it the memory of Uncle Robert to make Frances grit her teeth. *It doesn't matter if Jonah wants to wed or not. Even if he were looking for a bride it would make no difference, and that is very much the end of that.*

She forced the chewy gristle down her gullet. 'I'm of the same mind myself,' she stated firmly, fighting back the unsettling feeling that she was trying to convince herself as well as Jane. 'I've no taste for romance either. I'd never expect much of it in Marchfield, anyway—I fear you'll discover it would be embarrassingly difficult to find a man with anything good to say about me.'

Out of the corner of her eye she saw Jonah put down his spoon and push his plate away, but he didn't turn his head in her direction. Instead he seemed to be inspecting a long scar on the back of his right hand, smooth and silver now but when fresh must have glowed a livid, blood-filled red. Perhaps he was content to be talked about as though he wasn't in the room or perhaps he simply had nothing to add— although that indifference seemed to vanish at his sister's reply and he looked up sharply as Jane laid down her own spoon to twinkle across the table at her guest.

'I'm not so sure that's true. I could always ask Jonah for a summary of your virtues—you're one of the only people I've ever heard him speak well of.'

Reaching for his coffee cup with studied calm, Jonah shot his smiling sister a warning glance.

Of all the times she chooses to meddle...why now, when things were going so well?

He took a sip of the scalding brew, burning his tongue in the process, but at least it meant he didn't have to look at Frances. He could *sense* her confusion and catching a glimpse of her smooth cheeks filling with the rosy flush that became her so well wouldn't help his pretence of composure one bit. It was already a struggle to sit beside her as if her presence at his table meant nothing, when in truth each rustle of her skirts drew his attention like a moth to a flame, reminding him of the slender legs he knew—all too temptingly—were hidden underneath. Even the smell of her was an assault on his self-control, the scent of wild roses that came from her hair when he'd leaned down to whisper into her ear was so lovely he found himself wishing he could take another breath.

But I won't. He took a more measured sip, determined that neither vexing woman would see his unease. *I have to keep trying—assuming Jane's interfering doesn't destroy the progress I've made. If she frightens Frances away by making her think my intentions are anything other than cordial I won't be pleased.*

She was still watching him with that insufferable glint in her eyes and Jonah cursed himself savagely for his stupidity in allowing a single word about Frances to escape his lips. What had possessed him to speak of her at all, let alone with uncharacteristic approval? It was hardly surprising it had piqued his sister's interest. Jane would have learned of Frances in time and doubtless would have wanted to meet her even without his introduction. One damaged soul could recognise another—he might have saved his sister from the mire they'd been dragged up in but she could remember the misery of it as well as he could and her heart was still soft enough to feel for others' unhappiness and want to help. He'd sacrificed his own sense of compassion in order to keep Jane's intact— just as he sought to forfeit his comfort now to save her and the twins from ruin. He had to remind himself of that goal as Frances adjusted a stray sweep of hair, even that subtle movement capturing his attention at once to make one hand twitch briefly into a frustrated fist.

Get a hold of yourself, man. Repair the damage before it's too late.

He affected a shrug, hoping it was nonchalant enough to fool two pairs of sharp female eyes.

'I may have expressed some slight admiration for Miss Nettleford's farming endeavours. Anybody who labours as hard as she does deserves a degree of respect, in my opinion at least.'

Surely even the ever-wary Frances could accept a compliment for her work rather than her personal charms, Jonah thought as he waited to see if imminent disaster had been averted. If he'd praised the honeyed tone of her skin or glossy dark hair she'd be right to be suspicious of his motives, but any alarm she might have felt seemed to be soothed by his careful unconcern.

'Well. I suppose I ought to be grateful for such hard-won approval.'

He nodded as casually as he was able, while aware of the curiosity radiating towards him from the other side of the table. Jane didn't pursue the topic, however, perhaps taking her lead from her brother's stern glance, and the rest of the meal passed with far less dangerous conversation. His sister clearly enjoyed Frances's company, her sunken eyes growing brighter than he'd seen them in months as the two talked over a somewhat deflated sponge pudding, but as the evening wore on he watched with concern as the colour left her cheeks and he knew she was reaching the end of her energy.

By the time Jonah passed her the linen-draped crate Frances had brought, the effort of playing hostess had all but exhausted her. Fighting to keep her fatigue at bay, Jane gave a soft cry at seeing the roses, lifting them out to show the children.

'They're beautiful! Thank you, Miss Nettle-

ford. I'll put them in my best vase directly. You're
so very kind—I can't recall ever being given such
perfect blooms before.'

Frances shifted in her chair, her skirts brushing Jonah's leg to tempt him once again. 'You're
welcome, I'm sure. If I'm to call you Jane, though,
I think it's only right you must call me Frances.'
She looked down at the tablecloth, seeming almost shy faced with his sister's delight. 'And I
suppose you might, Lieutenant Grant, if you've
a mind to. Not that I'd assume…'

'Jonah.'

She lifted her head at his interruption, turning
to him for the first time in what felt like hours.
'Pardon?'

He hadn't meant to say it and Jonah felt himself tense at his momentary lapse of control. He
hadn't meant for his lips to move at all. Something in the unexpected sweetness of her bashful
face when confronted with Jane's praise, however, had made him speak without thinking, and
now he couldn't take it back, however much he
suddenly felt he was playing with fire.

It couldn't have been clearer she was more
used to unkindness than a genuine compliment
and her uncertainty was more affecting than he
liked, a fleeting glimpse of the vulnerability behind the impenetrable façade she presented to
the world. For almost his entire life he'd man-

aged to keep up the same façade, the merciless cut of his father's belt into the flesh of his skinny back enough to teach him—as Frances had evidently learned likewise—to keep any weakness close to his chest. More and more often he seemed to find similarities between himself and the enigma he had to try his hardest to wed, the harshness he'd taken such pains to cultivate threatened every time he saw fresh evidence she'd had to be strong too.

'Not Lieutenant Grant. Jonah. I'd like it if you'd use my name too.'

He saw uncertainty momentarily dimming the glowing greenish brown of her eyes and for a fleeting second she reminded him of a wild bird, beautiful but wary, ready to fly at the slightest provocation, never to be seen again. Would it feel like a loss if she did just that? Jonah wondered as he met Frances's gaze, aware of an uncanny tension growing between them as neither looked away. The shadows in the room had lengthened as the summer sun finally began to set, but he found he could think of nothing but the woman sitting so close beside him, their eyes locked in something unspoken, until his nephew's whisper broke through to shatter it like a dropped pane of glass.

'Look. Mama is asleep.'

The little voice shook Jonah from whatever

spell he'd been under, his good sense rushing back to replace the strange feeling that he'd been drowning in Frances's hazel stare. Tearing himself away, he saw Matthew was right. Jane's eyes were closed and her head had dropped back to rest against her chair, obviously worn out by the most company she'd enjoyed since Thomas had disappeared. She'd be mortified when she woke, he imagined, although he couldn't help but feel glad his sister had missed whatever just passed between him and Frances. If Jane had seen that long, bewildering look she would want to know what it meant—a question Jonah had no idea how to answer, his own confusion mounting as Frances abruptly got to her feet.

'I think that's my cue to leave. Your sister is clearly exhausted and I've been away from the farm long enough.'

Whatever just transpired had evidently unsettled Frances just as much as it had him. With a stiff smile for the twins she began to back towards the door, a little more quickly when Jonah rose likewise to follow her.

Out in the hall, Frances seemed much occupied in straightening her cuffs, attending more to the embroidery there than Jonah's face. 'Please thank Jane for her hospitality. She was very kind to invite me.'

Jonah resisted the temptation to seek distraction in his own sleeve. 'Of course. I only hope being in this particular house wasn't too taxing for you, given your...connection to the former tenant.'

He saw her swift sideways look towards the corridor leading deeper into the cottage, what lay beyond still unknown to his unsettling guest. 'Taxing, no. Provoking my curiosity...perhaps more than it should.'

'I can take you on a tour if you'd like. It only seems fair for you to see where your own father lived.'

She hesitated for a moment. Contemplation flitted across her countenance but was chased away by the shake of her head. 'Thank you, but no. I think too much might be overwhelming. I've seen the dining room—the rest of the house can remain a mystery a while longer.'

'If you're certain.'

A nod this time brought the subject to an end, although not the mixture of relief and damnable disappointment that washed over Jonah as he rubbed the back of his neck. Part of him had hoped Frances might accept the invitation to stay a little longer—but the more sensible majority prevailed to shoot it down. What he'd intended as an opportunity to make her more comfortable with him had turned rapidly against him and now he felt as though he was in danger of getting too close. That intense stare had stirred something in him, he couldn't deny it, and he knew he should draw the evening to a close before any more mistakes were made to threaten his best-laid plans.

'Let me fetch your bonnet.'

Almost glad to walk away from her, Jonah turned to where her neat straw hat hung against the wall. Probably he should have paid more attention to where he was going, but was too distracted by the warning bells chiming in his head to notice Frances directly behind him.

'You needn't act the maid for me. I can do it.'

She reached past him, suddenly at his shoulder and aiming for the powder-blue ribbons that hung down like a waterfall of silk…

…just as he did the same.

Jonah's fingers closed round hers to send a shock whipping through him as though lightning struck right where he stood.

By accident or fate he held Frances's little hand in his rough palm, feeling the calluses left by hard work and hardly able to comprehend how it had happened. He *should* let go at once as his coldly rational side demanded, but a gasp so like the one he'd heard as he'd bathed her injured leg had slipped from Frances's parted lips and as he looked down into her upturned face he couldn't recall when he'd ever heard a sweeter sound.

But he *couldn't* think like that. He *mustn't*.

She stared back and he saw her eyes widen at whatever she saw in his. In barely half a second they had blundered into something neither understood, the tension that had stretched out at the dinner table returning now to find them balanced on a precipice with only two ways to fall. Jonah could release her hand and pretend nothing had happened, praying Frances might do the same, or he could plunge into the abyss that called him to abandon all restraint, the perfect oval of Frances's face more tempting than anything he'd known before.

Jonah had never allowed himself to lose his wits in drink. Watching his parents' descent into that murky world had turned him away from it for ever, but as he pulled Frances to him he realised for the first time what true intoxication must be like.

And it felt *good*.

Everything about her was just so soft—warm skin and the gentle arc of her waist beneath his heated palm, her hair as he sifted it through his fingers and, perhaps most exhilarating of all, the tiny intake of breath he stole from her willing lips as he moved over them, exploring the unmapped sweetness no other man had ever been permitted to taste. Nothing existed but her mouth on his and Jonah felt the desire he'd tried so hard to fight well up with unstoppable force, his usual self-control no match for the merciless power of Frances's kiss. It was the very thing he should never have allowed and yet the urge to bring her closer drowned out all else, an instinct he had no choice but to obey as he held her tight against his chest.

She didn't try to escape, not even when his hand moved blindly from her hair to the sensitive nape of her neck to caress the slender curve with unsteady fingers. Instead Jonah's spirits soared as Frances tipped her head back to accept a deeper kiss, some vague part of him wondering how such an inexperienced woman could possess the skill to make a man's knees feel like water but not caring enough to ask. All he wanted was for her to stay exactly where she was, swaying like a reed in his embrace, so slender yet with a core of iron he'd grown to admire as much as her face—that unbending courage of the kind many a soldier could take a lesson from.

Their breathing seemed to have fallen into perfect harmony—or perhaps both had simply stopped entirely. Jonah certainly felt as though he was suffocating, the air in his lungs turning to flame as Frances's tongue ventured to dance with his so deftly he had to swallow a groan.

She was unmanning him more and more with every moment that ticked by, the boiling tide in his blood surging against a dam that could surely only hold it back for so long—

'Uncle Jonah?'

At the voice behind them Frances leapt away from him like a startled deer, eyes wide and her chest rising and falling just as hard as it had after she'd run from the bull. Even then, however, she hadn't looked as panicked as she did now, blazing scarlet from the neck of her gown to the very top of her head and one hand pressed to her bodice as if to shield herself from Margaret's sudden appearance.

'We were just… Your uncle and I, we were… We *certainly* weren't…'

Jonah's shock was no less than hers, although he recovered more quickly. 'I was helping Frances with her bonnet, Meg. Nothing more than that.'

His niece looked doubtfully from one tight face to the other. She might only be six years old but she wasn't a fool, Jonah knew, and the only way to stop any awkward questions was to change the subject without delay.

'She has to return to the farm now. There's a lot for her to do before the evening is over.'

He glanced over at Frances, a dead weight of regret already beginning to settle over his breastbone. She still resembled a cornered rabbit, refusing to look at him, her fingers clearly shaking as she scooped up her crumpled hat.

'Yes. Yes, there is. Perhaps…perhaps you and your brother might like to come and see it one day? Oh…'

From the expression that flashed through her eyes the words had obviously slipped out before she could stop them, too rattled and desperate for a distraction to think clearly until it was too late, but Margaret's face lit up at once.

'Can we? Truly?'

The rigid set of Frances's features increased but she had little choice but to attempt a nod. Jonah was all too aware of the power of his niece's smile. 'Of course. If your mama is agreeable to bringing you, nothing would make me happier than to show Barrow to you, your mother and Matthew. Now… I must bid you goodnight.'

His exclusion from the list told Jonah everything he needed to know, the desire to bury his head in his hands burning hot as Frances stumbled to the front door. It seemed she couldn't escape quickly enough, not waiting for him to open it for her as she wrenched it aside and all but fled out into the warm summer night, only pausing to throw him the briefest nod before rushing past with her bonnet obscuring her face.

He watched in silence as she unhitched her

horse and vaulted onto his back, as good a figure in the saddle as any general could boast. Jonah heard her low murmur and then the sound of hooves galloping away as swiftly as they could— and if Margaret hadn't been beside him he would surely have kicked himself hard enough to leave a bruise, cursing both his own weakness and the fact it had made Frances ride away from him as though trying to outrun the wind.

Chapter Six

Sitting on the edge of her bed, curtains still drawn against the pale light of a new day, Frances prayed yet again for rain. It was something she'd done many times over the years when her vegetables needed watering and the pump was running dry, but on this occasion her hopes had nothing to do with farming.

Please let it rain today. Anything to stop them from coming.

She felt another twinge of guilt and passed a hand over her tired eyes, wishing her own stupidity hadn't robbed her of much-needed sleep.

What was I thinking, asking visitors here? The very opposite of keeping my distance from others—and to ask those individuals in particular...

It wasn't the children's fault she'd invited them, only to regret it the next moment, but the thought of them arriving at Barrow that morning filled her with dismay, their little faces sure to conjure up images of their uncle far too vividly. Jane's note confirming their visit had done nothing to reduce the sense of constant dread Frances had suffered for the past four days, ever since Jonah had made her forget all Uncle Robert's lessons with the power of a single kiss. Even though the man himself was excluded from the party, seeing his family could only be the next-worst thing.

With a grunt Frances forced herself off the bed, feeling the all too familiar complaints of her overworked muscles as she staggered to the window and braced herself to peer outside. It was far too early for the sun to have risen properly and in the dim light it might *just* be possible for the sky to be a promising shade of grey…but, twitching the sprigged curtain aside, her hopes were immediately dashed.

There wasn't a cloud to be seen, the milky dawn breaking clear and dry, and Frances muttered a number of distinctly unladylike words under her breath. With no way out she'd have to endure the consequences of her actions, although the desire to wind back the clock taunted her as she dressed and pulled a comb through the wavy riot of her hair.

Catching sight of herself in her dressing table mirror just before leaving the room, Frances noted the shadows beneath her eyes, made darker than ever by four nights of next to no sleep. If she didn't put the events of the cottage from her mind soon she might lose her wits completely, the knot in her stomach pulling tighter as the memory of Jonah's intent face surfaced again to make her uncle's words echo harshly.

'Best to bide by yourself, Frances. Take heed of your mama's mistakes.'

He'd be so disappointed if he could see her now, and the knowledge raised a lump in Frances's throat so big the prospect of breakfast was impossible. Instead she thrust her feet into her work boots and left the house, Gyp hurrying at her heels, but even his pink-tongued grin was unable to lift her spirits as she moved mechanically to the chicken coop to collect the fresh eggs, the cackling of her hens falling on deaf ears and shame dogging every step.

I made a mistake in allowing Jonah to get so close—but that doesn't mean I have to do it again.

She should have known better but surely she wasn't the only one to blame. Hadn't Jonah made it clear he had no interest in forming an attachment, even his own sister believing that to be the truth? He hadn't been honest with either of them, clearly, and Frances felt a thread of anger begin to weave itself through her self-reproach.

Jonah was every bit as dangerous as Uncle

Robert had warned handsome young men could be, she saw that now, his pretence of friendship nothing but a lie. He'd come too close to creeping beneath her barriers with his pretence of decency and that persuasive kindness to his sister and Frances bridled to think he'd imagined he would succeed, although her defiance didn't completely eclipse the other feelings swirling inside her, regret and bitter disappointment settling like a rock, knowing how far she'd blundered down the wrong path before realising she'd been fooled.

She had kissed him, and she had enjoyed it, and there was nothing she could do to change that fact, no matter how much she sought distraction in backbreaking work or the repetitive tasks she busied herself with now, scattering grain for the hens and watching as they crowded round to squabble over every seed. All she could do was keep trying not to dwell on Jonah or his skilled mouth, for once glad Barrow's ceaseless demands left her little time to think.

The sun rose steadily, dawn coolness giving way to building heat, but Frances didn't stop to rest. The cows were checked and pigs fed before she turned to muck out Apollo's stall, jaw hard as she plunged her pitchfork vigorously into the dirty straw, and it wasn't until the yard's sundial read past ten o'clock that she wiped the sweat from her brow with the hem of her apron.

Jane and the twins will be arriving any minute. Just enough time for me to try to slap on a smile that might have half a hope of looking real.

She tried one out on Gyp, feeling her cheeks stiffen into an artificial grin that even the dog didn't seem to believe, before letting out a sigh. Perhaps by some miracle the Millards wouldn't come, leaving her to lick her wounds in relative peace without any reminder of the man who had inflicted them…

But no sooner had the thought crossed her mind than Frances heard light footsteps out in the lane and any chance of a reprieve was lost. Excited voices grew louder as she watched Matthew dart into the yard, followed closely behind by a much taller figure Margaret towed along by the hand—

Frances froze, the forced smile slipping from her lips.

Oh, no. Please, no. What is he doing here?

Jonah's face was even tighter than usual as he touched his hat to her, clearly aware his unexpected appearance wasn't welcome as he stopped a short distance from where she stood rooted to the spot.

'Good morning. I brought the children, as arranged.'

She stared at him, unpleasantly conscious of her heartbeat sounding loud in her ears. He looked straight back, infuriatingly handsome as ever for all his granite seriousness, and Frances had to curb the urge to let her eyes stray downward to that accursedly kissable mouth.

'The invitation was for Jane and the twins,' she managed through gritted teeth, determined to keep her composure despite more provocation than was surely fair. '*Not* you.'

Jonah glanced down at Margaret, still clinging to his hand. The little girl smiled back at him brightly with such complete trust it struck Frances beneath the ribs, for the briefest of moments making it hard to reconcile the child's faith in him with her own lack of it. It called to mind the unshakable bond she'd had with her own uncle before death had snatched him away, but she turned her back briskly on the unsettling thought. She'd been tempted into thinking there might just be more to Jonah than met the eye, perhaps something in him more worthy than the rest of the men who gathered around her like vultures, but this time not even Margaret's clear—and misplaced—adoration would be enough to fool her.

'My sister is unwell again today and cannot leave her bed. I suggested the visit be postponed but she asked me to go in her place.' He lowered his voice a fraction, the intimacy stirring the hairs on the nape of Frances's neck. 'I didn't think you'd appreciate my telling her why such a thing might not be…desirable to you. In the absence of any other explanation, I didn't have much choice but to agree.'

Frances felt herself redden at the implication but she coolly lifted her head. Jonah had imposed on her, deceived her and now thought highly enough of himself to imagine she cared what he did—and on her own property, no less?

That she *did* care was beside the point, she thought irritably. He needn't know it or flatter himself that she'd spent any time at all revisiting the kiss that had turned her whole world on its head and, drawing herself up to her full height, she allowed one cold shrug.

'I don't know why you think I'd mind you being here. It matters little to me what you do.'

Jonah's frown deepened. 'Frances—'

She cut him off, hating how good her name sounded on his lips. He was going to try to get round her somehow, probably with more tempting lies, and, quickly turning her full attention to the patiently waiting children, she hitched the smile back into place.

'So, what would you like to see first? Cows? Pigs? Or perhaps the orchard garden, where I need some help picking strawberries I couldn't possibly eat all by myself?'

Two emphatic nods decided on the latter and Frances began to usher them away, Margaret blessedly letting go of Jonah's hand to run ahead with her brother. One look from Frances was enough to tell their uncle he wasn't required to follow. He seemed to accept without argument, although he called after Frances as she strode away.

'Is there anything I can assist with while I'm here? It seems you have my niece and nephew well in hand without me and I don't like to be idle.'

Frances paused, one hand on the gate that led from the yard to the back of the house. A glance over her shoulder showed Jonah hadn't moved. He still stood beside the hay barn, so tall and comely he could have been taken directly from a novel, and her turmoil rose like a boiling tide.

'Do as you will, Lieutenant. It makes no odds to me.'

Matthew and Margaret's faces were pink with juice by the time Frances heard the faint chiming of her clock striking twelve, the sound floating through the open window of her kitchen to the orchard beyond. Where the past hour and a half had gone she barely knew, too many thoughts running through her mind to make much sense of any of them.

Straightening up, she lifted her full basket and looked around for the children, trying to sound more cheerful than she felt while their uncle's unseen presence jangled her nerves. 'It's time for luncheon, I think. If you run inside you'll find fresh bread on the kitchen table and butter and cheese in the pantry, and there might even be some jam. Go and help yourselves.'

The twins were off immediately, the lure of strawberry jam stronger than anything else, and Frances set her jaw. She'd have to go in search of Jonah now, she supposed, resolutely forcing back a flutter in her stomach at the prospect of seeing that tanned and handsome face.

The children can eat, see the animals and then leave. They can have a longer visit when Jane brings them, rather than their uncle lingering where he isn't wanted for hours on end.

With her mind made up, she carried her basket round to the front of the house and left it in the porch, turning to look over the sweltering yard. Jonah was nowhere to be seen. Her hens and geese roamed as they always did, while Gyp rummaged in the open-fronted hay barn hunting for rats, and Frances brought up a hand to shade her narrowed eyes as she wondered impatiently where he could have gone—until she heard a sound she recognised at once.

The unmistakable thud of an axe came again from behind the barn, ringing out above the rustling of the pigs in their sties against one wall of the yard. It was only a few steps for Frances to reach it and peer round the corner, although she soon wished she hadn't. The sight of what Jonah had found to occupy himself made any sharp words die in her mouth.

A pile of freshly split wood stood to one side of the patch of bare earth behind the barn, sunlight glinting off the axe's blade as Jonah raised it above another dry log. His brow was drawn into a frown of concentration and his hands gripped the handle with capable strength, but it was the state of his clothing that drew Frances's gaze like a falcon locking onto its prey.

Jonah's shirt hung open and loose from his powerful shoulders, forming the perfect frame to showcase a defined chest that even from a distance Frances could see gleamed with a sheen of sweat. Every ridge of muscle looked as if it had been chiselled from stone, only the sun-kissed smoothness of his skin a sign he wasn't carved out of granite as he brought the axe down, splitting the wood with no more effort than if it had been made of paper. A scattering of dark hair covered his chest, leading down like an arrow to the band of his breeches, and Frances's mouth dried to imagine—for the very briefest of moments—what might lie at the end of that *fascinating* trail. Every instinct screamed at her to look away, but she couldn't seem to obey as she watched him kick the chopped wood aside and wipe his forehead with the back of his hand, reaching up to make one bicep strain beneath the scanty cover of his sleeve.

Hastily Frances tried to gather her thoughts. It wouldn't do for Jonah to catch her staring, no matter how much her eyes wanted to drink in the sight before them with shameful greed, and she gave a loud cough before stepping out of the shadow of the barn and into the sun's full glare.

'There you are. I came to tell you Matthew and Margaret are at their lunch.' Frances scowled down at the log pile, carefully averting her gaze from Jonah's glistening chest as he turned towards her. 'You can have something too if you must, but not inside.'

Out of the corner of her eye she saw Jonah toss the axe down, the blade lodging in an upright stump by his dusty boots. 'Back to being banished from your house, I see. Not that I'd argue I don't deserve it.'

Frances's scowl grew deeper, a worm of uncertainty burrowing into her gut. If she wasn't very much mistaken she might have thought she caught a hint of regret in his low voice, almost as though he cared that her opinion of him had sunk from the tentative height his false friendship had raised it to, but it was difficult to think of anything else while his sculpted torso remained on such tantalising display.

She gestured in his general direction, still refusing—or daring—to look up. 'I wouldn't allow any man into my home dressed like *that*, no matter who he was. You are no different.'

Jonah's hands went at once to the front of his shirt, quickly fastening it across his enticing chest.

'My apologies,' he muttered. 'I didn't intend for you to see me like this. The sun is fierce today and I'd thought to keep myself cool while I worked…nothing more.'

She nodded curtly, painfully aware of a brazen little voice at the back of her mind that sighed disappointment the show was over. Swatting it away like a fly, she jerked her chin towards the towering heap of wood behind him, determined he wouldn't see her confusion growing like a weed at this puzzling activity on her behalf.

'What's all this?'

'I wanted to help. I saw the pile of logs to be split and thought it would save you a heavy job if I did it.'

'You think I'm not capable of doing that for myself?'

'On the contrary. My aim was to make some amends for my behaviour last week, not to insult you further. I'm well aware there's nothing on this farm you couldn't manage if you'd a mind to.'

Frances hesitated, her sharpness blunted by the unexpected candour of Jonah's stiff reply. The trace of something like regret she thought she'd heard before had grown more distinct— still difficult to detect in his gruff voice but there all the same, the faintest flicker of humanity beneath the ice, and it made a dent in the anger she'd held so close to her chest.

She couldn't have made it more obvious she hadn't wanted to see him that morning, freezing him out in both word and deed until only a simpleton could fail to get the message. Their kiss had been a mistake instigated by him. She'd been weakened by her pathetic longing for acceptance, his offer of friendship an obvious ploy to draw her in for his own nefarious aims…

And yet.

Frances swept another glance at the wood stacked at her feet, her confusion gaining strength. Jonah had chopped enough to last her well into autumn and possibly beyond, a task she had to admit she hadn't been looking forward to. Her back already ached and her hands were sore from relentless work and knowing she wouldn't now have to pick up her axe for months drew some of the poison from the wound Jonah's lips had burned into her heart. It was impossible to separate truth from lies when her own feelings were so unclear, her undeniable desire for Jonah clouding her usually clear judgement and making her more vulnerable than she was prepared to endure. Until their encounter he'd seemed so different from other men, his respect and apparent acceptance of her true self sowing the seeds of a tentative trust... But, for all she knew, her mother had once been in the same situation and chosen the wrong path, believing in an unworthy man when she should have turned and run. Trust had to be earned and Jonah had made her question whether he deserved it after all, his more admirable qualities potentially concealing the predator beneath, just as Robert had always warned.

Forcing herself to look at him, Frances balled her hands into fists. Doubt and suspicion crowded her mind, but Jonah's rich coffee stare cut through everything else to jolt her into speech.

'How am I to listen to a word you say when, for all I know, you're a man just like my father?' She lifted her head boldly, giving Jonah nowhere to hide. He didn't back down, simply watching her with that unflappable calm, and she couldn't help but admire the courage with which he met her searching eyes. 'How am I to believe you wanted anything other than to dishonour me—if indeed you think a woman like me has any further to fall?'

Jonah didn't look away from Frances's intent face, her provocative question left hanging unanswered. If he was to stand any chance of clawing back the ground he'd lost he would have to make a show of listening carefully to everything she said—although in truth his attentiveness was only part calculation.

A curious heaviness had lodged itself in his innards as he'd watched Frances ride away from him as fast as she could and he had the uncomfortable suspicion it was more than mere frustration that his plans had gone awry. The idea of her being displeased with him rankled somehow, especially now he knew how her lips tasted so warm and sweet, and this new comparison with her reprehensible father didn't exactly lighten the load. He was *nothing* like that man, nothing at all…or so Jonah told himself.

Frances's arms were folded in a resolute barrier across her chest as she waited for him to speak, the challenge in her face daring him to answer honestly, but he pressed his mouth into a tight line.

Everything I've done has been for Jane and the twins, not my own selfish satisfaction, he thought grimly. *Recommending myself to Frances was only ever out of necessity, the need to keep my family out of the gutter coming above all else. Courting her for some kind of cruel sport never crossed my mind for a moment.*

Jane's weak chest had worsened since they'd taken Rose Cottage, decades of neglect leaving patches of damp creeping up every wall despite the summer heat. She coughed more in the mornings and her tired spells seemed to come more frequently, and the worry for her that had plagued Jonah since childhood circled like an ever-present bird of prey. Her health—and possibly even life—depended on him finding the money to improve her situation and the twins' too, the shadow of his own impoverished origins lying long across his soul. He *had* to find a way back into Frances's good graces, even if his feelings had begun to blur into something he didn't fully understand, a notion he tried to set aside as her gaze never faltered and he attempted to find the right words.

'I'm nothing like your father.'

He saw Frances's mouth open as if to argue but he held up a hand before she could interrupt.

'From what I heard he courted your mother in secret, never intending anyone to learn of their connection, and when the situation became public he left her alone to bear her shame. I would *never* abandon a woman in that manner, nor would I give a damn what anybody said. Reputation means less to me than a tinker's cuss. I have never considered you fallen and I give you my word I never will.'

Frances's eyes narrowed, distrust still shining in their hazel depths. 'You speak of a *connection* but told me that was the last thing you wanted. You said you wanted to be my friend, and yet...'

She tailed off, finally looking away as a trace of pink entered each cheek, and for once Jonah knew exactly what must be running through her mind—the memory of him leaning in to seek her lips. The same thought sent a sudden pulse of longing through him, far lower down than was strictly polite.

'And I still do. My conduct at the cottage was regrettable.' He made his voice as flat as possible, hoping to conceal how his heartbeat had stepped up. 'I can only think my admiration for your fortitude overran its bounds, the line between appreciation and attraction blurring for a moment, before I realised my mistake.'

It was a pitiful falsehood and he knew it, but it was the best he could do while Frances stood before him, bathed in sunshine that lit every detail of her face as though a candle glowed behind it. Her jaw looked tight, the smooth line taut with strain, and it was damnably difficult to decipher her expression as she hid her thoughts behind a stubbornly blank mask.

Jonah ran his hand through his hair, thinking fast. He still had hopes for Frances and her farm, but now an unforeseen complication had joined the mix to make things ten times worse. He'd kissed her because he'd *wanted* to, because just the sight of her was enough to make his stomach twist with something he'd never felt before, but to admit it was impossible for a man determined to be untouchable. Allowing Frances to take up any space in his mind—or, a thousand times worse, his *heart*—went against every instinct for survival he'd held onto for more than twenty years. The prospect of exposing another vulnerability was unthinkable. To keep himself strong enough to protect his family he had to lock all weakness back in its box and learn to control himself…but Frances made that so *hard*, the repressed pain in her accusation piercing the underbelly of his apathy like a knife through butter.

It was *because* of his need to be strong that he recognised the same thing in Frances. The irony was so powerful that it stung. There was suffering concealed behind her harshness, the struggle of someone used to fighting every day in a world that tried endlessly to wear her down, and Jonah's insides knotted to realise she would *understand*. The weight of his responsibility to Jane, how his parents' abuse had convinced him that to care was to lay himself open for hurt—Frances would see the path of his thoughts with perfect clarity, a kindred spirit he still couldn't allow himself to accept.

She was too independent to be a burden, he knew now for certain. Instead, the danger she posed was of a different kind entirely. The worry now was how easy it would be to let her singularity sway him, her refusal to be anyone's victim touching a nerve inside him, threatening the foundations on which he'd built his entire life.

He lowered his voice, aware of its uncharacteristic gentleness but somehow unable to help himself. 'I have no intention of dishonouring you, Frances. I apologise wholeheartedly for making you feel otherwise.'

She frowned slightly at his tone, turning to look back at the barn so he couldn't see her face. The future of his family balanced on a knife's edge while she decided whether to accept his apology, and Jonah had to lean forward to catch her verdict when it finally came.

'I'll let no man make a wreck of me, Jonah,' she answered quietly, the note of warning clear.

'My uncle left the farm to me so I would never have need to tether myself to one who might only end up using me the way my mother was used. You can hardly blame me for erring on the side of caution, even if it comes as a knock to your pride.'

Frances glanced back at him over her shoulder, her eyes resting for a moment on the stacked logs he'd sweated so much to cut.

'I appreciate the wood, though. Thank you.'

Jonah smoothed down his cuffs, hardly noticing the dirt streaking the crisp white linen as he sifted through her statement like a miner panning for gold. She was still set as firmly as ever, then, on never letting a man get too close…

But she looked *so tired*. There were shadows beneath her eyes and her cheeks hovered on the edge of looking hollow, the life seemingly draining out of her by relentlessly hard work. If he could prove himself useful enough there might just be the possibility she'd still consider his proposal. Even Frances's pride was not enough to make her entirely blind to reason. It was the idea of a lover she rejected, not a labourer, and it could still be that all was not yet lost.

'I could come again tomorrow. There must be other things I can help with.'

Frances threw him a narrow look. 'If you did I wouldn't be here. I'm going to Cirencester market. My uncle and I would go a couple of times a year—we could get a higher price for our produce and I liked leaving Marchfield behind, even if only for a day. I shouldn't let my uncle's passing stop the tradition.'

She kept her arms folded but Jonah was sure he sensed a breath of hesitation beneath her studied composure.

'This will be your first time going alone?'

'Yes.'

'And that worries you?'

If he hadn't been watching for it Jonah might have missed the tiny raise of one shoulder. 'Perhaps. Only a little.'

A golden opportunity seemed to be presenting itself and Jonah spoke before allowing himself time to think. 'I could come with you.'

Despite the sharp lift of Frances's eyebrows he pressed on. 'It would give me the chance to prove myself. Even if you don't wish for my friendship I could at least be of some use to you, another set of hands if nothing else.'

'But what if that set of hands tried wandering? I've made my stance in that regard perfectly clear.'

'They won't.'

Jonah shook his head, even as the memory of how good it felt to trace the burning nape of her neck revisited to test his resolve.

The silk of her hair between my fingers...how softly her waist curved beneath my palm...

He gritted his teeth on a rising wave of yearning, his fingertips suddenly itching to feel the warmth of her skin once again. Once he made a promise he would have to abide by it, his assurance the only way to make Frances reconsider, but somehow he found himself reluctant to commit. Her strength and determination were growing harder to ignore every time he saw her and the respect they inspired did nothing to put his mind at ease. His thoughts were spinning now with treacherous notions he had no intention of indulging—especially since she'd reminded him with such crystal clarity that she wanted none of them.

'I'll keep my distance, and you have my word. The only way I'd ever kiss you again is if you asked me to.'

Frances snorted, yet there was a trace of dusky pink rose again on her cheeks. 'Don't hold your breath.'

'But are we decided? I'll accompany you to Cirencester tomorrow, giving my word I'll make no advances of any kind?'

She peeped up at him through long eyelashes that concealed the worst of her misgivings. By the quirk of her mouth he could tell a battle raged inside her mind, although which side had triumphed Jonah didn't know until at last she gave him one curt nod.

'Very well. If you're determined to be useful I won't persuade you otherwise.' She spoke casually enough and Jonah felt his innards clench—but with what emotion he couldn't quite tell. 'Be at Barrow for half past four—we leave at first light.'

Chapter Seven

R attling along the road to Cirencester, Jonah wondered yet again if he'd made the right decision to offer his help.

With every sway of the cart Frances's arm grazed his, a perpetual torture that after the first two hours was well on the way to becoming unbearable. The day had dawned humid and he'd long since rolled up the sleeves on his most workmanlike shirt, leaving no barrier between his skin and hers, and no choice but to grit his teeth on the torment of feeling her warmth so close but unable to reach out and touch. He'd made a promise and he'd have to keep it, although it seemed Frances was determined to make that as difficult as possible without even trying.

'We'll be arriving soon.' She didn't look away from the road, carefully navigating Apollo around the worst of the potholes. The sun was fully up now and the light glanced off the horse's glossy grey flanks, his tack jingling in accompaniment with the clip of his hooves. 'If you unload when we get there while I set up the stall, I'd appreciate it.'

'Of course. Whatever you need.'

Trying not to think about his burning right arm, Jonah watched the countryside gradually giving way to more buildings until they were in the town itself, houses and shops built from pretty Cotswold stone gleaming softly in the sunshine. Market day was clearly a busy one. Everywhere he looked other vendors were setting up shop, most simply resting long boards on top of barrels to create makeshift tables, but others raising cloth awnings to shelter them from the heat. The grumbling of chickens and honking of geese filled the air, along with traders' shouts, the scene reminding him of Marchfield's market square but on a far grander scale as Frances pulled Apollo to a gentle halt and scanned the gathering crowds.

'We'll pitch here. It's a good spot, the one my uncle always chose. Plenty of passing trade.'

She was off the cart before he had time to reply, her black skirts whisking over the side and away as she hitched Apollo to a nearby rail. In the next moment she was clambering up into the back to drag out an old table, heaving it down without pausing for breath and then hauling it across the cobbles. With every movement the sinews in Frances's slender arms flexed distractingly and Jonah realised he was staring far more than he ought at the slim but undulating muscles.

He stood up quickly, pretending he hadn't noticed the fragile shape of her shoulder blades straining through the back of her gown as she bent down to pull the table a few steps further away.

You're supposed to be here to help, he reminded himself sternly, *not sit around gawping. If you don't step in quickly Frances will realise she doesn't need you after all, and then you'll have wasted a chance to regain lost ground.*

With two of them working the stall was stocked swiftly, the table piled high with carrots, potatoes and squash and crates of eggs stacked neatly alongside, with baskets of cabbages placed on rugs on the ground and onions like pale moons tumbling from a sack. Preserves and fresh fruit were set next to them, strawberries glowing ruby-red and crisp apples with their rosy skins barely able to contain the juice within. Even if he hadn't been intent on winning her over Jonah would have appreciated all the hard work Frances had put into her goods, that tiresome admiration for her peeping out again like the sun from behind a cloud.

'Very impressive. I can't imagine many people will be able to walk by without stopping.'

Busy tying her apron, Frances glanced up, but she didn't seem displeased. Instead, Jonah's gullet squeezed as she gave him the closest thing to a smile she'd ever been gracious enough to bestow, a slight lift of her beautiful lips as she dusted her hands together like a woman on a mission. Even if he hadn't already been swayed by her forthright nature the arresting curve of her mouth would have stopped him in his tracks, all the more rewarding for how difficult it had been to earn and made lovelier still by what he knew lay behind it.

'It doesn't look too bad, does it? I only hope you're right.'

Curbing the desire to commit that smile to memory, Jonah leaned against the cart, folding his arms across his chest. Already potential buyers were being drawn to the colourful display and Frances stepped forward, taking up her place behind the table like a queen holding court.

'Can I do anything else?'

'Not at the moment, thank you.' She turned her head slightly, only her profile visible beneath her straw hat, but Jonah was sure he caught another enticing glimpse of an arc playing about her mouth. 'I can manage this part well enough.

If I have need of someone to frighten away my customers again, I'll let you know.'

Jonah had no opportunity to answer. After the first woman had taken her carrots, others pressed forward, Frances's stall rapidly becoming so busy she hadn't a moment to waste, and he watched with growing wonder at the change that came over her as she commanded her little empire among the bustling crowds.

She actually *spoke* to the women who came to buy, far more natural and friendly than he had ever seen her before as she showed them which potatoes were biggest or what apple might be most sweet. There was a cinder toffee for any child that peeped at her from behind their mother's skirts and a smile for every elderly lady that pressed a penny into her hand for a paper twist of seeds, and Jonah found he couldn't take his eyes off her as she called out to passers-by to come and see her wares. The usually tense, suspicious Frances receded into the background as this new creature emerged, a vibrant changeling left in place of the one he'd thought he was getting to know, vastly different but still just as fascinating as the other, two versions of the same person residing behind the face that made him want to stare. His confusion grew with every laugh that escaped her usually downturned lips as he leaned against the cart.

Is that how she would have been all the time if fate had dealt her a kinder hand? If she didn't feel she had to be always on her guard, ready to run the moment somebody gets too close?

It was a question without an answer, although he wasn't blind to the fact it applied just as fittingly to himself. In another lifetime he might have been raised with tenderness that left him enough to spare for another, his heart softer and more open to being shared. In *that* life, perhaps, Frances would be softer too, the two of them free to get to know each other without the caution on both sides that held them so determinedly apart. If things had been different then maybe they could have acted differently...but they weren't, and Jonah attempted to turn his back on such thoughts as he watched Frances go about her work.

'*Are you looking for onions this morning, madam?*'

'*Perhaps some strawberries, miss?*'

'*This cabbage has your name on it, I fancy. Will you come and see it?*'

She was clearly a gifted hawker. Time and again a coin changed hands, to disappear into the pocket of her apron, money that at one time Jonah would have considered small change before his fall from grace had forced him to reconsider. If he'd needed proof Frances and her farm were the best way of lifting his family out of poverty it was there in front of him, although the idea sent a skewer of discomfort through him all the same.

His face creased into a frown, deepening the one he always wore unconsciously. For a moment he'd almost forgotten the real reason he was there, the change in Frances so mesmerising it had chased out all other thoughts. It would have taken a man of stone to watch her and not be affected, her sudden whiplash alteration far too interesting to ignore—although stone was indeed what he needed to be if his hopes for the future were to come true.

Something I seem to find more and more difficult to remember.

Jonah rubbed his forehead, his hat doing little to spare him from the heat of the sun beating down as he leaned against the cart, Apollo waiting patiently a few paces away.

And to think once holding myself apart came naturally as breathing.

'Jonah?'

Frances calling his name cut through the clamour inside his head, ringing out above all else. 'Would you mind helping for a moment, please?'

He straightened up immediately, mildly bemused by the instinctive speed of his reaction.

Even as a lowly private he hadn't followed orders quite that quickly, but apparently the barest polite request from Frances was enough to make him stand to attention at the double.

'What do you need?'

She came closer, lowering her voice so he had to lean forward to hear her above the buzz of the crowds. Her face was pink and the smattering of freckles across her nose stood out endearingly clear, so distracting he had to force himself to focus on what she was saying.

'Could you bring out another sack of onions and whatever fruit is left? I'm almost out of preserves too. To think today has already been so profitable, and it's barely the afternoon!'

Jonah sensed Frances's excitement as she whispered to him, her enthusiasm snaking between the cracks of his usual cynicism to seek out any dregs of softness that might still lurk beneath. Once so impenetrable, it felt under constant threat now, the new sparkle in her eyes another weapon in the arsenal Frances had no idea she deployed more dangerously each time they met, and Jonah heard himself speak before he'd given his tongue permission.

'Surely that can't surprise you. I had no idea you were such a saleswoman. I think you could charm the birds from the trees if you chose.'

The compliment hovered for a moment, like

a bubble balancing on a needle's point, before Frances looked down at her hands.

'I don't mind talking up customers at this particular market. It's the ones closer to home I've no time for. We both know why.'

'Aye. We do. And we both know it's their loss.'

It seemed his tongue was determined to run away with itself. Frances slid him a sidelong look he couldn't quite understand and Jonah turned for the safety of the cart before any more incriminating words could burst free, his true feelings apparently so worryingly close to the surface they might spill out at any second.

He climbed over the tailboard and paused to take a swift inventory. A few barrels and crates still stood among the straw liberally strewn across the cart's floor and he crouched to retrieve three jars of gooseberry jam that had rolled under the seat. Kneeling on the wooden boards, he could hear the market all around but was screened from view of anybody passing by the high green-painted sides. Whoever called out to Frances could have no idea he was there, but the over-familiarity of their address made his ears prick up at once.

'Frances! Still the prettiest girl in Gloucestershire, I see. Not with Robert today?'

The voice was of the kind Jonah knew all too well and his brows knitted in a reflexive frown.

Loud, confident and demanding its object's full
attention, many of his fellow officers had possessed such a voice—men used to getting what
they wanted and allowing nothing to stand in
their way. The notion of history repeating itself
and yet another unwanted marketplace suitor
breezing up to Frances made his jaw tighten, but
he knew better by now than to intervene.

'No.'

'Ah. Is he ill?'

'Not any longer. He passed three months ago.'

'I'm sorry, I hadn't heard. My condolences.'

The man didn't *sound* especially sorry, and it
wasn't lost on Jonah that Frances had switched
back to her previously chilly form. Without
being able to see her, he knew exactly how her
face would be set with taut dislike, an expression she'd worn for him until he'd somehow been
able to melt the worst of the ice which stretched
out between them like a frozen lake. Treating
her like an equal was the way to do that, he'd
learned. Frances was more than worthy of respect rather than to be hunted like prey.

The newcomer, however, hadn't seemed to
notice his frigid reception.

'So you're here alone? That's dangerous for a
young lady. Perhaps *I* might be of some help to
you.' He paused for a moment, perhaps to give
Frances a smile Jonah knew she would not re-

turn. 'I'm sorry for the loss of your uncle but, I have to say, at least we have a chance to speak at last. He kept you so cloistered nobody was ever able to say more than two words to you.'

Still kneeling on the cart's floor, Jonah narrowed his eyes. *Of all the selfish, unfeeling wretches...*

If even *he* knew the other man had overstepped the line of what was considered civil then it must be bad indeed. A surge of pity and anger on Frances's behalf was about to drive him to his feet when he heard her speak.

Her voice was so cold it could have frozen the fires of hell. 'I don't need any help. I have a friend with me but, even if I didn't, I wouldn't accept the assistance of a man who considers my uncle's passing in any way convenient. You can keep your *two words* and spend them on somebody who actually wants them, because I can assure you I certainly don't, not now, not ever.'

There was silence, or at least it was as silent as the marketplace could be while life went on around the suddenly separate universe of Frances's stall. The chatter hadn't died down but the hopes of Frances's unwanted suitor clearly had, the sound of boots stomping away the only clue Jonah needed that the message had been received.

Distantly he realised he should stand up. If

Frances were to look into the back of the cart she'd wonder why he was sitting so still on the straw-covered boards, but her words rang in his ears so loud somehow his legs wouldn't move.

A friend, she called me.

A curious warmth welled inside him, chased immediately by a start of alarm. It was the very goal he'd been seeking, but now he hardly knew what to think, overwhelmed by the carousel of emotions he'd tried so hard so deny.

If his mind had been an artist's canvas, the painting would be a mess of different shades, colours clashing and bleeding into one another until no sense could be made of it at all. He ought to be pleased she'd admitted out loud how much her trust in him had grown, moving him another rung up the ladder towards achieving his ultimate aim of persuading her to accept his proposal of convenience, but it wasn't for that reason an unfamiliar ember glowed in Jonah's chest. Perhaps, by some miracle, she was coming to regard him as highly as he did her—perhaps seeing something inside him he thought life's harshness had long since snuffed out, his reluctant admiration of her having grown like a flower in a desert, despite the arid ground...

But the next moment the ember's tentative spark was doused as reality crashed over him like a flood, stopping any cautious hope dead in its tracks.

If Frances *was* coming to tolerate him, *like* him even, it would only make his life more difficult. Any encouragement from her would only make his own dizzying descent into madness worse, when the cold hard fact that she wanted no man's regard remained unchanged. Her fondness for him—if indeed he could call it that—would never be anything more than platonic, but it could set him on a hazardous path, stoking the fire that already smouldered inside him to new and worrying heights. He'd meant their acquaintance to remain one of mutual convenience and yet his heart was in real peril of betraying him into admitting the emotion he'd forced aside for so long. Falling for Frances would leave him open to hurt later on, when it became clear she would never feel the same way—the very thing he'd never wanted to happen, knowing for all his life that to allow others in was a recipe for pain.

He needed to pull himself back from the abyss before he stepped too close to the edge. Under any other circumstances he'd simply turn away, abandon his plans in favour of something less risky for his soul…although, as he slowly got to his feet, Jonah knew he had no choice but to stay the course. The wheeze in Jane's lungs grew worse by the day and the shadows beneath her eyes darkened, robbed of sleep by nights spent coughing green muck into a handkerchief so the children wouldn't see. If it was a choice between his sister's life and his own feelings Jane would triumph every time, and yet the prospect of growing closer to Frances cut deeper each time he thought of it, his gaze instinctively seeking her as he stood high up in the back of the cart to look over the side.

She was still standing behind the table, her back to him but tension written in the angle of her narrow shoulders. Her hands were screwed into fists at her sides as if she longed to run after the stranger and knock him to the ground, and Jonah was about to call out to her when she turned around, her face shadowed by the wide brim of her hat, and for the briefest half-second of agony his heart stopped.

Frances looked straight up at him, her eyes finding his and their brilliance refusing to let him break away. Something crackled in the air, like static or the strange silence before a storm, the bustle and noise of the market growing hazy as Jonah felt his heartbeat resume with a clumsy thump.

There was something in her tanned face he couldn't name, another unexplained connection like the one that had passed between them as they'd sat at his dining table and he'd pretended his pulse hadn't leapt up to the sky. Had she somehow read his mind? He had no idea what *she* was thinking, no idea at all—only able to keep staring into those hazel depths, beautiful but filled with such sadness and loss he felt it radiate from her, and hope they hadn't cut a window into his soul. Pity he knew she wouldn't want stirred in places he'd forgotten even existed.

But then she turned back to her table as though nothing had happened, and the sounds of the market all around them burst back into life…and Jonah could only wait for his breath to return as he wondered what the hell—if anything—that had *meant*.

Frances was exhausted by the time she flicked Apollo's reins to guide him into a faster trot, barely able to sit upright in her seat. The sun had already set but they still had miles to go before the spire of Marchfield's church appeared on the skyline, although it would be far too dark to see it by the time they reached home.

Jonah sat in silence at her side, an indistinct shape in the gloom. Whatever he was thinking was clearly nothing he wanted to share and Frances found she was grateful he had no gift for small talk. Seeing that idiot Charles Arden had tainted what might otherwise have been the first pleasant day she'd had since Uncle Robert died and she was in no mood for pointless chatter as she turned the unwanted encounter over in her head. It was probably a mercy Jonah hadn't overheard. He might have tried to intervene, causing more of a scene than she had herself in her cold, hard rage, and she had no wish to be as infamous in Cirencester as she was at home. Arden had presumed on his scant acquaintance with Robert as a fellow farmer to impose on her and the memory of his ruddy face, first leering and then indignant, made her upper lip curl.

To think he imagined it was only my uncle's presence that stood between us. Why are so many men delusional? Can they truly think they only need wink at a woman for her to desire them?

She scowled into the darkness. What he'd said about her uncle's passing was unforgivable, tearing into a wound that had barely begun to heal. The grief that sat within her as a constant chaperone flexed its claws and Frances pressed a hand where they raked beneath her bodice as if trying to cut out her heart. Usually she was alone when the weight of unhappiness became too heavy to bear...but a glance to her side helped lift the smallest fraction of the load.

There was something oddly comforting about Jonah's quiet presence. Perhaps it was the solid shape of him, sculpted muscle hidden beneath a linen shirt, or perhaps the calm he showed in every situation. Whatever it was, Frances realised she was pleased he was nearby, something she'd never dream of telling him but true nonetheless. He'd been as helpful as he'd promised to be and a little more of the tension unwound as she watched him out of the corner of her eye.

I'll admit I'm not sorry I took a chance in letting him redeem himself. It was a risk—but by his behaviour today there might just be the possibility he isn't a lying cad after all.

His profile was barely visible, only just lit by a thin sliver of moon peeping from behind the clouds, but she could just make out how he stared directly ahead. The dim moonlight blanched his face a ghostly white and for one puzzling heartbeat Frances thought his expression was haunted likewise, although when he glanced over she saw she must have been mistaken.

'Is something amiss?'

'No, no.' Quickly averting her eyes back to the road, she hoped Jonah hadn't caught her watching him. 'Just tired, that's all.'

'I'm not surprised. Sometimes today it seemed as though you had eight hands, the way you were able to do so many things at once.' He stretched out his arms, bringing his own hands up to rest behind his head. 'I can't recall when I've met anyone more capable, and that includes half the British Army.'

Glad the darkness hid her cheeks, Frances couldn't think of a reply. From any other man she'd have batted the compliment away like a fly, but as she urged Apollo over a rickety wooden bridge she had to admit Jonah was different. Somehow he had begun to tunnel under the ramparts she'd built to keep everyone out, waging a war of attrition she was starting to fear she might lose. Once such a prospect would have been unthinkable, laughable even, but now Frances had to wonder…

If he did manage to break through, would it still only be friendship he sought?

Frances tightened her grip on the reins. She'd been so sure that would be the extent of their connection, so adamant he wouldn't be allowed anything more, and his behaviour towards her ever since his promise had been above reproach. Jonah hadn't tried to kiss her again, or placed his warm hand on her waist, or even so much as snatched a glance at her figure, and as much as she tried to convince herself she was glad of it, one sensation kept returning to circle through Frances's mind.

Disappointment.

Her frown grew deeper and she sat up a little

straighter in the hard wooden seat, her aching back protesting.

I said no to him. And I meant it.

He'd respected her decision, as well he should, and if some ridiculous part of her tempted her to change her mind she would pay it no attention—even if the day had highlighted just how different he was from the other men she knew, Mr Arden's presence only emphasising Jonah's superiority in every way. When Jonah spoke to her it was as an equal, not a potential conquest, and he had never looked at her with the smirk so many others thought improved their chances. He'd worked hard without either complaining or expecting anything in return, hefting heavy loads all day beneath the scorching sun, and with a jolt Frances realised she might actually have been telling the *truth* when she'd told the other farmer that Jonah was her friend.

She blinked into the darkness, unsure how to feel about the revelation her subconscious had just dumped into her lap. It was so unlikely… and yet surely she couldn't deny…

Frances felt the sideways lurch of the cart before she heard Apollo's high neigh, its shrillness splitting the night's silence, and instinctively she hauled on the reins.

'Steady, boy! Steady there!'

Beside her, Jonah jerked forward, his hand

reaching at once to keep her in her seat, and Frances felt a burst of fire sweep the length of her body as his fingers tightened on the first thing he found to grab, the very top of her thigh, a place so intimate Frances thought she might have burst into flames if her attention hadn't been fixed on keeping the cart on its wheels.

Whatever had spooked the horse did a thorough job. He skittered to one side, throwing his head back and the whites of his eyes shining in the moonlight, and Frances felt a stab of fear alongside the fireworks in her gut. If she couldn't calm Apollo he might injure himself or break the cart, neither of which she could afford. With every wild thrash the danger grew and without hesitating she threw the reins to Jonah and leapt to the ground, only dimly aware of a sudden chill on her thigh where a warm hand had rested.

'Frances!'

Heedless of Jonah's concern, Frances cautiously approached Apollo's head. He looked down at her, wide eyes rolling, but he didn't pull away as she slowly reached out to take hold of his bridle.

'Shh, now. Shh.'

He snorted, still moving fretfully and his ears back, although he began to still as Frances ran a hand down to rest on his nose. Apollo grumbled, pulled a little and then relaxed, his huge body twitching but the crisis clearly passed.

'Shh, that's better. Good boy. Did something scare you?'

She looked around but the darkness gave nothing away. They'd stopped beneath a stand of trees, leaves rustling in the night air, and a shiver crossed her skin. Whatever had frightened Apollo would be long gone by now, disappeared into the shadows, although she had other things to worry about as she swiftly checked him over.

'Damn it! He's thrown a shoe.'

She heard Jonah jump down behind her but didn't turn around, too dismayed even to move. Exhaustion threatened to overwhelm her, like a hound after a fox. She was already so tired she could have cried and the prospect of what this would mean sent her heart sinking to her boots.

'I'll have to leave the cart and lead him the rest of the way back to Marchfield on foot.' Frances closed her eyes, resignation and despair making them even heavier.

Of all the times for Apollo's nerves to get the better of him...

'There's no blacksmith within miles of here and even if there was it's too late.'

Opening her eyes again, she saw Jonah step up to the horse's head and calmly stroke the white blaze. Even in the moonlight she could see the set of his expression and knew he was going to disagree before he'd even opened his mouth.

'It'll take hours to walk back and you already look dead on your feet. Why not sleep here and we'll go at first light? You need rest, especially after today.'

'Sleep here?' Frances froze in the act of patting Apollo's smooth neck. 'With you?'

It wouldn't be the first time she'd slept in the back of a cart, the stars casting a sparkling canopy above and straw prickling at her back—but then she'd been with Uncle Robert, not a man who drew her to him like a moth to a candle flame with no effort at all, and the thought of it made heat flare beneath her skin. To imagine Jonah lying so close was enough to make her dizzy, but Frances forced herself to remain calm. If she refused his aggravatingly sensible suggestion he would want to know why, and she would no more admit her increasing attraction to him than she would tear off her own arm. With no other choice, and midnight fast approaching, she had to agree, although it was difficult to prevent a strangled note from entering her voice.

'I suppose we don't have any other option.'

'Quite.'

Was it possible there was something in Jonah's tone as he gave his curt reply? Frances couldn't quite tell, busying herself unhitching Apollo and leading him off the rough road. It didn't take long to slip his reins over a low branch and make sure he was settled, and then there was nothing left but to slowly walk back to the cart, Frances's legs carrying her forward but weakening with each step.

As she climbed unsteadily over the tailboard Frances's stomach fluttered to see Jonah already stretched out in the straw, his long legs catching her eye despite the gloom. The floor didn't leave much room for two people, let alone one as tall as Jonah, and Frances had to take great care not to touch him as she awkwardly lay down and tucked her skirts around her. He didn't move, not even the slightest rustle of straw as Frances fiddled first with her hair and then tried to find a comfortable position on the hard boards, muttering a curse when her elbow banged against the side.

Finally she fell still, although a strange kind of nervous energy coursed through her and suddenly she didn't feel tired at all. All she could focus on was Jonah lying barely a hand's breadth away and she laced her fingers together firmly against the alarming urge to reach out and know for certain. Only the thin sleeve of his shirt separated his skin from hers and she wondered if it was the heat of his body she could feel, or whether the flush creeping over her was from her own desire to rise up on one elbow and trace the handsome line of his profile with one fingertip…

'Have you finished fidgeting?'

Jonah's voice drifted through the darkness and Frances started guiltily.

'Yes.'

'Good. Now we can both get some sleep.'

She heard the cart creak as he settled himself and then silence descended, the soft whisper of leaves the only sound as Frances determinedly closed her eyes. Her body was weary even if her mind insisted on whirring and she hoped sleep would come to claim her soon, the sole escape she had from the many temptations of Jonah's presence.

But it seemed fate was against her.

A midnight breeze stole over the cart, raising goosebumps on Frances's skin as it passed, and she huddled into a tighter ball. Wrapping her arms around herself, she clenched her teeth on a shudder, the thin fabric of her gown no match for the cool night air. In the daytime heat her short sleeves had been a blessing but now every little hair stood up on end and Frances could have kicked herself for not thinking further ahead and packing a shawl under the seat.

With her eyes still closed she heard Jonah shift slightly.

'Are you cold?'

'No.'

'Frances. I can hear you shivering.'

She was about to argue, to declare she was doing nothing of the sort, when he went on. 'You'd be warmer if you came closer. It's easier to share body heat the closer you are.'

Her eyes flew open at once. 'Come closer?'

'If you intend on sleeping at all I think it would be wise.'

He sounded unmoved by the prospect of her curling up with him—perhaps unflatteringly so?—but Frances didn't dare reply. There was no way her own voice could possibly be that steady, her innards twisting into a sudden knot.

Heaven help me!

It was enough of a trial lying next to Jonah as it was and now he wanted her to move closer still—nearer to his warm, firm body. The image of his glistening bare chest flashed through Frances's mind before she could stop it. She'd be able to run a hand over it if she were any closer, perhaps trace the fascinating terrain of muscle hidden beneath his shirt, and the overwhelming temptation to do just that stole any hope of speech from her nerveless lips.

When she didn't respond she heard him quietly clear his throat.

'You can relax, Frances. I remember my promise. You needn't fear.'

His sincerity pierced through the whirl of her thoughts with welcome calm. As cool and serious as ever, Jonah didn't waste words when they weren't needed, and his assurance was enough for Frances to grit her teeth on the worst of her panic. From any other man she wouldn't have believed such a vow for a moment, but Jonah had little in common with any of *them*, his contrast to the boorish Mr Arden like night and day. He had made a mistake in kissing her but he'd apologised and attempted to repair the damage, and she couldn't deny he hadn't put another foot over the line since she'd reminded him of where she'd drawn it.

He's my friend. Just my friend. I can remember that—as apparently he can too.

It was just one night, one measly night to control the disloyal longings of her lonely heart, something she should be able to do with ease after so many years of holding herself apart. Jonah was evidently set on respecting her boundaries even if she barely knew what they were any more, and eventually the exhaustion coursing through her body won over everything else.

Without a word she wriggled sideways a fraction, and then a little more, until she gently came to rest against the long length of Jonah stretched out on his back. She lay perfectly still, not feeling the hard floor beneath her any more or the prickle of straw against her skin, the slow rise and fall of Jonah's chest the only thing she could focus on as he retreated into whatever kind of dreams a man like him had. It was definitely warmer huddled at his side, her goosebumps gradually subsiding as the heat of his body crept into her bones and drove off the night's chill, and her aching muscles rejoiced to be allowed to rest at last.

But it was still quite some time before Frances fell asleep.

Chapter Eight

Nestled into the downy mattress of the feather bed, Frances couldn't recall a time she'd ever been more comfortable. The room was hazy and indistinct, its walls perhaps a soft grey, but not important enough to notice as she looked across at the man sharing her pillow, his arms around her and their legs a tangle of warm, heavy limbs. Her husband gazed back, his lips lifting in a smile that made her heart sing, and it seemed the most natural thing in the world to reach up and kiss Jonah's curving mouth.

And why not? It was only a dream, after all.

She felt him stir but she didn't draw back, instead pushing forwards until his arms tightened and he pressed her closer to his chest, his shirt smooth under her fingertips but the heat beneath it burning through. The clever dance of his tongue made her feel weak, unable to move as his leg slid between hers to pin her to the mattress, but the thought of escape never entering her mind. Her hand came up to cup the back of his head and hold him to her, the other tracing a scorching path down his back to force a growl from Jonah's throat, and when he deepened the kiss she wondered—distantly—*why* she'd been so set on avoiding matrimony if this was what it meant. Perhaps a man in her bed wasn't the worst thing in the world, although the revelation was crowded out at once by Jonah's lips teasing the sensitive spot beneath her jaw, the pulse there bounding wildly as he lifted his head again to smile down at her so wickedly she almost gasped before he stole it from her open mouth.

It was difficult to tell where she ended and he began, their bodies locked together so tightly not even a whisper could have slipped in between. Lying in Jonah's hold Frances felt safe, his capable strength shielding her from the pain and grief that usually sat inside her like a stone, and she revelled in the knowledge that for once *she* didn't have to be the one who was strong. Jonah's kiss was exciting, rousing her in places she'd never known she had, but more than that, he offered her sanctuary from life's harshness, and as she twined her fingers through his hair she felt her spirit lighten as if he'd lit a fire in her soul.

But then he started pulling away. Gathering darkness had begun to flood the room and the more Frances clung to him the further away he seemed, retreating so quickly she couldn't keep up. His voice calling her name echoed in her ears, closer and more distinct despite his disappearing into the gloom, and she felt herself being hauled upwards through the layers of her own unconscious mind…

She opened her eyes.

In the dim dawn light Jonah's face was mere inches from hers, his breath coming quickly and a look of uncertainty replacing the usual frown. One hand lay across her waist, and they stared at each other in stunned silence until both sat up abruptly at the same time.

'Did I…?'

'I'm sorry. I didn't realise you were still asleep at first. I was half asleep myself or I would have pulled away far sooner…'

She watched Jonah drag a hand through his tousled hair, the action doing nothing to slow the frantic thumping of her heart. Absolute undiluted mortification swept over her, horror for both what she'd done and might have mumbled in her sleep making Frances's cheeks flame hotter than the surface of the sun.

'It's me who should apologise. I must have been dreaming.'

About being married to you.

The awkward truth piped up unhelpfully and

Frances shoved it back before it could escape, embarrassment spreading like wildfire. If *that* little snippet got loose she'd combust on the spot, the mere thought making her prickle all over.

The frown was beginning to form once again on Jonah's brow. 'Please believe I had no intention of kissing you. I gave you my word and I never would have broken it if I hadn't thought… if we hadn't been so…'

He broke off to gesture vaguely in her direction, even his usual cool rattled, and Frances wanted to hide her face in her hands. It had only been half a dream then, no feather bed or marriage licence but a kiss right enough, the ghost of his arms around her and his mouth bearing down more real than she'd known. At some point during the night they must have slipped into an embrace and slept wrapped in each other, until her secret desires drifted to the fore, encouraged by the unwitting intimacy, and in sleep she'd acted as she longed to when awake. *She* had been the instigator—Jonah had come to his senses first and pulled back. She had nothing to reproach him for, although that didn't make it any easier to meet his eye.

'I know you wouldn't. Whatever just happened was my fault, not yours… Sleeping so close together must have confused me and then whatever it made me dream carried on too far.'

It was hideous to admit what had been running through her head but thankfully Jonah didn't press her any further. He squinted up at the sky. Pale early-morning light was filtering down through cloud that would hopefully take the edge off the day's heat.

'Of course. It never occurred to me it would be anything else.'

That seemed unlikely to be true but Frances seized the lifeline gratefully. If stern, no-nonsense Jonah ever learned she'd dreamed of being his wife he'd probably rethink his desire to be her friend, she realised as another wave of embarrassment rose up to engulf her. He'd probably run for the hills, the very thing she'd have done once upon a time before he'd arrived, making her question everything she thought she'd known.

She stood up, mumbling something about seeing to Apollo before clambering over the tailboard and down to the ground. The horse whinnied a greeting at her approach and she stroked the long nose before checking his shoeless hoof, pleased to find it undamaged. As long as they went gently the walk back to Marchfield would be fine, although the sooner they got going the better. There was still a full day's work to do as well as finding the time to ride back for the cart and Frances didn't know whether to feel relieved to hear Jonah come up behind her.

'I imagine you'll want to set off soon. Is there anything you need me to do before we go?'

She shook her head, noting he didn't try to come too near.

Perhaps he's anxious you might try to kiss him again, the same unhelpful little voice suggested, once again offering an unwanted truth. *It seems he's not safe from you while you're sleeping—how much more dangerous are you when awake?*

'Only watch Apollo while I fetch us all some water. There's a stream on the other side of these trees. I won't be a moment.'

Frances hurried away through the undergrowth, pausing briefly to retrieve the flasks and bucket from the cart. The image of Jonah's dream smile followed her all the way to the stream, something not even hastily washing her face with ice-cold water was able to wipe away, and by the time Frances returned a new anxiety had planted itself firmly. It would take at least another couple of hours to walk to Marchfield and she bit back a groan, wondering how much of it would be spent in strained silence now she'd thrown their burgeoning friendship into fresh disarray and Jonah's kiss still lingered on her lips, both the real and the dream merging into one.

They set out as soon as Apollo was fed and

watered, Frances leading the horse gently along the uneven road. He would have followed her even without the rope but she was glad of something to occupy her hands as Jonah walked beside her, not saying a word but his presence making her fidgety nonetheless. It was so hard to know what he was thinking behind that stern mask, giving no clue whether he felt as embarrassed as she did by their passion that was no less intense for being accidental. The longer they walked beneath the stirring trees the more a sense of unspoken tension grew, feeding off their silence like a leech gorging itself on a wound.

After about half an hour of wordless torture Frances couldn't take any more.

'Will Jane have been worried when you didn't come home last night?'

Jonah glanced over with the look of one roused from being lost in thought. 'I'm not sure worried is the word. Curious perhaps about what could have delayed us, but she knows better than to worry about me by now.'

Determined not to allow another unbearable pause to settle, Frances stumbled on. 'I know I'll be glad to get home. I may even allow myself a glass of plum wine after this mess.'

'Is that a treat?'

'It is to me. My uncle and I would have some

to celebrate every time we had success at market.' She carried on talking, realising she was gabbling to fill the silence but unable to help herself. 'I think a stressful time is just as deserving of a reward. Do you not like it? I've heard some men say it's too sweet.'

'I couldn't say. I've not so much as taken a sip of strong drink in my life.'

Frances's brows rose. 'What? Never?'

She watched a flicker cross Jonah's face, a slight tightening of his jaw, almost lost among the undulating shadows of the trees. He looked down at her seriously, searching her expression as if weighing whether her question deserved an answer, and Frances found herself wishing she hadn't asked.

Eventually he gave a tiny movement of one shoulder that might have been a shrug. 'My parents were slaves to anything in a bottle. Whisky, gin, wine…it didn't matter as long as they had enough to become insensible. Their need for drink came even above feeding and clothing their own children and I resolved from a very young age that I wouldn't follow that path.'

Frances's stomach plummeted. Of all the answers she'd expected, *that* hadn't been one of them. Such frank honesty had come from nowhere but Jonah seemed unmoved, only a fierce glint in his eyes advising her he wanted none of the pity that had begun to circle inside her.

'I had no idea. I'm sorry… I shouldn't have asked.'

One corner of his mouth quirked in a half-smile that captured Frances's attention at once. 'Natural curiosity. I'd have been surprised if you hadn't.'

He certainly didn't sound annoyed and Frances couldn't stop another glimmer of interest. She knew next to nothing about Jonah's past and the desire to learn more called to her irresistibly, inviting her to dig a little deeper beneath that forbidding exterior even as another part warned her against it.

'And Jane…?'

Jonah didn't slow his stride. 'I took care of her the best I could. She's only four years younger but from the moment she was born I felt responsible for looking after her, knowing from bitter experience that our parents would not.'

Jonah's eyes narrowed, but not with anger at the woman walking at his side. Instead he seemed to Frances to have retreated into memory, his shoulders tensing as some private moment replayed through his mind. What he saw she had no way of knowing, but it couldn't be pleasant, the undeniable pity in Frances's chest glowing hotter as he stared straight ahead.

'I shudder to think what might have become of her if I'd left her to their *tender mercies*. There's no doubt in my mind that if I hadn't taken us both out of that cesspit she would be dead by now, killed by their selfishness and indifference.'

A hard edge had crept into his tone and Frances nipped at her bottom lip, unable to look away from his granite-carved face. So tall and unbending, it seemed impossible he'd once been a neglected child fearful for his little sister, but his determination must have sprung from somewhere and a flood of compassion flowed through her when she thought of what he must have endured. She never would have guessed he'd faced such hardship, her own difficult childhood holding up a mirror to the apparent cruelty of Jonah's, and she only stopped herself just in time from reaching out for his tightly clenched hand.

Just as on the fateful night his lips had first touched hers, Frances felt something stir at Jonah's obvious concern for Jane. Clearly it was rooted even deeper than she'd realised, again calling to mind Uncle Robert's devotion to her mother and then to the niece he'd tried so hard to shield. It seemed some of the same fierce loyalty ran in Jonah's veins and the curious feeling of security she'd experienced in her dream came back to make her wonder if perhaps her subconscious had made the connection long before her waking mind. Uncle Robert had always made her feel so safe. Could it be that Jonah might have been the same as a husband, if his ruinous childhood hadn't made him so determined not to share that strength with anyone other than his family?

Oblivious to Frances's burning sympathy, Jonah drew himself up to his full height as if to challenge any more unwanted memories. 'I'm not ashamed of where I came from. In my opinion a person is what they make of themselves, not what they were born. Given your own parentage, I imagine you feel the same way.'

Frances inclined her head. 'I do. My mother was not what people say she was, but even if she had been—am I not a separate person? None of us can change the accident of our birth. We just have to make the most of what we have.'

Jonah nodded, a sudden accord stretching between them where only minutes before tension had reigned supreme. The sun was beginning to burn away the clouds, splashing bright patches of blue across the sky, although Frances barely noticed it above the whirl of thoughts that twisted like a hurricane at finding she and Jonah had more in common than she'd known.

He only had one person to love growing up, just like I did. Perhaps people said unkind things about him too, forcing him to shut them out and turn himself to stone as I thought I had to.

Apollo trotted placidly behind her and she reached back to rub his velvet nose, revelling in the familiar warmth of his breath against her palm. At least he was uncomplicated, everything else seeming to shift in unexpected directions and leaving her not knowing which way was up. Jonah just kept walking with the same long stride he had for the past hour, as if nothing had changed, leaving Frances to wonder what else might link them in ways she hadn't foreseen.

He certainly knew what it was to feel rejected and alone, dedicating himself to the only person he cared about and who cared about him in return, and he clearly felt Jane was his to protect, just the way she felt about Barrow. The more Frances thought about it the more parallels leaped out at her, another question rising to balance on the tip of her tongue.

'Is that why you don't wish to marry? Because you feel you have responsibilities elsewhere?'

Jonah's frown deepened, the lines scoring his brow making him look older than his years. 'More or less. My parents succeeded in curing me of any romantic notions when I was very young. It's difficult to entertain the idea of caring for another when all it seems to bring is more trouble.'

His gaze was fixed on some point in the distance although what he saw in the waving grass and gritty road escaped Frances. It didn't seem to please him, though. His jaw looked tighter than ever and his gait was stiff, and Frances wondered if she'd finally pushed him too far as the end of his sentence was carried off by a rising summer breeze.

'Very difficult indeed.'

The sun was sitting high when they finally saw Marchfield in the distance and Jonah could have sighed with relief as they turned into the town's main street. It had been the most confusing twenty-four hours of his life and he wanted nothing more than to find somewhere to sit alone and think, needing to unpack the series of events he hadn't been able to stop wondering at for the whole long walk home.

She called me her friend, gave me that strange look—and then she kissed me, after swearing and declaring that would never happen again. So what in the nine circles of hell does that mean?

Snatching a glance over at Frances, he couldn't resist lingering on her mouth, reliving the moment he'd been woken by the insistent pressure of those soft but determined lips. Still halfway between reality and dreaming, he'd responded with eagerness that made him grimace now he was fully awake…but even so he couldn't quite manage to regret it. She was the most aggravating, contrary woman he'd ever met and yet somehow she was steadily burrowing beneath his skin, even coaxing out tales of his childhood he never would have shared with anyone else, and he chided himself now for revealing far too much.

She didn't need to know all those details about Jane. You just wanted her to imagine you weren't completely heartless—and perhaps come to see you as something more.

The truth was like a hornet's sting and for the first time he felt a glimmer of doubt at the very edge of his grim certainty.

When the right moment came and everything fell into place…would he be able to bring himself to make the final move, the situation having turned out to be so different from what he'd predicted?

Too shaken by the stark thought, Jonah barely noticed the people walking past, more than one of them turning to stare at the admittedly eyebrow-raising sight of a dishevelled Frances leading her horse alongside the most handsome man in town. Any other time he might have realised her uncombed hair and slept-in dress were a scandalous giveaway that she'd been out all night, but instead he stared blindly ahead, his chest growing heavier with each step. For perhaps the first time in his life the strong, severe

Lieutenant Grant was questioning his abilities, and he found he didn't like the novel sensation one little bit.

Living together as man and wife would present the ultimate temptation—and torture. To see Frances every day while knowing her feelings for him were no deeper than those she held for her dog was a prospect that made him flinch, even as another part of him tried to deny the truth. Presented with such continuous reminders of her allure, his treacherous feelings could surely only grow, however—the very thing he'd been so resolved to avoid ever since the first time he'd laid eyes on her determined scowl. If not for Jane and the children he'd cut his losses and run, making sure to guard his battered heart from an attack the assailant wasn't even aware they were waging.

But I don't have a choice.

Out of the corner of his eye he saw Frances gently rub Apollo's chin as they walked, still kind even when half-dead from tiredness. She was *supposed* to be a means to an end but somewhere along the way all that had changed and now the prospect of getting even closer to her poured salt into a wound only she could have cut into his heart, unknowingly thrusting a dagger into the last vestiges of softness he'd tried so hard to hide. Once he hadn't cared for anyone's good opinion but now that had changed too, the knowledge of how much power Frances was gaining over him twisting his innards without mercy.

'Uncle Jonah! Frances!'

He looked up at the sound of two little voices and saw Margaret and Matthew waving from the corner of the street, jumping up and down in excitement, and he tried to relax the tension of his jaw as they ran to meet him.

'We were looking out for you!'

'Yes, we've been waiting for hours!'

As the church clock had only just struck eight Jonah didn't *quite* believe that, but it was a relief to have a distraction from the discord inside his head. Margaret seized his hand and Matthew fell into step beside Frances, his usual shyness apparently overcome after his visit to Barrow Farm.

'Mama said to invite you to breakfast. Will you come?'

Jonah watched Frances lay a hand on his nephew's blond head, the tenderness of that one tiny move almost enough to make him stumble. 'That's a kind offer but I really must get back to the farm. Please tell your mama I'll send some preserves over soon, though. Perhaps you and your sister could collect them when you come to see the new piglets.'

Margaret piped up at once. 'She said she'd like to see you. She said she hoped you were well after spending so much time with Uncle Jonah. Mama thinks after that you deserve breakfast at the very least.'

A sound suspiciously like someone suppressing a laugh came from Frances's direction and Jonah caught the tail-end of a smile disappear behind her hand. The eyes above it were bright and he was suddenly helpless, whatever unpleasant thoughts rampaged around his head fading into the background at the beauty of her lips.

'I'll come to say good morning then, but I won't stay. I've been away from the farm for too long already and I don't want the animals to miss me.'

Unsure whether to throttle his niece or reward her, Jonah led the way to Rose Cottage, attracting more attention than ever now the twins were in tow. He noticed Miss Fletcher and her sister coming the opposite way and threw them the smallest nod good manners allowed, irritation flaring as he saw how their hungry gazes devoured every detail of Frances's bedraggled dress and hair that clearly hadn't seen a brush. No doubt they'd have plenty to say but he paid them no mind as Jane appeared at the cottage's open front door.

'Well! I'd almost given you up for lost!'

She smiled although Jonah could see how she held the door frame for support, wrapped in a shawl despite the mild weather that made his own nape feel damp. Her laugh had a hoarse edge and as Frances looped Apollo's reins over the fence Jane coughed violently into a handkerchief, folding it quickly so the children couldn't see what was left inside.

'It was my fault. My horse cast a shoe on the way back from Cirencester and we had to spend the night at the side of the road.' Frances came up the path, her face clouding over. 'But are you unwell? You looked flushed and that cough…'

'Oh, I'm fine.' Jane waved one hand in the dismissive gesture Jonah knew so well, ushering the children into the house with the other. 'A summer cold, that's all. A couple of days will see me right.'

Jonah was about to argue when another coughing fit made his point for him. Jane clung to the door as she wheezed into her handkerchief, eyes streaming and her skinny shoulders hunched, and Frances took her arm.

'You should be in bed.'

'I can't afford to lie around. There's a house to take care of and the children need their breakfast.'

'All things Jonah can do.' Frances spoke gently, her concern stirring embers in Jonah's stomach. 'You know better than anyone he's capable enough.'

The compliment warmed him right down to his boots but still Jane hesitated.

'They're my responsibility. I can't expect Jonah—'

'There's no shame in accepting help, Jane. Something your brother is teaching me.'

He thought he saw an echo of Jane's rosiness gleam in Frances's cheeks, the colour far more pleasing in hers than his sister's. Frances didn't look at him but she didn't need to, her praise of him hanging in the air until Jane nodded reluctantly.

'Perhaps you're right. I suppose the sooner I'm well again the sooner I can return to running the house as I ought...' She turned to Jonah. 'If you're sure you could manage?'

'I think I can cope with feeding two children.' He folded his arms across his creased shirt, trying to look as capable as Frances apparently thought him. 'Go back to bed.'

Jane sighed, quite possibly with relief. With a squeeze of Frances's hand she drifted back inside the cottage, her white shape moving down the corridor towards the stairs, and Jonah rubbed the back of his neck as his sister's ghostly figure disappeared.

'I think you did the impossible. Jane would never have listened to me alone.'

'Sometimes it takes a fresh voice to talk sense into people.' Frances peered up at the azure sky, giving the distinct impression she was avoiding meeting his eye. 'I'll bring down the recipe for a chest poultice and some honey for her throat. Don't worry. Between the two of us we can make her well again.'

She shot him a swift glance, sharp but reassuring at the same time, and Jonah felt his heart turn over. The idea of having someone to share his burdens was so unfamiliar he didn't know what to say, the embers in his stomach smouldering hotter at the compassion in her face.

With a brief nod Frances turned away, almost reaching the bottom of the path before Jonah found his tongue.

'Thank you for your kindness. I appreciate it, truly.'

'We're friends now,' she replied, carefully untangling Apollo's reins from the fence and beginning to lead him away. 'You said it yourself. Friends help each other…don't they?'

He watched her go, her footsteps weary but head still high, until she turned the corner of the street and was gone from his sight.

Jonah leaned against the cottage's porch, briefly closing his tired eyes. He'd go inside to tend to the children in a moment but for now he just wanted to savour the quiet, hoping to make some sense of the commotion inside his head. Far too many thoughts jostled for his attention, emotions he'd always tried to block out forcing themselves to the fore, and he pinched the bridge of his nose as he tried to order them.

Frances's kindness to Jane... Offering to take some of the weight from my shoulders, so for once I needn't bear it alone...

Genuine gratitude welled up, only to turn to ash a half-second later, Jonah wincing as a stab sliced through his chest. The growing sweetness of Frances's true nature contrasted ever more bleakly with the hopelessness of his own feelings, every gesture on her part increasing the treachery of his. With each smile or kind word she made it harder for him to imagine living with her while pretending to keep himself so determinedly apart, but one look at Jane standing in the doorway had told him everything he needed to know. If he didn't act to move the family back up in the world his sister would die. Her condition was worsening by the day and soon it would be too late. He was trapped between the two women, disaster waiting for him whichever way he turned. In that moment Jonah couldn't have been less pleased to feel a tap on his shoulder.

'Lieutenant Grant. May we speak with you?'

Opening his eyes, Jonah had to bite back a grunt. Miss Fletcher and her sister stood close beside him, arm in arm as always and aglow with self-righteous vigour that made him want to turn away at once.

'Miss Fletcher. Mrs Campbell. Is there something I can do for you?'

'More something *we* can do for *you*.'

He ran a hand over his face, already weary of their unwanted company. 'Ladies. I'm very tired. If there's something you'd like to say to me, perhaps you could tell me quickly.'

Mrs Campbell glanced about as if worried eavesdroppers might be hiding behind a blade of grass before leaning in confidentially, lowering her voice to murmur into his ear. 'We saw you walking through town with Miss Nettleford. It hasn't gone unnoticed that she's been courting your attention. We would advise you to exercise more caution.'

His brows rose in surprise but Miss Fletcher pressed on, nodding ominously. 'We told you her history when you first arrived, but perhaps we hinted too delicately, never wanting to speak ill of anybody. You understand.'

Jonah's eyes narrowed. What nonsense was this?

'I'm not sure that I do. You'll need to be more explicit.'

Clearly this was the response they had been hoping for. Both sisters took a step closer, faces alight with barely concealed malice, and Mrs Campbell's affected whisper grew louder. 'Frances Nettleford is notorious, Lieutenant. Not only for her wanton mother but for her rudeness, her pride, her complete refusal to behave in a manner befitting any decent young lady...'

She hardly paused for breath, evidently warming to her theme, and Jonah felt a steady pulse of anger begin to heat his blood. Standing beneath the sun, he was hot enough already but their venom made him boil in a different way entirely, all the confusion and uncertainty of the past few days mixing in a dangerous melting pot.

'She's been known to encourage the advances of any number of men, both married and single, and is altogether so disreputable as to make herself infamous for miles around. Her face is fair, I'll allow, but I'm afraid concealed behind it is a gateway to a *moral abyss*.'

Miss Fletcher pursed her mouth primly, now so cloyingly sweet she could have rotted Jonah's teeth. 'You mustn't think that we enjoy talking about this, Lieutenant. We felt it our duty to warn you, being only recently come to town and perhaps not fully aware of the kind of woman she is. Your poor sister will be sensible of the peril of allowing her daughter to spend any more time with Miss Nettleford, I imagine, now you know the truth.'

Jonah looked down at them, the two malevolent creatures who'd come to see him with the sole aim of blackening Frances's name, and the ire building inside him reached new heights.

How can they speak of her like that? How can they talk about her as though she were nothing more than mud on the bottom of their boots?

The injustice of it was more than he could stand. It was because of precisely such unkindness that Frances felt she had to build a wall around herself, never allowing anybody to get close. If she hadn't been subjected to a lifetime of such cruelty and rejection she might have considered opening her heart to him rather than maintaining her distance, perhaps accepting the fledgling emotion he was finding it harder and harder to control... The thought that individuals like the sisters before him were responsible for ruining their potential chance at happiness made him want to growl.

If not for them Frances might not have known so much suffering. If not for them things might have been different indeed.

His tumultuous feelings were pushing him closer to the edge, and the frost in his tone belied the fire in his blood when he finally trusted himself to speak.

'Madam, you have no comprehension of the truth. The only women I would prevent my niece from spending time with would be you and your sister, two people so lacking in both sense and judgement that even a passing acquaintance would be damaging beyond repair.'

Miss Fletcher's mouth opened, her sister's face blanching with speechless shock, but Jonah didn't spare them.

'I'm proud to call Miss Nettleford a friend and so is my sister. If Margaret grows up to be even half as strong and self-reliant as Frances then I would be pleased beyond measure. In fact, I don't know of anyone else I'd rather she drew inspiration from. Now, I'll have to bid you good morning and beg to be excused.'

Mrs Campbell stood rooted to the spot, fixed in place by her stupefaction, and Miss Fletcher had to tug repeatedly on her arm to draw her away. With what felt like lava coursing through his veins, Jonah followed their stumbling progress, both sisters obviously far too stunned to speak as they brushed past a figure standing at the end of the path—someone Jonah recognised at once, an instinctive thrill leaping up at the sight.

'Frances?'

She stared at him, one hand clutching the rickety fence, and Jonah cursed beneath his breath to think she'd heard the cruelty spilling from two pairs of lying lips.

'I… I only came back to ask if you'd send one of the children to the farm later to fetch some soup. I thought it would be easy for Jane to manage with her sore throat.'

The explanation came uncertainly and Jonah strode forward, ready to do his clumsy best to console her.

'Damn it, Frances. How much of their gibberish did you hear? You must know not to take them seriously—'

Something in her expression cut him off. The rest of his sentence faded away as she looked up at him, her hazel eyes clear and sparkling like pools of crystal water. For the first time he noticed an amber ring encircling each pupil, so pretty that whatever he'd been about to say seemed suddenly unimportant compared to the unnamed emotion he saw in her gaze.

'I don't care what they said. I've heard it all before. It's what you told them…'

'What about it?'

But she didn't reply with words. Before he even knew what she was doing, Frances had risen up on her tiptoes and Jonah's heart stopped to feel her press a kiss to his stubble-roughened cheek. Then she was gone, leaving him to stare after her retreating back with his mind blank as a puddle of spilled milk.

Chapter Nine

It took almost three days for Frances to make up for the time she'd lost and when she eventually fell into bed on the third night, long after the clock had struck twelve, she was asleep as soon as her head hit the pillow. Too tired even to dream, she lay perfectly still beneath the covers, dead to the world until something roused her groggily from the deepest reaches of sleep.

Unwilling to open her eyes, she wondered with vague irritation what had disturbed her. Even without looking she could tell the room was still dark, dawn hours away and her snug little bed as warm and comfortable as ever, and she was about to turn over and retreat back into unconsciousness when a movement at her feet made her sigh.

'Ah. It was you, was it? Go to sleep, Gyp. It's not time to get up yet.'

Pulling her covers higher, Frances waited idly

for the dog to settle. It wasn't like him to wake her, though, and when he pawed at her leg again, this time with a low, worried whine, she sat up.

'What's the matter?'

She peered through the darkness at the dog's white face—darkness that somehow wasn't quite as complete as it should have been. A strange glow peeped in at the edges of her curtains and before she'd even flown out of bed to rip them open she knew what it meant.

'No!'

A cry froze in her mouth as leaping flames reflected in her bedroom window. The whole yard was lit by the fire raging from the stable at the far end. Smoke curled towards the sky, orange tongues dancing above the roof and the smell of burning wood filling the air, although Frances hardly noticed as she fled for the stairs, slamming her bedroom door behind her to keep Gyp from following. Distantly she heard him set up a howl but she didn't stop, not even to throw on a pair of shoes as she ran barefoot through the kitchen and out into the blazing night.

'It can't be…'

She stood for a second, staring up at the glowing building with wordless horror squeezing her in a merciless grip. Silhouetted against the starry sky, the stable looked monstrous, its window like a single flashing eye daring her to come closer, and for a moment she faltered before its mocking glare.

What should she do? Anguish rising, Frances wavered, trying desperately to think clearly. Her first instinct was to rush inside and drag Apollo to safety but her legs felt like water, fear coursing through her veins alongside a ferocious kind of energy she'd never felt before. If she didn't make up her mind soon it would be too late—but then she heard the sound that tore the decision from her hands.

She caught the horse's screams even above the crackle of the flames, high and terrified, and turning her blood to ice. If she didn't get him out he'd die alone, thrashing and burning until his last breath, and without another glimmer of hesitation Frances pulled the neck of her nightgown up to cover her nose and mouth and wrenched open the smouldering door.

A solid wall of heat forced her back, the smoke making her eyes water at once. She could barely see. Harsh orange light filled every corner and ash tumbled through the air, the once familiar space disorientating and her heart pounding so hard it made her head spin. Narrowing her eyes against the soot and flames, she forced her way inside, bunching up her skirts to stop them catching on a beam that had fallen to smoulder at her feet. Wildly casting her eyes around the empty stalls, her stomach roiled with sick dread, but then a movement seized her attention, an indistinct shape barely visible, rearing up amid the deadly clouds.

'Apollo!'

He didn't seem to hear her, Frances's voice hardly more than a choking rasp as she struggled to find enough air. Sweat ran down her back as she took another step forward, one hand out as if she could ward off the heat and noise and the other pressing the nightgown to her face, never looking away from Apollo as he skittered and plunged, trapped at the back of the stable by a flaming bale of straw. He didn't look like her beloved docile boy at that moment. With his eyes rolling and lips drawn back from his teeth he was more like a wild animal, dangerous in his terror, but the sight of him was enough to push Frances on without a thought. If she could just reach him, just let him see her face, he might calm enough to let her lead him out…or so she hoped, with no other plan to fall back on.

A sudden shard of agony in one bare foot had her suck in a ragged gasp, immediately regretting it when the lungful of smoky air made her cough until she could scarcely stand. Through streaming eyes she saw a large burn shining on the sole, the pain of it making her see stars. For a half-second she wondered if she was going to faint, the heat and her fear combining with that hateful throb to send her crashing to the ground, and it was only a hand suddenly clamping around her arm that kept her upright as her vision began to blur.

'I've got you.'

Somebody was lifting her—somebody with the strength not to put her down even when she struggled, fighting against them as she was slung over a broad shoulder and carried out of the blazing building with no trouble at all. She tried to shout but no sound emerged. She could only cough as she felt a cool breeze on her scalding cheeks and knew she would never see Apollo again.

Jonah laid her on the cobbles, careful not to place her down on her injured foot—because of course it was him, Frances realised with distant resignation. With his back to the flames he was all in shadow, just as he'd been the day he'd rescued her from the bull, although this time Frances couldn't summon much gratitude for his pulling her out of the lion's den. He put a steadying hand on her shoulder but she shrugged it off, her head swimming and torment clawing at her insides.

'No… Apollo…' She managed a pitiful wheeze, each word a monumental effort with a chest filled with ash. 'I can't leave him…'

She tried to stand but her legs gave way at once, the agony in her foot lighting up every nerve, and with a strangled cry she crumpled back down onto the ground. Tears of pain welling up, she set her jaw, gathering the strength to crawl to the stable if she had to, when she felt Jonah's hand at her shoulder once again.

'You can't be thinking of going back for him? You'd risk your own life for a horse?'

Frances nodded, eyes burning from more than just the smoke. How could she expect Jonah to understand? To him Apollo was just a horse. To her he was all the family she had left, the farm and its animals the only link with her uncle now he was gone for ever. If Apollo died it would unleash her grief all over again and she'd rather die than feel that despair, sucking the joy out of her just as she was beginning to wonder if there might be more to life than merely existing.

Jonah looked down at her now, his face streaked with soot, and she watched it harden with grim determination at whatever he saw reflected in hers.

'Stay there.'

'Wait… Jonah…'

Dawning realisation hit her like a physical blow and she reached out at once to grab hold of his hand, but he turned away, striding towards the stable before she could finish calling his name. Only able to watch in mute horror, Frances's stomach dropped as he pulled a cravat from his pocket to press to his face, bracing himself on the threshold and then stepping inside to disappear amid the rising plumes of smoke.

Frances sat frozen to the spot, the dampness of the cobbles beneath her seeping up through her nightgown to chill her to the bone. The burn on her sole hurt like nothing she'd known before but it couldn't overshadow her terror as she sat on the ground, eyes fixed on the whirling flames and counting the seconds until Jonah resurfaced, the alternative too awful to bear. *She* should be the one in danger, not him. If he didn't come back she would never forgive herself, the idea of never seeing that stern face again slicing her heart in two. Once again he'd appeared from nowhere at the very moment she'd needed him most and the thought that it might be the last time almost made her retch up her supper, the intensity of her fear finally forcing her to admit the truth.

I'm falling in love with him.

A strange sense of release washed over her but there was no time to dwell on it. A shadow had darkened the stable doorway and Frances thought her chest might burst as she made out a hazy shape stumbling through the thick black fug, a grotesque creature that seemed to have six legs...

With a choking cry she pushed herself up,

forcing her shaking legs to bear her weight even as they threatened to give way. Her injured foot shrieked when she tried to walk and she swayed with sudden dizziness, unable to go to meet Jonah as he carefully led Apollo towards her and away from the blazing wreckage. There were no words to describe how she felt as she threw her arms around the horse's neck and breathed in the singed smell of his hair. Relief so powerful it nearly floored her swept through her body and she clung to him for support as her vision grew dark, her mind breaking free from her body to float away on the spark-scattered breeze. As if from a great distance she heard Jonah say something but she couldn't quite tell what it was, everything growing fuzzy as finally she allowed herself to give in to the pain in her foot and adrenaline in her veins and folded gently in a dead faint onto the ground.

When her eyes opened it took Frances a moment to understand that she was back in her bedroom. She lay on top of her covers, still wearing her torn and smoky nightgown, and she was about to try to stand up when Jonah appeared in the doorway.

'Don't. You need to rest.'

He came into the room, ducking slightly to fit through the low door. In one hand he carried a candle and in the other a glass of water, both of which he set down on the little table beside Frances's bed, before folding his arms across his soot-blackened chest.

'The fire's out. I was able to douse it before it spread any further.'

Frances slowly nodded her aching head, a growing awareness of the agony in her foot making it difficult to fully focus. She opened her mouth to speak but winced instead, her throat feeling full of rusty nails. Her voice was hoarse when she managed to force out one word.

'Apollo?'

'Safe in the orchard for now. I can move him somewhere more suitable in the morning.'

Closing her eyes briefly, she let out a deep sigh. Apollo was alive and Jonah had come back unharmed, or so it seemed, a quick glance showing nothing worse than streaks of dirt and a scorched shirtsleeve. Another tidal wave of relief engulfed her, her hand shaking as she pushed back her tangled hair. Jonah watched her every move like a bird protecting its eggs, a complicated mixture of gratitude and guilt rising inside her as she saw the concern in his handsome face.

He could have died because of me, and Apollo along with him. They both could have perished in the flames and it would have been my fault.

A cold, wet nose pressing against her hand

made her look down. Gyp was observing her likewise, perhaps even more worried than Jonah, and Frances was pleased to have an excuse not to meet Jonah's eyes as she smoothed the dog's ears. The conclusion she'd come to as she'd watched the fearless Lieutenant walk into the flames came back with a vengeance, the truth of it something she could no longer fight. She was growing to love him, coming to care for the man behind the severe mask, whose steadfast respect for her had proven him so different to every other young man, and by her own foolishness she had almost caused his death.

'I must have left my lantern behind when I checked on Apollo before going to bed. I knew I was starting to make mistakes, being so tired all the time, but to think what could have happened...'

She couldn't bring herself to finish, allowing the sentence to tail off as sheer dread gripped her. Despite every good intention, every vow to live by the rules Uncle Robert had set out to keep her safe, she'd fallen under Jonah's spell, leaving her weak and vulnerable, and now *this*. If any harm had come to him she didn't know what she would have done. Her voice cracked as she realised just how close to calamity she had unwittingly sailed.

'I could have killed him and apparently you as well. I know better than to be so careless and yet I can't seem to get things right. If my uncle could see what I've become...'

To her shame tears sprang up to sting her red eyes and she stared down at the dirty lap of her nightgown, hoping Jonah wouldn't see. Her uncle's face flashed before her, disappointed and disapproving of both her feelings and the fire, as well as the terrible image of Apollo's frenzied panic. If Jonah hadn't come there'd be no chance the poor creature would have survived and Frances screwed her eyes shut to think how badly she had failed. Barrow and all its inhabitants were hers to protect now. Instead she'd done the opposite, placing them in danger because she couldn't manage the task of keeping them safe.

Without invitation, Jonah sat heavily on the end of her bed, jogging Frances's arm as she reached for her water. Peering at him over the rim of her glass, she saw him frown down at his hands, a fleeting thrill running through her, despite her despair, at the intimacy of him treating her bedroom as if it were his own. A little closer and she could have touched him with her outstretched foot. Belatedly, she noticed the burn there was covered with a strip of fabric torn from the bottom of his singed shirt. He must have bound it while she lay insensible and the thought of him once again tenderly treating her wounds sent her memory reeling backwards to recall the scene in her kitchen when his gentle touch had torn a gasp from her unwilling lips. Those very same lips had brushed his skin three times since then, each kiss another attack on Frances's defences until they lay in pieces, with Jonah having no idea of the triumph his gruff kindness had won over her once guarded heart.

And I can never tell him. Frances forced down another sip of water, the taste of it acrid on her tongue. *He's been clear enough that he has enough to worry about without any romantic entanglements...and what man would choose to add to his burden a woman who courts disaster wherever she goes?*

Still studying his hands, Jonah shook his head, thankfully oblivious to the whirl of Frances's thoughts.

'What you've become is a woman whose bravery your uncle would be proud of. Who else would think to risk their life trying to save a horse, apart from you?'

Frances set aside her glass. His words reminded her of what she'd overheard him telling Miss Fletcher only a few days before. It had been so unexpected yet poignant that she hadn't been able to help herself from showing how much it had meant. His stubbled cheek had scratched her mouth and she felt a ghost of that friction now as she fiddled with the torn lace at her cuff.

'*You* did. You went back into the fire for him, and he isn't even your horse.'

'I didn't do it for Apollo, although I'm glad he's safe. I did it for you.'

A blanket of silence fell over the room, the only movement that of Gyp settling against Frances's legs. Automatically she stroked the dog's head although her mind had stuttered to a halt, uncertainty pushing out any idea of what to say next. Jonah sat like a statue, still not lifting his head to meet her eyes, and it was impossible to read his face in the shadowy light of the lone candle beside her bed.

'Thank you. I never would have asked you to do such a thing, but I'm so grateful you appeared out of the blue—again. How is it you always seem to sense when I'm in trouble?'

Jonah lifted one impressive shoulder as if to shrug off her gratitude. 'I haven't been sleeping well of late and was sitting out in the garden when I saw smoke in the distance. I'm only glad I got here in time.'

Resisting the urge to ask what was keeping him from his sleep, Frances surreptitiously rubbed her eyes. Unshed tears still clung to her lashes and she gathered Gyp closer, burying her face in his warm fur. It was all too much—the fire and almost losing Apollo, imagining Uncle Robert's disappointment, and now all the feelings Jonah stirred to buffet her like a tree in a storm. Pulled this way and that, she didn't know where to turn, confusion and distress rising inside her until she felt Gyp's fur grow wet and realised the dam of her tears had given way.

'Frances?'

The uncharacteristic gentleness of Jonah's voice speared her right through the vulnerable place reserved only for him, but Frances didn't look up. There was no way she could show him her emotion when he'd risked so much already, her distress another weight she refused to place on his back. Cuffing the wetness from her cheeks with a rough hand, she glared down at her fingers, the nails black with soot, a reminder of how close to real disaster her foolishness had taken him, and her anguish forced the truth from her mouth.

'My uncle placed too much faith in me. What more proof is there that I can't take care of Barrow alone?' Blindly she smoothed Gyp's damp ears, the little dog's unblinking adoration somehow making her feel worse. 'I'm exhausted and surely it's only a matter of time before I make another stupid mistake that might end up costing a life.'

Out of the corner of her eye she saw Jonah stiffen a little. *Probably my snivelling causing him discomfort*, she thought harshly, in no temper to spare herself the contempt she knew she deserved. There couldn't be an inch of his hands he hadn't inspected by now but still his gaze was turned downward, making it harder to catch his low reply when it finally came.

'What if you weren't alone any more? What if you had someone who would always help you?'

She huffed a dark, humourless laugh. 'That would be a miracle.'

'Not necessarily.' There was a pause and then Jonah finished his sentence, ten words that dropped a lit match into the bonfire of Frances's heart.

'If we were to wed, that person could be me.'

Jonah had fought in more skirmishes than he could remember, but forcing himself to look up into Frances's stunned face was harder than walking into any battle, his heart hammering so hard he thought it might break through his ribs.

She stared at him, the candle's wavering flame reflected in her wide eyes, and his breathing grew shallow as he watched shock turn to confusion in their hazel depths.

'Are you asking me to *marry* you?'

'Yes.'

'But…why?'

There was such complete bewilderment in her expression that he almost turned away. It was a question he couldn't immediately answer and yet he had to find some way to persuade her, all his efforts over the past weeks paving the way for this very moment.

The chance he'd been waiting for had finally arrived, but it felt hollow as his stomach tied itself in knots and bitterness climbed his gullet. Looking at Frances in her ruined nightgown Jonah had never doubted himself more, only Jane's increasingly skeletal figure pushing him on down the road he'd long since realised had no happy ending for him.

Only if Frances rejected his offer would his heart remain safe, he thought bleakly. He would be spared the torture of marrying a woman he'd fallen for quite accidentally, never having intended to see her as anything other than a way out of the mess Thomas Millard had left behind. He wouldn't be forced to spend the rest of his days pining after his own wife if Frances refused his hand, knowing she would never care for him in the way he did for her and feeling his hopes dwindle with every passing year. If allowed to distance himself he might begin to forget the feelings she'd managed to stir in his jaded soul.

But if I don't marry Frances—it could very well spell the end for Jane.

Jonah fought back the desire to pace the room, on the horns of a dilemma. The insistent little voice inside his head spoke the truth and he couldn't deny it. If he didn't sacrifice himself to shield Jane from her fate, just as he had with his body when they were young, it was likely that she would die. It was the same situation it had been all their lives, and for what could have been the thousandth time he reminded himself of what he'd always known. To care was to open oneself to pain, allowing a chink in defences through which life might thrust a dagger, and it was far better not to run the risk. He'd allowed himself to stray from his convictions and now his growing weakness for Frances would bring nothing but heartache—the very thing he had always been so careful to avoid.

Tears still shone on Frances's cheeks and Jonah almost gasped as the desire to wipe them away hit him like a physical blow, in spite of his hopelessness longing to take her in his arms and hang whatever might come next. Instead, however, he made himself speak.

'It makes sense. You said you're struggling to run the farm alone. I could take some of the strain if I was at Barrow too.'

She opened her mouth and closed it again, clearly at a loss for words. In the dim light he thought he saw a pink glow creep up from her neck but he couldn't be certain, streaks of ash hiding whatever flush might lie beneath.

'But you don't want a wife. You told me that yourself.'

Frances glanced at him with a measure of her old caution, making his heart turn over. Once she would have rejected him outright and her hesitation was enough to give him hope, even if some contrary part of him wished she'd turn him down flat. 'And my uncle left me Barrow so I might be safe from relying on anyone but myself—especially a man.'

Jonah sat up a little straighter. Tension pulled every muscle and his shoulders ached with the strain of having to pretend he didn't want to cut their conversation short and walk right out of Frances's bedroom, the sound of blood roaring in his ears making it hard to think.

'It's true neither of us have ever sought romantic connections, but everybody needs someone sometimes. Even you. I imagine your uncle would have understood that.'

He saw her swallow. Sitting back against her pillows, she looked so small suddenly, like a lost soul with nowhere to call home, and compassion spread through Jonah's gut. That she was even considering his offer told him the depths of her despair in a way words never could, the urge to hold her seizing him again and refusing to let go.

The sinews in her neck moved again and he realised she was holding herself under tight control. 'You have enough to worry about. I won't add to the burdens you already have to carry.'

Leaning forward, Jonah fought the instinct to bury his head in his hands. Letting them hang between his knees, he looked at the floor, staring down at his scuffed boots as he tried to find the will to carry on with his own destruction.

Is that how she sees herself? As a trial rather than the treasure she really is?

Surely it was impossible. Surely she knew any man fortunate enough to win her hand would be lucky beyond belief. Out of the corner of his eye Jonah saw her tuck her tousled hair behind one ear, the perfect line of her cheekbone gleaming in the candlelight. The unconscious beauty of her countenance only underlined what was hidden behind it. Her once icy demeanour had given way to sweetness he hardly dared believe she deigned to share with him now, and her limitless courage raised her even higher in his eyes. Still pretending to study the ground, Jonah recalled the heart-stopping moment he'd found her in the stable, surrounded by flames, injured but determined to keep going, and then her face after he'd pulled her out, so resolved to return for Apollo even if it meant she had to crawl back on her hands and knees…

'You're nobody's burden, Frances,' he said

quietly. 'It would be no hardship for me to have you as my wife. In fact, it would be an honour.'

He lifted his head and let her see the sincerity in his eyes. It was a relief to tell the truth at last, both to her and to himself. The feelings he'd tried so hard to kill refused to die and he had no choice but to admit Frances's good opinion mattered more than almost anything else in his entire life, knowing he must marry her to keep his family safe. It was the cruellest irony and his chest squeezed so tight he could barely breathe as Frances finally met his eye over the top of Gyp's white head.

'You'd help me with the farm? Truly?'

'Yes.'

'And that's the only reason you asked me. For the farm's sake. Not for…me?'

The bitterness on Jonah's tongue almost choked him as he shook his head.

Oh, Frances. If only you knew.

He knew what she wanted to hear. He couldn't tell her that the idea of sharing her bed made the earth shift on its axis, or how ardently he wanted her to be the first and last thing he saw each day. From the very beginning he'd vowed to be honest about his intentions, allowing no comparison between himself and the lying brother-in-law responsible for his family's distress, but surely there were some truths better left unspoken. A silence wasn't exactly a lie, or so Jonah tried to believe, steeling himself to walk the fine line between what he could and could not reveal.

'I know how you feel about marriage. In that way we're well suited. Think of it as a business arrangement if that makes things easier to bear. You need help with the farm and I need money to support Jane and the children. I would have no further expectations than that.'

Frances's eyes were huge in the dim light and as she passed a hand over her face Jonah saw her fingers shaking.

'I need to think about it.' She rubbed her forehead, leaving a smudge of soot behind to join that already marking her smooth skin. 'It's not a question I ever thought I'd be asked. Not by you...not by anybody.'

'I understand.'

Jonah tried to find something resembling a smile but found his lips were too stiff. All at once the desire to be anywhere but Frances's bedroom forced him to his feet, unable to bear the tumult of his feelings a moment longer, and he felt her eyes on him as he moved for the door.

'I'll leave you to rest now and think things through. Take all the time you need.'

Jane was waiting for him when Jonah got back to the dark cottage, sitting at the kitchen table with one hand pressed to her chest. From the number of handkerchiefs crumpled in her lap she must have suffered one of her coughing fits and even in the scant moonlight coming through the thin curtains he could see the ruddiness of her cheeks as she looked round.

'I heard you leave. Where have you been in the middle of the night?' Her voice was hoarse but she seemed not to notice as a frown crossed her shadowy face. 'And what on earth happened to your shirt?'

Jonah felt his shoulders tense. An interrogation was the very last thing he wanted in his current state and he tried to sound as unmoved as possible despite the snakes writhing in his stomach. 'There was a fire at Barrow. I saw the smoke and went to help.'

'A fire! Is Frances…?'

'She's safe. Her foot was burned but, apart from that, she and her animals are all unharmed.'

'Thank heaven.'

Jane exhaled deeply and Jonah heard the congestion of her chest even from across the room. It sounded worse than it had mere hours earlier when she'd retired early to bed and he was too distracted by fresh unease to guard himself from an ambush.

'If there was no great calamity, why do you look so grim?'

He scoffed, although privately he could have kicked himself for letting his feelings show in his face. 'As opposed to my usual beaming good humour?'

'You know what I mean.' Jane picked up one of the cleaner-looking handkerchiefs and began to pleat it, looking down so innocently Jonah's suspicions were aroused at once. 'Perhaps you were worried about Frances. Perhaps you need time to recover from your fright and whatever happened while you were at the farm.'

A sensation like cold water creeping down his back made Jonah stiffen. He had no intention of telling her exactly what conversation between him and Frances had left him feeling so confused, but evidently he would have to work harder if he wanted to conceal it until the time was right.

Jane watched him from beneath her lashes, a strange smile lingering that Jonah didn't trust.

'Do you love her?'

Jonah started. 'What?'

'Frances. Do you love her?'

The unexpected attack cut far too close to the bone and Jonah realised he'd taken a step backwards when he bumped against the wall. 'Where did that come from? Of all the ridiculous questions—'

'Is it ridiculous, though?' Jane regarded him

closely, head held to one side like an inquisitive bird. 'You speak so highly of her and are always the first to offer your help. I've never seen this side of you before and it makes me wonder.'

'It's no secret that I respect her.'

'That much is obvious, but not what I asked.'

The wall behind him was cool against his palms—palms that prickled with sudden sweat. He wanted to brush Jane's question aside but couldn't seem to think, his mind too full of the night's events to leave room for anything other than confusion and regret and a growing awareness of how much he hated the trap he'd made for himself. His sister still studied him with that damned smile and he knew he sounded even terser than normal as he turned away.

'I'm going to bed.'

Jane nodded, a knowing gleam in her eyes at her brother's evasive reply as, for the second time that night, he left a woman to her own thoughts in a darkened room. But what else could he say? It wasn't as though he could tell her the truth…

That he knew the answer was *yes*.

Chapter Ten

Frances felt her knees grow weaker with every slightly limping step she took towards the front of the church until she feared they might give way completely.

Empty pews stretched out on either side of the aisle but she couldn't tear her eyes away from Jonah's face, so handsome in its seriousness. The sight only added to the butterflies swooping through her stomach. She'd had three weeks to get used to the idea and yet now the fateful day had finally dawned, bringing with it the first hint of autumn carried on the breeze, and she could still hardly believe what she was about to do.

Tie myself for ever to a man—the very thing Uncle Robert spent my whole life warning me against.

She tried not to think of him as she approached the altar, legs shaking but head held high. It was to protect his legacy that she had made such a drastic decision and Frances clung to that thought, feeling her heart racing beneath the bodice of her best gown. He'd be horrified if he could see her now, Jane and the twins beaming as she prepared to throw herself into Jonah's keeping, but what was the alternative? There wasn't one—or at least she hadn't found one in the agonising days before she'd given Jonah an answer to the question she'd never imagined he'd ask. She'd tried to run Barrow alone and it had nearly ended in tragedy, the almost healed burn on her sole leaving permanent proof, and she had no choice but to seize the only lifeline she had been thrown.

Jonah seemed taller than ever standing beside the stooped Reverend Moir, whose warm smile was as genuine as Jane's. Only the two about to be wed looked grave, Frances's lips too numb to move and the man who would be her husband wearing the same mask that always hid whatever stirred behind it. If she needed any more evidence their wedding was based on convenience she only had to look into Jonah's set face. There was none of the joy one might expect from a love match, although when he took her cold hand her breath caught at the reassuring caress his thumb traced on her palm.

'You look beautiful.'

His voice was too low for the witnesses to

hear but it lit Frances's cheeks on fire and she had no hope of curbing the leap of her pulse at his murmur so close to her ear. It wasn't lost on her that he looked well himself in his sharp red uniform, an array of medals gleaming on his chest, and she wondered briefly if any woman could have asked for a handsomer husband. Her own cream dress was simple but a circlet of blue harebells peeping from among her curls lent a fresh prettiness she didn't dislike, a small posy of wildflowers in her free hand the only other ornamentation a country girl needed.

'Thank you. You look very smart yourself.'

The Reverend beckoned them nearer his lectern and Frances stumbled forward, hardly able to believe what she was doing, but Jonah's hand on hers making it impossible to back away. His fingers were so strong yet gentle at the same time, their warmth helping to thaw some of the frozen anxiety that mounted as she realised it was almost the moment of no return. Robert had told her never to walk this path, but surely Jonah was different from her father in every way. He had never tried to deny her nor hide their connection, even after being warned. Instead, he'd been *proud* to call her his friend in front of the whole town. Her trust was hard-won but Jonah had managed it, by some miracle breaking down the defences she'd been so careful to build…and more than that, if she was honest, the most un-ladylike anticipation spilling through her body at the thought of what the night would bring.

I wonder if it'll be like my dream.

Frances braced herself as Reverend Moir began to speak, Jonah's hand scalding now as if made from molten metal.

I know he doesn't want anything but friend-ship from me...but I confess I'm intrigued to find what it's really like to share my bed with a man.

Less than an hour later and the deal was done.

The church bells pealed overhead as Jonah led Frances out into the sunshine, Jane and the children following behind. It wasn't much of a procession but even if there had been a hundred people Jonah would still only have had eyes for his new bride, radiant in her pale dress and crowned with flowers that made her look like a fairy queen. Her fingers in the crook of his arm were a little unsteady but she managed to find a smile for the twins as they danced around her and the lead weight crushing Jonah's chest was briefly lightened by admiration for her nerve.

She went through with it. I never should have imagined she wouldn't.

For the entire three weeks required for the banns he had half hoped she'd change her mind, torn in two by such conflict that for the first time in his life he'd been tempted to reach for a bottle. Sleepless night had followed sleepless night, Jane's cough echoing in the darkness, but it was his spinning thoughts that had kept him awake until the sun came up and he was forced to endure another day. More than once he'd determined to call the whole thing off, but Jane's chest rattled worse than ever and now the children had begun to wheeze from the damp seeping through the cottage walls, and he had to accept Frances and her farm were the only way of keeping his family from being laid in the churchyard through which he now walked. It could only be a matter of time now until his heart crumbled to dust, legally bound and sentenced to yearn after the new wife who would never return his love.

Frances peeped up at him, a shadow of uncertainty *just* visible behind the smile she so resolutely wore.

'So. No escape for either of us now.'

'It would seem not.'

He arched what he hoped was a light-hearted eyebrow even as he felt something inside give a sharp stab. Jane's questioning had forced him to confront the true extent of his feelings and now they wouldn't leave him alone, his pain and his delight wrapped up in one woman who had no idea she was either thing. He ought to feel relief that his plan had worked and the way was clear for him to pluck his family from the gutter, but that release refused to come, instead the knife in his gut twisting at the way the sunshine high-lighted every fleck of amber in her pretty eyes.

Those eyes weren't on him at that moment, however, and following Frances's gaze Jonah saw a row of graves standing to one side of the path. She slowed a little, her face suddenly clouding, and she didn't need to say anything for him to understand.

Two headstones were placed closer together than the rest. The first was cross-shaped and more weathered, a light film of green soften-ing its edges, while the other was rectangular and much newer, although the name Jonah read carved into each bridged any differences be-tween them.

Marina Nettleford. Robert Nettleford. Fran-ces's family.

She stopped in front of them, still holding Jonah's arm, and he felt her fingers grip harder. The line of her jaw tightened as she looked down at the graves and her smile faltered, some new emotion chasing out her courage.

'I don't imagine my uncle ever thought he'd be at my wedding, and yet…there he is.'

Frances nodded towards the fresher-look-ing stone, her voice quiet among the rustling of fallen leaves that littered the ground but the re-

strained pain in it like a dagger to Jonah's soul.
A swift glance was enough for Jane to make the
connection and usher the children away, Frances
not seeming to notice as she slipped her hand
free of Jonah's elbow and stepped forward to
trace the worn letters on the cross.

'Mama too. What a touching family occasion.'

She spoke dryly but something sparkled on
her eyelashes and she quickly turned her face
away so Jonah couldn't see. Her fingertips wandered over each carved letter, a practised gesture
Jonah realised she must have done a thousand
times on a thousand lonely days, and he was
almost engulfed by a tide of pity only Frances
could command.

Carefully, as though trying not to frighten a
wild bird, he moved closer. He wanted to reach
for her but something in the rigid set of her
shoulders told him to stop, the idea of intruding
on her grief leaving a sour taste in his mouth. All
of a sudden she was like an island, untouchable
in her sorrow, and the urge to do something—
anything—to console her was more than Jonah
could bear.

A gleam of inspiration struck him. Gently he
took the posy from Frances's hand and drew out
two roses, their petals pearlescent in the morning light and laden with a scent that reminded
him of the first time he'd kissed her in Rose

Cottage's dark hall. She'd almost fallen into his arms then and he could recall every detail of how her waist had curved beneath his palm. A fierce longing filled him, wondering if she'd grant him the same favour again on their wedding night, but he pushed the ungentlemanly thought aside as he knelt on the ground.

In silence he laid a flower at the base of each gravestone, solemnly bowing his head over the grassy mounds. Frances said nothing, only watching without comment, but her eyes were dry when Jonah straightened up and she settled her hand back into the crook of his arm without hesitation as if his presence was a comfort.

They stood together, neither speaking as they gazed down at the two roses glowing white against green. It wasn't much of a tribute but it seemed to mean something to Frances, a touch of her old self resurfacing when she threw him a sidelong look.

'Well. If I didn't know better, I might think you were sentimental after all.'

He huffed a dry laugh, relieved some of the unhappiness had drained from her face. 'Perhaps I am. You're forbidden to tell anyone, though—I'll only deny it if you do.'

With one last long look Frances stepped back onto the path, allowing Jonah to guide her away. He could have sworn he heard her sigh, although when he glanced down she merely frowned, the hand holding her posy resting on her stomach.

'Shall we go back to Barrow? I missed breakfast chasing after an escaped hen and I hear the wedding cake calling my name.'

The mental picture of Frances dashing after a chicken in her best gown could have made him smile but Jonah kept his face grave, her sadness of moments before still imprinted on his mind. 'Good idea. I won't have it said I'm the kind of husband who's happy for his wife to go hungry.'

They reached the churchyard gate and Jonah stood back to let Frances go ahead of him. Jane and the children waited at a discreet distance, although it was an entirely different, and infinitely less welcome, collection of bystanders that caught his eye.

Mrs Campbell, Miss Fletcher and a gaggle of their fellow gossips hovered by the stone wall, dissolving immediately into rapid muttering as Frances passed by. She didn't so much as glance at them but Jonah saw her hesitate, the stiffening of her spine at the loud whispers a clear giveaway that she didn't appreciate the attention.

Can't they leave her alone even on her wedding day?

Jonah's face darkened like the sky before a storm. That those vultures had come solely to gawp made his blood boil, none of them bothering to offer congratulations or anything other than avid curiosity as though Frances were a creature in a zoo. Out of the corner of his eye he saw Mrs Campbell fall back nervously at his approach but he strode past without stopping, not slowing until he reached Frances and found her little hand.

She peered round at him in surprise, cheeks reddening as his fingers slipped between hers and held on tight. It was far more intimate than a chaste hand on his arm and Jonah felt his throat dry at her palm pressed against his, their fingers laced like two halves of a puzzle finally made whole.

'What—?'

'Ignore them. Pretend they're not even there.'

Behind him he heard the whispering grow in pitch at this most interesting development but he couldn't find the will to give a damn. They could talk all they liked. He would never take notice of their spite and he hoped Frances wouldn't either, her worth as comparable to theirs as gold was to tin.

'That's easy for you to say when half the town swoons every time you walk by.' She tried for a smile, that pretty blush still illuminating her cheekbones in the most distracting manner imaginable. 'They think I somehow tricked you into marrying me—that welcoming committee is only looking for proof of what they believe already.'

Jonah drew her closer to his side, wishing he had the nerve to bend and kiss her parted lips. A complex mixture of defiance and uncertainty danced in her eyes and he couldn't fathom how anyone could be so resolved to think badly of her, when her courage and spirit were there for all to see and admire. It was those very qualities that had broken down his walls, giving him proof that caring for somebody other than Jane didn't have to be a burden. Frances added to his strength rather than draining it, something he ached to tell her even as he knew he never would.

'You don't need to listen to them any more. You're my wife now and I promise to stand between you and their malice for the rest of my life.'

Something flickered over Frances's face, there and gone in less than a second but leaving the distinct impression he had touched close to the bone. She turned to face him full on, their fingers still twining together and his chest gave a squeeze as she looked frankly into his face.

'I think you've realised by now that I don't need a man to stand in front of me,' she murmured, quietly holding his gaze. 'But knowing you're willing to walk at my side means more to me than anything else you ever could have said.

For that I thank you, and what's more—I promise I'll always do the same for you.'

Jonah nodded, a fraction too sharply and hurting his neck, but he hardly noticed the pain.

They were the prettiest words she'd ever spoken to him and for the smallest, most short-lived of moments his spirits flickered upwards. What did she mean by them? Was there a chance she'd come to walk at his side in the way that he craved, he wondered, and allow them to make the kind of life together he hadn't known he wanted?

For that single precious second he allowed himself to dream, a happier future stretching out before him like a magic carpet—before the harsh truth came crashing back to make his soul wither.

Of course not. You know that and yet you still continue to dream like a child of things that will never be.

Frances offered him a small fleeting smile that left sparks in its wake, and began to lead him away from the women watching from close by. He followed like a lost dog, helpless in the face of his growing love for the wife for whom suffering had shattered any chance of surrendering her heart. She'd never made a secret of it, her uncle clearly the only man she'd ever think it safe to love, and Jonah cursed every single person who had treated her badly, sealing his fate.

He was a fool for wanting a happy-ever-after and an even bigger fool for hoping it might come true…but foolish hope was all he had, and he clung to it as he and Frances walked—still hand in hand—to meet Jane and the twins.

It was almost midnight by the time Frances slowly climbed the farmhouse stairs, her body tired but mind more awake than she'd felt in months.

Wedding or no wedding, there had still been work to do and she hadn't seen much of Jonah after Jane and the children had departed after the celebration breakfast, Matthew still halfway through an enormous slab of cake and Margaret proudly carrying what was left of Frances's posy. Jonah had disappeared up to the top field to mend a fence and Frances had carried on work around the yard, although in truth her legs had carried her with little input from her brain. All she could think of was Jonah, his face as they'd said their vows, the heat of his hand as he'd tried to shield her from Miss Fletcher's venom…and what he might do later, the prospect of their wedding night terrifying and exciting in almost equal measure.

Now as she reached the upstairs landing Frances felt her heart hammering against her ribs. He'd gone up before her and the thought of what waited behind her bedroom door made her hands shake, the flame of the candle she carried quivering and her shadow distorting against the wall.

She wasn't *completely* clueless about what was to come—she'd seen animals in the act of making young more times than she could count—but quite how that compared with what happened in a bedroom Frances couldn't quite say. The men who had imposed on her in the past had been after something dark and selfish but surely Jonah wasn't like *them*? He might not feel the same way towards her as she did him but even a business arrangement needed to be sealed, and at the very least her new husband could be relied on to treat her with respect—if not the same desire that ran in Frances's veins and made her stumble as she took a deep breath and pushed open the door.

He stood at the window, looking out over Barrow's yard with his powerful shoulders outlined in moonlight, shoulders still covered by a shirt, something Frances noticed with undeniable disappointment. With his back to her, she was glad of the chance to gather her nerve, although Jonah turned at the tell-tale sound of creaking floorboards.

Hesitating by the door, it was as though she'd lost her tongue. She stared at him and he looked back, his expression half-hidden in shadow but apparently waiting politely for her to speak. They'd been alone many times before but now the moment had come for them to take the final step Frances couldn't seem to move, pinned to the spot by rising uncertainty mixed with longing she felt in her bones.

Say something. Don't just gawp like a simpleton.

She swallowed down with difficulty. Both she and Jonah were still fully dressed and she wondered if he'd expect her to change into her nightgown in the same room, a thought that made her breath catch sharply.

'Well. Here we are.'

'Here we are.'

Jonah's voice was significantly more composed than hers and Frances almost winced at her own gawkishness. They might have been complete strangers. Meeting his eye was suddenly impossible as she tried desperately to ignore the loud beating of her heart and find something to say.

'Do…do you remember the first time you were in this room?'

'I ought to,' he replied patiently, as if she'd spoken sense rather than awkward rambling. 'It was only three weeks ago and that evening is rather stamped into my mind.'

'Oh. Yes, of course. A stupid question.'

A pause threatened to settle, the silence broken only by the mournful cry of an owl somewhere out in the night. Gyp was asleep downstairs by the dying sitting room fire, so Frances couldn't even draw comfort from his presence as she combed her blank mind, all rational thought apparently abandoning her at the prospect of Jonah in her bed.

He moved away from the window, coming a little closer but not enough to touch, although even those few paces made Frances's legs weaken. Folding his arms, he observed her narrowly, his scrutiny raising the hairs on her nape.

'Are you nervous?'

'What makes you say that?'

'You're lingering in the doorway as if ready to run.'

A hot flush roared up from Frances's neck. 'Not in the slightest. I don't know what you mean.'

She took a couple of unsteady steps further into the room, turning briefly to close the door behind her. When she looked round again Jonah was still watching her, his curiosity replaced by a strange gentleness.

'You don't have to do this. I wouldn't think any less of you if—'

Frances shook her head at once, half mortified

by the speed of her instinctive denial. 'I know what happens on a wedding night.' *More or less.* 'You may not have entered into this out of any kind of feeling but if a thing's worth doing it's worth doing properly.'

She saw Jonah's eyebrows rise and felt her cheeks burn a flaming crimson, glad of the candle's forgiving light. Perhaps she'd been a little *too* insistent. The helpless desire for Jonah that sang in her blood had crept into her voice too, and she feared he'd heard the emotion concealed behind a businesslike façade. Frances faltered, embarrassment coming to warm her all the way down to her toes.

'Unless, of course, you don't want...?'

Her sentence petered out as Jonah moved towards her, his footsteps the only sound in the silent night. Taking the candle from her unresisting hand, he placed it beside the bed, leaving no obstacle between them as he came to stand so close before her she had to tip her head back to look up into his face.

'Oh, no. I wouldn't say that.'

Carefully, giving her plenty of time to pull away, he brought a hand up to cup one burning cheek, his fingertips tracing the line of Frances's jaw to make her stiffen with sudden, *delicious* anticipation. His eyes sought hers with a wordless question and she answered it the same way, allowing her lashes to flutter closed as Jonah bent to conquer the last distance between them.

Frances's breath hitched as his lips touched hers, so gently at first she barely felt their caress. They were every bit as warm and soft as she remembered but knowing how much more firmly they could bear down made her shiver with impatience, wishing he would read the silent cues of her body and give her what she wanted, *more*. From somewhere deep in her core a fierce longing rose, a side of herself Frances barely recognised as she wrapped her arms around Jonah's neck and pulled him closer still, rejoicing in finally acting as she'd yearned to for so long. He came willingly, with a growl that made her heart leap, and a strong arm encircled her waist to give Frances nowhere to hide.

His hand slid from her jaw to cradle the back of her head, twining in her hair and pulling just enough to set every nerve on her scalp ablaze. Jonah held her to his hard chest with merciless resolve, the muscles beneath his shirt like granite—but there was nowhere else Frances would rather be, accepting her imprisonment gladly without ever lifting her mouth from his. A trace of stubble on his chin scratched her lips, making them burn, although the friction only made her feel more alive as they stood entangled in each other, two sets of lungs heaving and the room's temperature shooting skyward with every snatched breath.

Suddenly Frances gasped, feeling Jonah's lips curve into a wicked smile beneath hers. His hands had wandered downwards, ghosting over the hidden curves as they went until they gripped the backs of her thighs and jerked her off her feet, lifting her to lie flat against the front of his body with his mouth perfectly placed to tease the spot where her pulse raced beneath the thin skin. If it was *more* she'd wanted then Jonah was certainly happy to oblige. Frances's head was swimming as he dropped scalding kisses from her collarbone to her ear, nibbling on the delicate shell to set stars twinkling before her closed eyes and with her head thrown back she surrendered completely to the sensations blazing in every sinew.

Her hands were in his hair, fingers tunnelling through tousled waves and clenching when he gently bit down on her lobe. Some part of her questioned whether a man and a woman in a platonic marriage ought to behave with such abandon but the thought had no chance to take root, Jonah choosing that precise moment to run the very tip of his tongue along the edge of her ear. The tiny movement obliterated any hope of thinking rationally and Frances shuddered, good sense and caution disappearing behind a thick fog of desire.

She heard Jonah's low murmur, the strained hoarseness of his voice more rousing than she ever could have imagined.

'Can I...?'

He didn't even need to finish before Frances found herself nodding, shamelessly eager for whatever came next. She might have agreed to anything if it meant Jonah would keep his hands on her, the pressure of his palms on her thighs shocking and scandalous and *wonderful* beyond measure. However many times she'd imagined a scene like this, whatever she'd seen in her most unladylike dreams, nothing could compare with the reality of Jonah's tongue dancing with hers or the breathless relief of letting herself go, her hunger for him a tide that carried her further and further out to sea.

Still holding her firmly to him, Jonah turned for the bed, stumbling slightly and taking her with him as he lay back against the pillows. Her skirts were rucked up between them and Frances thought she might faint when warm fingers slid beneath to stroke the secret skin no one else had ever discovered, her choking sigh making Jonah snatch an equally ragged breath.

Something was building low down and when Frances's eyes drifted open she saw a shadow of the same nameless rush in Jonah's rapt expression. His colour was high and his eyes glazed, although from somewhere he found the willpower to pull back when he saw her watching.

'Frances? Do you want me to stop?'

His voice was still rough with want and Frances weakened further at how good her name sounded on his lips. She tried to speak but all words had vanished, leaving only action with which to reply.

Snaking an unsteady hand downwards, she took hold of his shirt and pulled it free of his breeches, her breath coming faster than ever at his answering groan. Pushing it up, she ran her fingers over the diamond-hard ridges of muscle she found there, the same light dusting of hair she'd noticed that day in Barrow's sunlit yard unexpectedly coarse beneath her questing fingertips, and she marvelled at how much darker it was than the chestnut waves on his head. Sliding her palm higher, she felt Jonah's heart jumping in his chest just as fast as hers as his light touch explored the tied ribbons on the back of her gown.

One eyebrow flickering higher, she smiled against his mouth. 'Do you need me to help you with that?'

'I think I can manage.'

The deft fingers tugged a little more and then her bodice loosened, the bows at her neck and waist coming apart to allow Jonah's hand inside, and Frances's heart stopped when she felt him begin to unlace her stays. Once he'd undone those, all that would lie between them was her shift, a prospect that soon became reality when, with one last burning glance to gauge her reaction, Jonah slid both gown and corset down over her shoulders, Frances impatiently wriggling free of her tangled skirts and dropping them onto the floor.

She pushed herself up now, one leg on either side of Jonah's reclining body, and she saw his eyes darken as he devoured the sight of her in nothing but her scanty shift. Even in dim candlelight it was almost transparent and Frances couldn't help another smile to finally realise her power, the spell a woman could weave over a man. He was transfixed, a muscle in his jaw working furiously, and when she slowly undid the ribbons that held her shift closed she feared he might lose his head.

Throwing aside what last vestiges of shame or restraint might remain, Frances let it fall open, the fabric settling with a whisper around her hips, and Jonah balled his hands into fists. A sound more animal than human escaped from him and the desperate look he threw her made every last inch of her skin combust into flame, the naked need in his face something she couldn't resist a moment longer.

Leaning forward, she claimed his lips again and felt his hands lock fiercely around the bare skin of her waist, refusing to release her even when she murmured into his ear.

'I've never done this before, Jonah. You'll have to show me how.'

He laughed then, a low, broken note so charged with molten want Frances's knees almost gave way. One hand still gripping her waist, the other came up to graze her ribs, wandering higher until Frances choked on her own breath, and it was Jonah's turn to smile at the strangled gasp.

'It would be my pleasure.'

Chapter Eleven

Jonah swung the mallet again, the dull thud of wood against wood ringing out across the field. The fence he'd started fixing the day before was almost halfway finished and a sense of satisfaction rose as he cast a critical eye over the strong posts he'd worked so hard to drive into the ground. Barrow's bull watched him mildly from a safe distance, placid now he was alone in his bachelor paddock, and although Jonah didn't trust him enough to turn his back he still sought the other male's opinion.

'Well? Will it please Frances, do you think?'

The bull didn't answer but Jonah imagined he saw approval in the huge black eyes before shaking his head at his folly. The desire to please his new wife was tipping him into madness, it seemed, and he snorted to himself as he wiped the sweat off his brow that a rising autumnal breeze hadn't yet dried.

She was never far from his mind though, even backbreaking labour not enough to distract him from the thoughts of Frances that had harried him since the first moment he'd awoken that morning to find himself alone in her—*their*—bed. Only a still-warm furrow in the mattress proved she'd been there at all and he had lain motionless as snippets of the previous night flickered before him, the smell of her hair and the fevered heat of her skin burned into his mind for ever. Even now he could feel her breath on his neck and hear her cries as they both reached the point of no return, her arms locked around him and neat nails digging into his skin with unconscious need. The taste of her lingered on his tongue and his lips longed for another chance to explore the sweetness of hers, a heavy ache beginning to develop lower down as Jonah's memories ran riot and he had to take a moment to bring himself back under control.

He tipped his head back to stare up at the sky, watching soft white clouds pass across it. Had Frances enjoyed it as much as he had, the night he realised was the best of his whole harsh, unhappy life? He'd been with women before, of course, but never like *that*, feeling as though he was drowning in her half-closed eyes and her gasps like an angel sighing, the seamless melding of their bodies effortless as if they'd been designed with no other purpose in mind. It was so natural, so thrilling yet familiar, but even more than that—if he'd had any doubt he loved her before, he certainly had none now.

Screwing his eyes shut, Jonah groaned.

Last night didn't help much in that regard. If anything, it's made things a hundred times worse than they were already.

Like a stubborn weed, his love for Frances had forced its way under barriers and through tiny cracks in its determination to grow towards the sun and there was nothing he could do to stop it, he accepted ruefully. His heart belonged to her now and always would, their wedding night the final nail in the coffin in which he'd bury the indifference he had cultivated since he was a child. Without knowing it, Frances had smashed every last brick in the walls he'd tried to build up between them, leaving him to wonder how he'd lived for thirty years without her at his side. Another thirty stretched out now, but the knowledge they would be spent in the constant torment of wanting something he couldn't have lay heavy on his soul, a future of one-sided devotion all Jonah had to look forward to now he'd taken such an irreversible step. It would be an endless cycle of delight and agony to share his life with Frances and yet never have his feelings returned, forced every day to deny the emotion he had never intended to allow.

He was gripping the mallet's handle far too hard. His knuckles ached beneath the strain and, flexing his fingers, he looked out across the field, his stomach suddenly twisting as he made out a familiar figure climbing over the five-barred gate.

Jonah watched Frances come towards him, his heart beginning to set up a steady thump beneath his shirt. In one hand she carried an enamel jug and in the other something wrapped in cloth, her skirts rippling about her legs as she walked and her hair bound up in a simple green ribbon that contrasted prettily with the dark waves. She was just as beautiful in her worn working clothes as when dressed as a bride, and he found he couldn't look away as she drew closer, with Gyp following hot on her heels.

She stopped at the fence, sizing it up with one practised glance, and Jonah felt a gleam of pride at her decisive nod.

'This is looking good. You've certainly been busy.'

'No time like the present to start earning my keep.'

The corners of Frances's lips lifted a little—the same lips he had kissed mere hours earlier, the thought of it making his breath suddenly unsteady. They had parted so readily under his, the sweetest gasps coming from them and so soft surely no man could resist tasting and then coming back for more. Their rosy warmth was an addiction he had to surrender to, the temptation to bend down now and seek them again so strong it almost brought him to his knees...

Offering silent thanks that Frances couldn't read his mind, he propped the mallet against the fence and stretched his arms above his head, feeling the tension in every muscle from wrist to shoulder. He couldn't help but notice Frances followed the movement, the appreciative flick of those hazel eyes more gratifying than any words and stoking the embers already glowing from having her standing so close.

Clearly she hadn't meant to stare. With a little shake she held up what she carried in each hand, the mystery of the jug and cloth-wrapped bundle about to be solved. 'I thought you might be glad of some breakfast. It's only bread and cheese but the milk was fresh just half an hour ago—it should still be warm.'

As soon as she suggested it Jonah realised she was right, a hollow feeling joining the other sensations already gnawing beneath his shirt.

'Thank you. It hadn't occurred to me how hungry I was until you mentioned it.'

Frances smiled knowingly. 'My uncle was the

same. He'd get so distracted when working that if I didn't remind him about mealtimes he could go all day without eating a thing.'

She sat down on the grass, leaning back against the strong new fence and untying the parcel to reveal a cottage loaf and thick slab of cheese. Patting the grass, she gestured for Jonah to sit too, cutting off a generous slice of bread as he took his place beside her.

'Here. No forks or plates—you're a farmer now and we have to make do with roughing it.'

She passed the slice to him and he took a bite, making himself chew although his mouth dried as frustration tightened its grip. Frances sat so close and yet his previous thoughts of the futility of his feelings wouldn't leave him alone, crowding round in an attempt to drown out any pleasure he might have found in her presence. All he could think was what lay ahead of him, the light of the present moment thrown into shade by contemplating the darkness of days yet to come, and he cursed himself with every dry swallow.

I know it's hopeless, but if I could have but one hour with Frances where I didn't feel the impossibility of a happy future eating me alive...

Glancing to the side, he watched her tear off another wedge of bread and break a piece of cheese onto it before putting it to her mouth. She seemed to be savouring every bite and Jonah wanted to do the same, although it was the moment, rather than the food, he wished could last for ever.

The truth was he wanted to simply enjoy being with her, watching the breeze move over her tanned skin, knowing the unspoken pleasure of seeing the woman he loved bathed in sunlight as though illuminated from within. Sooner or later his heart would be worn to a thread by unrequited longing, he knew, but surely it couldn't be a sin to pretend otherwise for the briefest time, fixing the scene in his mind to revisit after all else had fallen apart? For one fragment of time he had everything he needed within his reach, Frances finally at ease in his company and even the sun seeming to smile down on them as if blessing the scene.

They ate in companionable silence, neither feeling the need to fill the quiet that descended over their spot near the fence. Frances appeared content to sit at his side, once brushing an insect from his shoulder with such natural ease they might have been married for years rather than a day, and Jonah treasured the precious minutes as they slipped through his fingers. The soft cooing of birds in the hedges and Gyp's gentle snores were the only sounds, the fields spreading out around them in a blanket of green that made Jonah feel he and Frances were the only two people in the world. With her eyes closed and face turned to the sun, she looked more relaxed than he'd ever seen her before, a pretty young woman in place of the bone-tired wraith he had first met weeks ago.

He had to pretend he hadn't been staring when Frances opened her eyes and slid him a smile that made his heart leap painfully.

'I've just realised I didn't bring cups either. We both have to drink straight from the jug…if you've no objection?'

'None at all.'

She lifted the heavy jug and took a deep draught, letting out a satisfied sigh as she offered it to Jonah. He took it from her and raised it to his own mouth, the intimacy of placing his lips where Frances's had just been not lost on him, nor the accursedly *interested* feeling stirring in his gut.

The milk was delicious, rich and creamy and unmistakably fresh, and for a second it managed to pull Jonah's attention away from the woman sitting so near he could have touched her. He was caught a little off guard then, when Frances cleared her throat with studied nonchalance, crumbling a small piece of bread into fragments on her skirted lap.

'I suppose, after last night, it would be silly to

be coy about sharing a drink when so many other things have passed between us. Do you think?'

Covering his surprise with a cough, Jonah put down the jug.

She wants to talk about last night?

The stirring in his innards grew stronger, moving a little lower down to places he had no intention of involving in any decent conversation. Frances was inspecting her handiwork but he sensed her listening, far too sharp to be distracted by a pile of crumbs.

'I would agree. I think the time for us to be reticent with each other has long gone.'

She nodded, still not looking up from her lap, and Jonah couldn't quite tell if he'd said the right thing. The temptation to ask a question of his own reared its head and he tried not to sound too eager as he laid a hand on Gyp's sleeping back, readying himself to take the plunge.

'Was it to your liking? Last night, I mean.'

Out of the corner of his eye he saw Frances's fingers stop mid-dabble. 'Surely you know the answer to that.'

'A man shouldn't assume. For all I know, you were glad to get the single required occasion out of the way so you need never suffer my advances again.'

The sharp line of Frances's profile was just visible at the very edge of his vision and Jonah saw a hint of pink creep into her cheeks, his pulse beginning to skip faster at that familiar blush. It told him she was thinking something, but not *what*, forcing him to wait until she decided to grace him with an answer.

'That isn't quite my way of thinking. I don't see why two friends shouldn't enjoy the…the *advantages* of marriage, as well as its mere conveniences. Do you?'

She shot him a swift sideways glance from beneath her lashes, and he had to bite back a harsh breath. If she was saying what he thought she was then Frances had just suggested a repeat performance of the most wonderful night of his life, the very idea lighting a fire in Jonah's blood.

A small part of him held back, however. A glimmer of disappointment at Frances's exact turn of phrase echoed at the back of Jonah's mind to take the edge off the heat winding through his insides.

Two friends. That's how she described us.

He brushed a piece of grass off his knee. That first surge of anticipation was subsiding as quickly as it had come and cold reality replaced it, his delight rapidly turning to ash.

What else had he expected? She might find his body attractive—that much was obvious— but that was clearly as far as it went, any romantic nonsense his folly and his alone. Love and

lust were two very different things and just because his feelings had changed didn't mean he
had any right to hope for the same from Frances.

*Just as she's always said. You can never say
she's ever told anything other than the absolute truth.*

She was clearly waiting for him to say something. Her heap of breadcrumbs was getting
taller by the minute and Jonah made sure his
voice wouldn't betray his disappointment before he replied.

'Certainly, if both parties were satisfied with
the arrangement.'

'I understand.' Frances inclined her head with
careful unconcern that didn't fool him for a moment. The colour in her cheeks was feverish and
if he hadn't been keeping himself under strict
control Jonah could have reached out for her
there and then. 'It seems we reached the same
conclusion. For my part, I wouldn't be *opposed*
to further exploration of what marriage entails,
as we find ourselves in that position.'

'Nor would I.'

His insides gave an unpleasant tweak but
Jonah stubbornly ignored their complaint, the
prospect of holding Frances in his arms again too
enticing to resist. Like a siren's song it called to
him and even knowing he would eventually be

dashed against the rocks he couldn't block it out, his heart pulling him onwards with no choice.

They sat for a while longer, although the companionable silence of before seemed in danger of being replaced by something quite different. A strange charge hung in the air, Frances's hands noticeably clumsier than usual as she gathered what was left of the food and knotted it in the cloth, and Jonah could have sworn he felt her start when his fingers brushed hers passing over the empty jug.

Jumpy as a wild cat. Maybe she thought that conversation just as interesting as I did.

He stayed leaning against the fence when she stood up and slapped the dirt from her skirts, Gyp waking with the movement. The dog gave a great yawn and Jonah ruffled the wiry ears, trying not to stare as Frances stretched her back and the graceful arch highlighted the shape of her bodice with tantalising clarity. He knew exactly what lay beneath those layers of fabric now and he gritted his teeth as a memory flitted through his mind, so heated it almost drove him to his feet.

He'd give himself one day, Jonah decided, helpless in the face of his weakness for Frances that he feared might drive him mad. Tomorrow he'd go back to dreading what relentless disappointments the future might bring, but just for today he would set aside the knowledge of what was to come and live with her in the here and now. While the sun shone down and Frances glowed like a bronze statue he wanted to drink it in, trying to memorise every detail of her glossy hair and beautifully curving lips as she smiled over her shoulder and began to walk away.

'Come back to the house at dinnertime. Don't forget.'

Frances's mouth turned down with distaste as she surveyed her hands, soot clinging to every last inch. Catching sight of herself in the mirror propped up on the kitchen dresser, she saw her face was little better. Black streaks covered her cheeks, a particularly grimy smear on her forehead where she'd pushed back her increasingly untidy hair. At least the ruined stable was getting better, however, and the progress she'd made that afternoon in clearing out the ash and charred wood had made it worth looking like a chimney sweep. A couple more days and she could see about fixing the roof, Apollo finally able to return after three weeks living in a hastily emptied store behind the barn.

She looked at the clock.

Almost four. It'll be a while yet before Jonah comes back.

If she was quick enough she'd have time to

bathe before he returned from the fields. She was almost amused by the unfamiliar imp of vanity that murmured in her ear. Like as not, Jonah wouldn't care two straws whether it seemed as if she'd been down a mine but the insistent voice whispered again, its argument *slightly* strengthened by the trail of soot that followed Frances across her otherwise pristine floor. A hot bath would wash her clean and perhaps soothe the ache in her muscles that never left her alone… as well as maybe, just *maybe,* distracting her from the conversation that morning that now made her flush hot.

Could you have made it any clearer you want him again? If you're not careful he'll think he married a wanton after all, just like everybody warned him.

She grimaced as she set her biggest copper kettle to heat over the fire. It was fortunate Jonah was so determined to ignore the sly mutterings about her, if he'd ever really considered them. If he'd looked at the evidence in front of his own eyes there was no way he could have missed how she truly felt. She needed to work harder to conceal her growing weakness, both for his sake and her own. It was more important than ever now they shared a bed as well as a roof, and the knowledge that he wouldn't want her love sat as a constant ache in the very depths of her chest.

'He married you to be helpful, as a favour between friends,' Frances chided herself out loud in the empty kitchen. 'You know full well he never really wanted a wife. Don't make him regret his kindness just because you can't control your heart.'

It was easier said than done, however, when memories of the previous night came in a never-ending stream, and Frances bit her lip as a particularly vivid image of Jonah's rapt face flickered through her mind. The feel of him, the masculine scent of his body, the skilled touch in undiscovered places that had made her fall apart under his questing hands...

What woman alive could have shared that experience and not fallen even deeper? Her feelings were so strong now Frances knew there was no hope of escape.

With a sigh she sank into the old chair beside the hearth, staring into the steam rising from the kettle but seeing nothing but Jonah's dark smile in the curling mist.

I should be grateful for what I have rather than strive for what will only end in disappointment. I have a good man for a husband and the future of Barrow is safe now—surely it would be greedy to wish for more.

She smoothed down the lap of her filthy apron, only vaguely noticing the dirt ingrained beneath her nails. Her conscience gave good advice and she knew she had to follow it, that clear guidance her best chance of avoiding even more heartache than already hounded her every step. If she just kept busy, kept going without ever stopping to think, perhaps one day this madness would end—although even as the thought occurred Frances knew it was nonsense. She felt suddenly wearier than ever as she pulled the simmering kettle from the fire and made for the stairs.

The old tin bath waited in a corner of her bedroom and with one foot Frances pushed it over to stand in front of the hearth. The room was already warm but she poked the fire regardless, the flames dancing merrily as she poured the first load of water out to splash against the bottom of the bath. It took another two hot kettles and one cold to fill it, although it was worth the trudging up and down when it was ready and Frances finally stepped inside, lowering herself into the scented water with a contented sigh.

For a while she sat without moving, leaning back against the rim with her eyes closed and the water lapping at her half-submerged shoulders, simply enjoying the relief of heat on exhausted muscles. The green ribbon holding her hair back had already loosened and still with eyes shut she pulled it free completely, allowing the thick waves to fall into the water, where they drifted around her like seaweed, floating in time with the gentle ripples her breathing sent across the surface.

Lifting one lazy eyelid, she was annoyed to see she'd left her rose oil wash ball on the little table beside the bed—a bed she swiftly looked away from before any more arousing memories could disturb her peace—but couldn't seem to find the will to get out of the bath to fetch it. She would eventually, although the warmth was creeping into her aching bones so pleasantly that her head started to nod.

Frances only realised she was dozing when a sudden noise from behind made her sit up sharply, the unmistakable sound of creaking floorboards sending her heart crashing forwards into her ribs.

'I'm sorry. I didn't realise—I came upstairs to change, but...'

Jonah stood in the doorway, looking every bit as surprised as Frances felt. Caught too off-balance to cover herself, she could have sworn she saw him glance down at her naked shoulders before respectfully averting his eyes, fixing them on an interesting point on the ceiling, but too late to stop a wild thrill from running the length of her spine.

'I'll come back later.'

He made to leave, although not before Frances saw something in his face that made her stomach flutter with scandalous delight. In the split-second before he turned away his gaze had darkened, the already chiselled line of his jaw tight with strain, and a look of such plain want had passed over his countenance that she heard herself call out before she realised she'd even opened her mouth.

'Wait.'

Jonah stopped at once, not even a pace from the door. 'Do you need something?'

He spoke politely enough but Frances couldn't hold back a helpless shiver to see how difficult it was for him to look into her eyes. He seemed to be fighting the urge to let his gaze wander, gentlemanly good manners at war with a far more feral instinct, and she knew herself to be teasing him when she sat a little straighter, letting one more tantalising inch of skin show above the waterline to make Jonah's taut jaw almost snap in two.

'Before you go…would you pass me that wash ball?'

Jonah followed the line of her pointing finger towards her table next to the bed and she saw his eyes linger on the pillows, thoughts of the previous night clearly not far from his mind either. They certainly crowded hers, her breath coming quicker as she saw him hesitate. The air was suddenly stifling with unspoken tension as he slowly came into the room.

It crackled between them like bottled lightning, Frances aware of every movement of Jonah's body and not wanting to look away. In three deliberate strides he was beside the bed and a memory of him in that very spot flitted through her head, when his bare chest and wicked smile had made her blood burn in the darkness. The longing to see him like that again crashed over her like a tidal wave, so insistent Frances couldn't bring herself to feel any shame—only hopeless desire, rising to a sharp peak when he turned towards her, the little ball seeming tiny in his hand as he lifted it to his nose.

'So this is why you always smell of roses.'

'That's right.' Frances realised her voice was husky, choking to think he knew the intimate scent of her skin. 'I make the oil myself from blooms in the orchard.'

Jonah nodded but it seemed he'd hardly heard her. His attention appeared fixed on other things entirely as he approached the bath, holding out his hand for Frances to take the wash ball, and his jaw so hard now it could have been carved from stone. The atmosphere hadn't lightened one bit, still as heavy and brooding as a storm cloud waiting to burst, and she could hardly bear another second of her heart racing away with breakneck speed. If one of them didn't act soon she feared she might lose her wits completely— or perhaps she already had, all thought abandoning her as a wild impulse commanded her to move.

She rose slowly from the bath. Jonah's lips parted on a harsh breath as her eyes sought his and she saw the surprise in them turn to such raw hunger that it made her tremble. Water cascaded over the hills and valleys of her body, the secret geography Jonah had only just begun to map with his hands and mouth, and she longed for him to continue his studies as her pulse leapt beneath skin crying out to be touched.

He didn't keep her waiting long.

Jonah came towards her and she reached out at once, their lips meeting with a passion that surpassed any before. The heat of his kiss eclipsed everything else, the room fading into the background as his tongue danced with hers, leaving no time to do anything but arch against his chest and know she had nothing left to lose.

He didn't love her, Frances was well aware of that, the knowledge even now sitting in the pit of her stomach, never letting her forget…but he desired her, and if that was the best Jonah had to offer she would take it with both hands. It was a pale substitute for real love and doubtless one day she would regret her choice, but with his hands tight on her hips and his fingers pressing into her flesh it was very difficult to care.

Wordlessly he swept her off her feet, cradling her against him without ever breaking the scalding seal of their lips. One blind kick of a booted foot sent the door slamming shut and then they were completely alone, neither interested in anything but the other as the afternoon turned to evening and all thoughts of what work was left on the farm disappeared from Frances's pleasure-drenched mind.

Chapter Twelve

Frances peered up at Jonah from beneath the brim of her bonnet, the white edge of her new cap almost hiding her from view as they walked through Marchfield's busy streets. He hadn't said a word since they'd left Rose Cottage, looking more serious now than she'd seen him for the entirety of their two-week marriage, and it wasn't hard to understand why.

He turned so pale when the twins came to wake us, banging on the farmhouse door as if they were chased there by wolves. They must have been terrified to find their mother so ill when they woke this morning and Jonah seemed hardly less frightened himself once he knew why they'd come.

He'd been out of bed and pulling on his breeches before Frances had time to realise what was happening. Jane had taken a turn for the worse during the night, the children managed to explain between sobs, and was coughing so hard she could barely breathe. One short nod was enough to tell Jonah to leave the twins at Barrow and go immediately to help and he'd left at once, only a lingering glance passing between them that held too many emotions to fully decipher. All Frances knew for certain was that for the first time she saw a glint of fear in Jonah's dark eyes, and that the sight drove a knife through her. It was the same sick dread she knew she must have worn on her own face while Robert lay dying and her heart ached with both worry for Jane and compassion for Jonah, about to confront a nightmare she'd have done anything to spare him.

Now they walked together in silence, Jonah's frown etched so severely it seemed carved in stone. The children had been desperate to return to their mother and by the time Frances had brought them back to the cottage the doctor had been and gone, leaving Jane breathing more easily at last and Jonah brooding beside the kitchen hearth. The glower hadn't left his face since, increasing if anything when Jane had insisted he and Frances go home, and a deep unease spread through her as she waited for him to speak.

He didn't seem inclined to, however. His gaze was fixed dead ahead as if lost in his own thoughts and Frances had to gently squeeze the arm she held to get his attention, the first time she tried to ask him a question receiving no sign he'd heard.

'Jonah… What did the doctor say?'

The glance he cast her was carefully blank, the restrained pain in it cutting her to the quick. 'The same things they always do. They rarely deviate from the script I've heard a hundred times before. Weak chest since birth, very little to be done…'

He broke off and Frances watched a cloud pass over his countenance, plunging it further into the darkness that already reigned. He seemed to hesitate, as if debating whether to say out loud whatever was circling through his mind, and she didn't interrupt as he retreated once again into the murk of his thoughts.

Eventually Jonah spoke. His voice was low and there was a note of something Frances couldn't quite identify, although the reluctance matched his expression.

'He did make *one* further recommendation, but…'

'But what? What was it?'

She looked up at him quickly—*just* quickly enough to catch a puzzling flicker of regret. It came and went like a flash of lightning and then she could sense the shutters coming down again, the smooth unsmiling mask he so often wore firmly back in place. Whatever he'd been about to say had clearly been abandoned, although Frances felt her curiosity stir at the swiftness of his retreat.

'It was nothing. Just some stupid notion.'

Resuming his unseeing forward stare, Jonah led Frances down the street, evidently determined to ignore her questioning gaze. His unhappiness was tangible, however. It radiated from him despite his silence and she felt it like a physical touch to her skin and Frances racked her brain to think how to comfort him. In his quiet pride he'd doubtless deny anything was wrong but she was no fool. His suffering was plain as day and it hurt her to see it more than she ever would have guessed.

Jonah had made a home for himself in her formerly guarded heart, the two weeks of their marriage among the happiest of her whole lonely life. Now when she woke in the morning it was to find his tousled head beside her on the pillow rather than an empty space, their bodies seeking each other's warmth in the night and unconsciously twining together in a sleeping embrace she was always reluctant to end. It was somehow easier to fall asleep with him beside her, his gentle breathing a soothing sound in the darkness... Or perhaps it was more that what came before simply exhausted her, every night since they'd wed following the same path of wandering hands and burning kisses, giving and taking until both fell into a sated sleep…

Glad that Jonah's focus was elsewhere, Frances gave herself a shake. It was hardly the time to be thinking such things when Jane was so ill, the only friend she had in the world apart from the distant man at her side. The acceptance and kindness she'd been shown by her sister-in-law was a testament to her nature and a lump rose in Frances's throat to think of the injustice of one so good being forced to endure so much. Margaret and Matthew had already lost their father and now it seemed their mother might follow, Jonah and the children left behind to try to swallow their grief at the loss of so sweet a soul.

Her chest felt full and Frances pressed a hand to her bodice, hoping Jonah wouldn't notice her distress. He didn't need anything further on his list of worries and she resolved not to add to it, although the next moment her already down-turned lips twisted further.

'Oh, no. Not him…and at a time like this…'

A man was coming towards them with a purposeful stride and her heart leapt to feel Jonah draw her a fraction closer to his side, immediately protective at her obvious dislike despite his own far worse cares. He seemed to grow taller somehow and she couldn't help a flicker of satisfaction when the newcomer hesitated for a moment before continuing his advance.

'Good morning, Miss Nettleford. A pleasure to see you again.'

She glowered at the older man as he bowed, dropping the very smallest of curtseys in return.

If only I could say the same. Of all the people to meet at this moment, why did it have to be you?

'Good morning, Mr Reeves.'

Forcing herself to attempt to sound civil, Frances tightened her grip on Jonah's sleeve. The man in front of her was someone she was in no hurry to see again, with no desire to recall the previous occasion they'd met, but Jonah's quiet presence was a comfort as she pushed the memory away.

'I don't believe you've met my husband, Lieutenant Grant.'

Jonah touched his hat although Frances saw his grave expression didn't change.

Mr Reeves made an attempt at a smile from beneath his greying moustache. 'An honour to meet you, sir.' He bowed again, sunlight glinting off the expensive black silk of his hat.

The more Frances looked, the more she saw evidence of the other farmer's wealth. His land sprawled for miles either side of Marchfield's boundaries, making a fortune for its imposing owner. Barrow stood as a stubborn little island among Reeves's territory, for years refusing to be gobbled up by the estate stretching out around it. Robert had rejected all offers to sell and Frances would too, determination to keep hold of her birthright stronger than any price.

Mr Reeves looked down at her keenly now, seeming friendly, but Frances was not fool enough to fall for his pretence. 'How are things at Barrow? I heard you were having some difficulty obtaining enough help to run the place alone.'

He paused to furrow his brow sympathetically, the falseness of it raising Frances's hackles like a wary cat. 'My offer still stands, you know, if you're struggling. You can always come to me if the burden your uncle placed on you has grown too great.'

Frances pressed her mouth into a thin line, anger beginning to simmer. Was there no end to the man's scheming, the same every time she had the misfortune to cross his path? He had no right to comment on her situation and the idea of him questioning her uncle's judgement, especially when she had more pressing things to consider, made her set her jaw defiantly.

'I'm more than capable of keeping Barrow as Robert would have wanted. It is not and never will be for sale.'

'Come now.' A shadow of bad temper crossed Mr Reeves's face although he swiftly reined it back, attempting another compassionate frown. 'If it's a question of money, Miss Nettleford... Vulgar as it is to discuss, I've made it clear all along you could name any price.'

'The money is irrelevant. No sum could persuade me to part with my farm and that's my last word on the matter.'

Frances straightened her spine. Jonah still hadn't said a word, a silent statue at her shoulder, although she could sense from the stiffness of his posture how much he wanted to intervene. He didn't, however, clearly aware by now that she could fight her own battles, and it was with quiet pride in her husband's faith in her that Frances raised her head.

'And my name is no longer Miss Nettleford. It's Mrs Grant.'

She saw Mr Reeves's sharp eyes dart to Jonah and back again, perhaps thinking the better of pressing her any further while a wordless giant stood beside her. 'My apologies. Having known you since a child it's something of an adjustment.'

He made it sound as though he'd been a treasured family friend rather than a thorn in Robert's side but Frances made herself smile blandly.

'Of course. We all have things that are difficult to accept, but we must try our best. Especially when there's no hope of changing them.'

The thinly veiled dig hit its mark. The other farmer's eyes narrowed but he had no choice but to incline his head politely. He would never stop wanting Barrow and they both knew it, and the air was heavy with unspoken tension as Frances and Jonah moved away, Mr Reeves watching them go with a look of calculation on his face that made her deeply uneasy.

Once they were a few long strides away Frances muttered between gritted teeth, 'Insufferable vulture. If I were a man I would have knocked him down.'

'Who is he?'

'Another farmer. He owns every scrap of land around Marchfield apart from Barrow and he hounded my uncle for years to sell our plot to him too.'

Jonah nodded, straight eyebrows drawn tightly together. Frances walked quickly but he kept pace with her easily, cutting through the crowds around him with no trouble at all. 'But your uncle wouldn't consider it.'

'Never. Not even when he was offered ten times what the place was worth. I thought Reeves had finally accepted defeat but then my uncle died and left Barrow to me.'

Frances steeled herself against the memory

that had assailed her before, one she'd much rather forget. 'He came the day after the funeral. Can you believe it? The only family I had left, in the ground for less than twenty-four hours, and that scavenger came sniffing around, no doubt thinking I was an easier target than Robert. I soon made him see the truth.'

Her eyes had been swollen from crying, red-rimmed and raw, when Mr Reeves had arrived at the farmhouse with his hat in his hand and empty words of condolence that meant nothing at all. Putting a fatherly hand on Frances's shoulder had been his first mistake and then sitting in Uncle Robert's chair his second, but it was trying to turn Frances's grief and uncertainty to his advantage, as leverage to persuade her to sell, that had sealed the deal for ever in her mind. She would never part with Barrow and she'd told him straight, a kind of agonising satisfaction coming over her as he'd left in high dudgeon, and she knew her uncle would have been proud.

She'd slowed her pace, not realising until they came to a halt outside the baker's shop. The smell of fresh-baked bread was mouth-watering but Frances could taste only bile, her voice low as she slid Jonah a grimace.

'That's why I call him a vulture. Circling around, hoping to benefit from death. He saw an opportunity to profit from my loss and I'm not sure I can forgive him that.'

Jonah looked away and she wondered what the expression was that she'd seen cross his face whip-fast. It was akin to a flinch, like someone recoiling from something they didn't want to see, but it was gone so quickly she couldn't say for certain she'd seen anything at all. The people around them still bustled past, the autumn breeze now carrying with it a slight chill, and with a shiver Frances moved closer to the welcome warmth of Jonah's shoulder as if it could chase out the unhappiness of the past.

He glanced down at her, whatever he was thinking once again concealed behind that blankly handsome façade. 'Are you cold?'

'A little.'

At once Jonah turned them around, murmuring a brief word of apology to a passing couple as he steered her across them, and Frances tutted to herself as her lace cap drooped momentarily over her eyes. Blinded for a half-second, she paused to fix it, too intent on the wretched thing to pay much mind to anything else—so she missed Jonah's swift glance over his shoulder at Mr Reeves walking on the other side of the street, as well as the look of pain that crossed his face before he could wipe it away.

* * *

He could hardly bring himself to look at Frances for the rest of the day and only when she asked if she had offended him did Jonah manage to force some pretence of normality. The arrival of the twins around lunchtime, sent out so Jane could sleep, saved him from having to make excuses. Frances was mercifully distracted by Margaret's incessant questions and Matthew's desire to see the bull, and for the first time in weeks he was glad when she left him alone.

Eternal damnation on you, Thomas Millard. How did it come to this?

Sitting just outside the kitchen door, Jonah reached for the whetstone beside him, mouth grim as he began to grind away at the axe in his other hand. Usually such a job would take all his concentration but he couldn't seem to focus on anything other than the conflict raging inside his head, two opposing sides warring against each other with him caught in the middle.

Jane's doctor had been marginally better than the others he'd encountered over the years. The taciturn man had examined her closely and asked intelligent questions, and when he'd taken Jonah to one side and quietly made his recommendation for a cure it had cut the ground from beneath Jonah's feet.

'If you want your sister to see another winter

you'll move her now. She needs a bigger house with a decent garden to take the air and none of this damp that rises through the walls to get into her lungs. If she isn't taken away soon I'm afraid you will most certainly lose her.'

'I don't have the funds to buy a bigger house that quickly. Is there truly no time...?'

'To save the money? Of course. But not then to save your sister, if you tarry that long.'

The doctor had snapped his case shut, looking sober, and Jonah had tried not to fall back against the wall. With his head spinning, he'd shown the doctor out and then sunk into one of the chairs beside the cottage's kitchen hearth, where Frances had found him after who knew how many hours spent staring down at the flagged floor. The same thought had repeated itself over and over, insistent as the beat of a drum. He had to buy a better house for Jane, and for that he needed money. His only option was to sell the most valuable thing he possessed.

Frances's farm.

Just as in the first moment the realisation had hit him, Jonah now felt a wave of cold revulsion sweep over him from head to foot as he sat beside the kitchen door. That the thought had even entered his head was already a betrayal—and the fact he was considering it was almost more than he could bear.

What would Frances say if she knew what I was thinking?

He ran the whetstone across the blade once again, pressing down savagely as he asked himself the desperate question.

What would she say if she knew the choice I have to make?

Barrow had passed to him the moment Frances had signed the marriage register. As her husband, everything she owned had reverted to him and by rights he could do as he pleased, disposing of what had once been her property however he saw fit. If he sold the farm he'd be free of the worry for his sister that haunted him like a restless ghost, at last able to live without the fear that any day could be the one her weak lungs gave up the fight. It was the aim he'd been striving for since they were children and it could finally be within his grasp if he were only to take the opportunity fate had handed him. He would surely never get a better chance to make things secure for his family once and for all.

Jonah rubbed a callused palm over his face.

I might live without that fear...but how would I live with the fact I tore Frances's life to shreds to save Jane's?

The prospect sent a ragged blade into his very core. Both women would hate him. That hardly mattered when he thought of the pain his actions would cause if he chose to follow that path. Jane would feel guilt and Frances betrayal. Even knowing he'd be acting to save Jane's life gave Jonah no reprieve from the nausea that writhed in his gut. If he could turn back time and tell Frances his troubles when they'd first met then perhaps things would be different... but he couldn't... Gripping the axe so hard the handle creaked, Jonah clamped down on a groan.

'It's not even as though I can invite them all to live at Barrow farmhouse,' he muttered bitterly beneath his breath. 'There's room enough and it's a palace compared to the cottage, but Frances only accepts *me* here out of convenience. There's no way she'd allow my whole family getting under her feet as well, considering she only married me for lack of any other option.'

The thought stung although the pain didn't make it any less true. Frances was under no obligation whatsoever to take in every waif and stray her business arrangement of a husband dragged in his wake. She might feel friendly towards Jane and have grown fond of the children but that was a very different prospect to having them live under her roof, especially when her connection to them was built on nothing stronger than mutual necessity.

Mr Reeves had at least saved him the difficult task of asking around privately. Probably he could have Barrow sold within a few weeks and then buy a new house just as quickly, returning Jane and the children to the standard of living they used to enjoy. Her chest would grow more robust away from the damp cottage and death would no longer haunt her steps, its scythe no longer hanging over her blonde head. All of his family's problems were a hair's breadth from being solved and he ought to congratulate himself on pulling them through, somehow managing to keep their heads above water thanks to his quick thinking and willingness to sacrifice his own inclinations in favour of theirs.

Grinding the stone against the dull blade, Jonah's lip curled.

You coward. Lying to yourself won't make this any easier.

The contemptuous little voice echoing in the back of his mind was right and Jonah didn't try to deny it. Marrying Frances had turned out to be no sacrifice at all in the end. In fact, completely the opposite. He'd gained infinitely more than he'd given and his chest ached to think it was she who would lose everything, not least the trust she'd finally given him. Her loathing of Mr Reeves was crystal-clear and it could only add to the enormity of the betrayal when she discovered the other farmer had at last got his hands on her land, Jonah's actions severing any connection between them with one cruel snap.

He was holding the stone too tightly, his inner turmoil making his movements jerky and imprecise. The axe turned in his grip against the whetstone's crunch, and he swore as the newly sharpened edge skated across the base of his thumb, blood rising at once in a thin red line.

'Damn it all!'

Dropping the axe and stone, Jonah brought the gash up to his mouth, tasting the iron tang as he sucked away the blood. No doubt he'd be left with another scar to join the collection already littering his hands, although this one would be a permanent reminder of a time he already wanted to forget.

He screwed his eyes closed, wishing it was as easy to stop his thoughts. The slash to his thumb stung but it was nothing compared to the bleak hollow in his gut, a terrible sensation as if he'd been disembowelled while still alive.

What if there's another way? What if I could save Jane without hurting Frances?

The question repeated itself on a loop as Jonah strained every sinew to think of an answer, even though he knew it was hopeless. The same puzzle had taunted him ever since the doctor's grim prognosis and there was still no solution. Every day he delayed was another day she spent in that cursed cottage, the damp seeping into her lungs and drowning her from within, and all the agonising in the world couldn't change the fact that if he continued to hesitate he'd soon be ordering a shroud.

Taking his thumb from his mouth, he inspected the red-lipped gash grinning back at him. It wouldn't need stitching at least, although that was little comfort when everything else in his life seemed to be falling apart.

'Have you hurt yourself?'

The sound of Frances's voice made him sit up sharply, his eyes seeking her of their own accord. She was emerging from the orchard, a basket of late apples in one hand and a rake in the other, and the guilt sitting in his stomach bared its teeth at the concern in her tanned face.

'It's nothing. Just a scratch.'

He watched her tip the apples into a barrel to sort later, some of them destined to overwinter in the already stacked larder. She wouldn't be able to make use of it for much longer, he realised with another stab of remorse, wishing he'd done a better job of concealing his thoughts when a frown creased her brow.

'You're quite sure it doesn't hurt?'

'Hardly at all.'

Frances put down her basket and leaned the rake against the side of the house, giving him only a split-second to regain control. It was nowhere near long enough and he feared she'd be able to read his mind as she studied him closely, one hand on her hip—but then her face softened.

'You're worrying about Jane.'

She came to sit beside him on the bench, clearly interpreting his uneasy silence as agreement. 'The children told me she was sleeping as they left. Surely that's a good thing?'

Jonah rubbed the stubble on his chin. She was half right about the torment raging inside him—the half he could talk about without giving too much away.

'Jane's health has worried me for years. Her chest was weak even when we were children. Coughing spells and periods of malaise are nothing new, but they seem to be getting worse, and with winter approaching I confess to growing concerned.'

'But the doctor? You think he can do nothing?'

'No.' Jonah shook his head, looking away from the sympathy in Frances's eyes that he knew he didn't deserve. 'I've tried every one of them, from respected physicians to country wisewomen, but none of them can help. She might have stood more of a chance if our parents hadn't neglected her from birth, although thinking of that is a waste of time. I did the best

I could for her, in the early days when we still held hopes of a cure…'

Frances listened to him tail off. 'You shouldn't rebuke yourself. It sounds as though you did everything in your power to make her well. But is there nothing else? You mentioned the doctor suggested one thing left to try?'

Jonah gazed down at the ground, dimly noticing his once-shiny boots were now speckled with mud. With her usual precision she'd put her finger firmly on the very thing he wished he could avoid without even realising.

'Perhaps. There might be one avenue left, but the cost is high indeed.'

'Cost means nothing,' Frances countered frankly, so firm Jonah couldn't help but lift his head. 'I would have done anything to keep my uncle alive and I know you feel the same way about Jane. Family is more important than anything else in the world and if there's anything— anything at all—you can do to keep yours intact, you should take the chance.'

There was still vivid compassion in her face but Jonah's heart sank to see a shadow of grief flicker behind it, the sadness he suspected was never far from her mind. She fought it back with the courage he'd come to admire and yet when she reached for his hand Jonah had to wonder if she was seeking to comfort herself as well as him.

'Remember that. Once somebody's gone you can never get them back—no matter how much you might want to. The only time we have is now.'

A chill wound through Jonah's veins despite the warmth of her palm. 'You really think family is more important than anything?'

Frances's face was solemn as she nodded, sealing her own fate without having a clue she was in danger. 'Anything. Not money, not houses, not land…only the ones you love. Without them you have nothing.'

She looked at him steadily, as if willing him to understand the gravity of his situation, and Jonah ached to gather her to him and never let go. With only a few wise words she had helped him see the stark truth and the two sides sparring in his head fell silent, both acknowledging which faction had finally won the war.

She's right. Jonah clenched his fist on the desire to cradle his head in his hands, the immediate pain in his thumb warning him to stay on his guard. *If I can do something to help Jane then I have no option but to try, even if it means Frances will hate me for the rest of her life.*

His love for her sat in his chest like a heavy chunk of ice, chilling him more and more with each breath. It was completely different to the bone-deep loyalty he felt to his sister. Jane had been his responsibility since he was a child and he couldn't abandon her now, she and the children the only family he had left and just as precious as Frances described. If their situations were reversed and it was her uncle who hovered at death's door perhaps Frances would do the same, Jonah thought despairingly, seeing the resolve that still lingered on her face, but they'd never know. His wife was all alone in the world with nobody but him to care for her, and the inescapable prospect of shattering her spirit broke his heart clean in two.

A creeping numbness began to steal over him as he stared down at the cobbles beneath his boots, Frances's little hand still resting lightly on top of his. Vaguely he wondered again if she might allow Jane and the twins to move into the farmhouse, solving all his problems with one neat act, but the next moment he knew it was no use. She didn't love him. If she'd felt the same way about him as he did her it might have been possible but, his mouth feeling as though it were filled with sand, Jonah had to acknowledge the truth. Frances had married him for help, not to take in an entire family as though she ran a charity instead of a farm, and surely there was no way around that simple fact. He was a convenience to her, or at the very most a mere friend, certainly not a soulmate and most definitely in no place to ask of her a favour too big to be considered.

Slowly he turned his hand over, Frances's palm sliding gently into his. Without looking at her, he allowed his fingers to lace with hers, callused but slender and crying out to be kissed, and he bit down on a ragged sigh, thinking it might be the last time she ever let him get so close.

Out of the corner of his eye he saw her concern, but when she spoke her voice was determinedly cheerful. 'The children are building a den in the orchard. Will you come to see how they fare?'

Jonah glanced across at her, taking in the now familiar set of that beautiful face. He wanted to remember that moment, her hand in his and her sun-kissed cheeks rosy, far prettier in her workaday dress than a princess in any fine gown. She'd brought so much joy to his life and yet he had to give her up almost as soon as he'd found her. His soul felt crushed to know he must inflict such undeserved pain on Frances, who had already suffered more than most yet still managed to find a smile.

'I'll be there shortly.'

He made his lips form the words, sick guilt circling as he released her trusting hand. 'If you'll excuse me there's a letter I need to write first.'

Chapter Thirteen

Reining Apollo back into a slow trot, Frances turned off the lane into Barrow's yard, hunching her shoulders slightly against a persistent draught trying to steal down her neck. A hot cup of tea called to her after such a chilly and, as it had turned out, pointless ride, although the thought was relegated to the back of her mind as she saw Jonah appear around the side of the house.

As always, the sight of him was far more interesting than anything else but a glimmer of uncertainty hovered as she took in the impressive build beneath his blue coat. He'd been behaving strangely for the past few days, distant and disinclined to talk, and more than once she'd had the unpleasant feeling he was avoiding her company. It seemed every time she entered a room he left it and although her bone-deep fatigue had put a temporary halt to their nightly intimacy she couldn't help but wonder if he thought the disruption a blessing rather than a nuisance.

He looked up at the sound of hooves on the cobbles and Frances's unease grew as she saw something flash across his face, a mixture of surprise and almost—strangely—guilt, immediately calling to mind the image of a criminal caught in the act. In truth he didn't seem especially pleased to see her, his eyes sliding away from hers, and her smile faltered as she pulled to a halt and slipped down off Apollo's back.

'Good morning.'

Jonah nodded a return greeting but there was still no answering warmth as he came towards her. Even his steps seemed reluctant, so different now from the proud stride she'd grown to love that Frances had to fight a frown.

'Frances. You're back earlier than I thought. I hadn't expected to see you until this afternoon.'

'Mr Dixon was ill. He offered to keep our appointment but I assured him this month's accounts could wait until he was feeling better.'

He nodded again and Frances knew she hadn't been mistaken. It seemed he wanted to look anywhere but directly at her and her stomach churned at the new coldness she didn't understand.

Holding Apollo's reins, she tried again to bridge the inexplicable gap he appeared so determined to keep between them. 'Are you going somewhere? You never mentioned leaving Barrow today.'

'Yes. Into town.'

Apparently some point over the top of her head held a mesmerising fascination for him. Instead of looking at her, Jonah studied the stable's ruined roof, only meeting her eyes when something stung him into elaborating further. 'Just to call on Jane. Nothing more exciting than that.'

'Oh? Well, give her my best regards.' Trying her hardest not to let her worry show, Frances mustered another smile. 'There's some blackcurrant jam in the larder she might like too, if you wouldn't mind taking it. It would be gentle on her poor throat.'

Jonah's face tightened. If anything, he looked more pained than he had before and Frances's confusion grew as he scuffed one boot across the cobbles, muttering a taut reply in the direction of the open gate. 'Thoughtful as always.'

'And why not? If one has the chance to be, why not take it?'

He didn't answer her question. His eyes remained firmly averted, fixed on the gate as if plotting his escape, but an unidentifiable emotion moved in them and when he finally looked down Frances couldn't think what to say.

She gazed up at him, the first stirrings of desire beginning to ripple beneath her skin at his unwavering stare. There was an intensity in it that she couldn't comprehend and the uncanny sensation of being measured came over her, of being held up to the light and examined to see what lay inside her soul. She hadn't said anything worth such scrutiny, she was sure, and yet Jonah barely blinked as he pinned her to the spot with those coffee-coloured eyes, so dark and inviting she didn't realise he was moving until he held her face in his hands.

His mouth came down and she yielded to it instantly, her lips welcoming his like a cool drink of water after a drought. Her heart, low enough to have sunk to her boots only seconds earlier, catapulted upwards, her pulse and breath quickening at the unexpected kiss that drove out one set of confusion only to usher in another.

Where did this come from?

The thought was vague and Frances couldn't spare it much attention as Jonah's hands cupped her heated cheeks and stole all reason from her unresisting mouth, her knees weakening as his tongue moved skilfully over hers. Usually a kiss like this was reserved for the darkness of their bedroom, dim moonlight making Frances bolder than she'd ever dare at any other time. She'd always thought Jonah's passion was solely in the heat of the moment, at night his more instinc-

tive desires overcoming the gentlemanly deco-
rum he showed during the day, but now as they
stood entwined in the bright autumnal sunshine
Frances wondered if she'd been wrong.

*Could it be he wasn't just carried away?
Could it possibly be...he's come to feel something more?*

Beneath the weight of that breathtaking
thought Frances almost stumbled and she reached
out for Jonah's coat, taking hold of his lapels and
holding on tight. His hands cradled her face with
a fierce tenderness he hadn't shown before, gentle yet firm as he delved deeper to light sparks in
Frances's insides, and when his thumb moved to
caress one burning cheek she feared she might
crumple to the ground. It was a kiss unlike any
other and her spirit soared to wonder what it
could mean, coming out of nowhere and so far
removed from anything friendly that her hopes
flew up to the sky.

When Jonah finally drew back he still didn't
release her. Instead he softly held her face tilted
up towards his, her tumultuous emotions qui-
eting a little at the strange message she read in
his expression. Their breathing was still fast but
time seemed to slow as he looked down at her
with something so close to pleading that she felt
fresh confusion rise, only his earnest entreaty

stopping her from asking what could possibly be wrong.

'Frances. I need you to hear this.'

He bent his head lower so there was nothing to interrupt the intense lock of their eyes, brown fixed on hazel with unflinching force. The hands on her cheeks were so gentle she could easily have pulled away but Frances didn't move, bewilderment keeping her still and quiet as Jonah went on.

'If in the future I should do anything to make you doubt my regard and respect for you, I beg forgiveness now. Your courage and kindness are an example I shall strive to copy every day, although in truth I know I will never possess even half a measure of either. I just… I want you to know.'

He stepped back. Her face was immediately cold where his palms had warmed her skin. For a second she couldn't find any response, her heart hammering too loudly to allow for any thought, and Jonah had turned away by the time she found her tongue.

'Jonah? What—?' she called after him but he didn't seem to hear. With long strides he crossed the yard and was through the gate before Frances could summon any more words, only able to watch him disappear as her brain tried desperately to make sense of what had just occurred.

Apollo stood placidly where she had left him and Frances laid a hand on his neck, still staring—a little dazedly—at the point where Jonah had vanished from her sight.

'What did he mean? Regard and respect… and that kiss…?'

The horse bumped his nose against her shoulder but didn't offer any wisdom. Apparently Jonah's motives weren't any clearer to him, and Frances nipped at her lower lip as possibilities crowded round to murmur into her ear.

Could it be the thought that had whispered to her as Jonah's lips sought hers was right? That something in Jonah's heart had changed, his feelings now following the same path her own had followed for longer than she really knew?

The idea set her alight but she hardly dared think of it directly, worried too much attention might scare it away. His baffling words echoed again, sweet but so unexpected she hardly knew what to make of them, and the kiss that had come out of the blue was nothing she could begin to explain. No other reason made as much sense as the one that kept pushing itself forward, although Frances forced herself to keep calm.

'Let's not move too fast. We ought to look at the facts before we leap to any conclusions.'

Apollo seemed to agree and Frances stroked his velvet nose, noticing a slight tremor in her fingers. The excitement running through her veins made it very difficult to keep still and she took a deep breath, the sensation of Jonah's mouth still a ghostly presence on her own lips.

'He kissed me in a way he's never kissed me before, without any preamble or intimacy to make him lose his head, and then spoke of his respect and regard for me that is surely more than a friend would feel. That's a fact.'

The horse snorted in such a way that Frances was certain he understood the importance of the matter. Her own mind buzzed with too much activity, a deafening roar that made her dizzy, and she didn't know if she could trust herself to find the right answer among the myriad thoughts running circles through her head.

He kissed me. He admires me. But he's been so distant of late...

Her fledgling hopes stuttered as she recalled how reluctant he'd been to spend any time with her over the past few days, cold water abruptly pouring over her dreams. They'd barely spoken and only that very morning he hadn't looked happy to see her when she'd arrived back at Barrow, evidently planning to slip away from the farm without having to see her. The contrast between his new-found reserve and the scalding intensity of his kiss was disorientating and Frances's stomach gave a lurch to wonder which version of her husband showed the real truth. On the one hand he barely offered a friendly glance, while on the other he behaved like a man very much in love, two conflicting sides fighting against each other so confusingly Frances's head began to ache.

She pressed two fingertips against her brow, smoothing the furrowed lines. How was she supposed to know what went on behind that stony mask? Any other man would be far easier to read, but Jonah had always been an enigma, his motives just as much of a mystery as his past.

A new thought occurred to scoop her spirits back up off the ground, a blinding flash of inspiration that made her snatch a breath.

Perhaps he *had* come to feel something more—and that was the very reason he'd been so determined to keep away?

Frances stood very still, not even an inquisitive chicken coming to inspect her boot nor Apollo's mildly impatient huff making her move.

I always told him I didn't want a man, even when I knew that was no longer strictly true... If he thinks I wouldn't return his affection, surely it would be natural for him to try so hard to conceal it?

Blindly she took hold of Apollo's reins and began to lead him towards the orchard, although she was hardly aware of where she placed her feet. The possibility glowed like red-hot coals, warming her to the bone, threatening to knock her off already unsteady legs.

Am I being foolish? Or could that be the truth?

Automatically she took off Apollo's saddle and tack and turned him out into the orchard, her mind firmly on other things. The sounds of the farm around her were curiously dim and nothing registered as she moved in a dream back to the house, Gyp appearing from behind the barn to escort her inside. Dropping into her armchair beside the kitchen fire, she absently lifted him onto her knee, the warm weight of him settling onto her lap but Frances a million miles away as her brain tried to untangle the knotted threads of her thoughts.

'If he's finally come to feel the way for me as I do for him then it will be more than I ever dared hope. Who could have imagined the kind of man Uncle Robert always warned me about would be the very one to bring me such happiness?'

Her heart fluttered in her chest like a soaring bird and Frances pressed where she felt it thrumming against the bodice of her gown. There was still a chance she was wrong and until she knew for certain it would be stupid to get carried away…even if the temptation to throw caution to the wind grew more and more tempting with every tick of the kitchen clock.

'I'll wait until he comes home. If I have to, I'll ask him myself.'

She stroked Gyp's obliging head, a combination of excitement and dread welling up in an unstoppable wave. She wouldn't know peace until she had the truth from Jonah's lips, the ones that had caused her so much confusion and unexpected delight she never would have guessed she could feel, but if his answer wasn't the one she longed for then it wouldn't only be her pride that was hurt. Her heart would break if Jonah's regard for her was indeed only that of a friend and growing fear nagged at her as she sat beside the fireplace, only Gyp anchoring her to the chair stopping Frances from pacing around the room. She had no choice but to wait until he returned and then take her future into her hands, plunging headlong into uncertainty and unable to think of anything else as the minutes crept past.

By the time an hour had passed, however, she couldn't take any more.

Putting aside the stocking she was attempting to darn, Frances looked—yet again—at the kitchen clock. It felt as though time was going backwards and she laced her fingers together in her lap, trying to talk sense into herself before she did something rash. She'd already tried to settle to reading but the words jumped about in front of her eyes and now apparently even mending was beyond her, constantly pricking herself with the needle held in unsteady hands. Try as she might to distract herself, nothing could outweigh thoughts of Jonah and, with the sensation of standing on the edge of a precipice, she made up her mind.

Apollo seemed resigned but not surprised when she saddled him again and turned his head for town. It was a good thing he knew the way as Frances could hardly think straight, carried along more by helpless instinct than any rational thought.

I'll go mad if I tarry much longer. One way or the other, I have to know.

Anxious anticipation spurred her on and she tapped Apollo into a canter, closing the distance between her and Marchfield with every beat of his hooves. Patience had never been a virtue of hers, Frances had to admit, passivity wasn't part of her nature and she wasn't about to change now with so much at stake. There was every chance Jonah might be horrified by her confession but asking was the only way to know for sure, all the uncertainty of the past weeks building up to the moment when she'd lay her secrets bare. She had no right to expect honesty from him while she kept her own feelings locked up tight, although the prospect of revealing all made a weight drop down into her stomach.

If I tell Jonah I love him, that will be the final thing Uncle Robert prayed I'd avoid. I'll have turned my back on everything he taught me and if I'm hurt I'll only have myself to blame.

It was a fact that she couldn't escape and Frances's gut gave a wrench as the image of her uncle's beloved weather-beaten face flickered before her. All he'd ever wanted was to spare her the misery his sister had endured. He was a good man and she owed him everything, more papa than uncle, and Frances knew she would treasure every memory she had of him until she herself had faded away.

But she no longer wanted to dwell in the past.

Mama and I are two different people, Frances thought grimly as the cold breeze sought an entrance to her gown.

Marina had made her choice and her daughter would too, and with her hands gripping the reins to steady her thumping heart Frances rode fast until she arrived in Marchfield and her father's cottage came into sight.

She looped Apollo's reins over the gatepost and took a moment to gather herself before stepping onto the path. Her pulse was thudding at a frightening speed and her palms were damp despite the autumn chill, and she closed her eyes briefly to summon the courage to lift the rusted knocker. The moment of reckoning was almost upon her and once she leapt there was no coming back, but there was no chance of her turning away now. The decision had been made and she'd keep to it, although she felt her hands shaking as the cottage door scraped inwards.

'Why, Frances!'

Jane's smile was welcoming although her face was almost as white as her neat lace cap. 'What a pleasant surprise! Jonah didn't mention you were coming too—I wonder that he didn't stay to meet you?'

Frances blinked, aware she must look like a stunned rabbit in her nervous state, but completely unable to help it. 'He isn't here?'

'Not any longer. He only stopped in for a few minutes. He was going to see a man in town, apparently. But come in! You know you needn't wait for my brother's presence to visit.'

Jane beckoned her inside and Frances obeyed with mute obedience, too rattled to do anything else. All the tension and anxiety that had built up inside her bursting chest came crashing down and the anticlimax was almost too much to bear, her nerves frayed and heart still pounding so hard she was surprised Jane couldn't hear it. The very last thing in the world she wanted was to pretend to be normal over a cup of tea but the genuine pleasure on her sister-in-law's face forced Frances to dredge up a weak smile.

'I must have misunderstood. I knew Jonah was coming to call on you, but not that he was going elsewhere afterwards.'

'Don't give it another thought. I'm glad of the company.'

She followed Jane's slight figure down the hall and into the kitchen, where a handsome copper teapot sat on the hearth. A chair stood on either side of the fire and Jane dropped into one of them, trying—but failing—to conceal her fatigue.

'Are you well? Is everything as it should be at Barrow?'

Frances dismissed the question with a shake of her head. Nervous energy still swirled inside her but she pushed it back, seeing the shadows beneath Jane's eyes, even deeper than they'd been already and her cheeks hollow and gaunt.

'Think nothing of that. How do *you* fare? Is your throat any better?'

'It's good of you to ask. Perhaps a little. All the delicious gifts you send are keeping me well-fed at the very least.'

Privately thinking she'd seen more fat on a chicken's beak, Frances found another smile although worry crept up to join the commotion already rioting through her mind. Jane looked worse than she'd ever known her before, practically a skeleton in a woollen shawl, and when she tried to reach for the teapot Frances got hastily to her feet.

'Let me do that. Really, I ought to leave so you can rest, but I can make you a cup of tea before I go.'

Jane sat back in her chair. 'I'm so tired of resting and allowing everybody else to run around after me. If only I were stronger…'

'I don't mind, truly. You stay where you are.'

Jane sighed but didn't argue, watching as Frances took command. Before long both women sat with a teacup and it was Frances's turn to watch as her sister-in-law took a sip, her wrists so fragile even lifting a cup seemed an effort.

The conversation she'd had with Jonah outside the kitchen door came back to her now, his face grave as he'd told her some of Jane's history. What was the one thing he had mentioned he had left to try in keeping his sister alive? In the moment Frances hadn't thought to ask, too concerned with his obvious unhappiness, but now she had to wonder…

What could it have been? And what did he mean by it having too great a price?

The question captured her attention and it was some seconds before she realised Jane was studying her over the rim of her cup, her eyes sparkling with interest despite the purple rings beneath.

'So. How are you enjoying married life? It certainly seems to agree with my brother.'

Frances started. 'Has he said—?'

'He doesn't have to. I can see a change in him and I don't think it can be mere coincidence that it dates from when he met you.'

Jane took another sip, her bright blue gaze missing nothing—including, no doubt, the ready blush that made Frances's face flush hot. 'There's a lightness to him now that was never there before. That has to be your doing.'

Frances looked down at her lap, too flustered to think quickly. The desire to believe Jane's praise was strong but a little voice urged caution, warning her not to get carried away.

'I wouldn't give myself that much credit.'

'I would. A marriage of friendship was how he described it at first… I don't know how much I believe that now.'

Jane's smile was knowing, as if she had the gift of understanding a man's unspoken thoughts. Perhaps that same wisdom would come to Frances in time, once she'd been married for as long as Jane had, although the idea of ever knowing for certain what lived behind Jonah's inscrutable façade seemed unlikely.

Frances studied her fingernails, bewilderment

nudging her into honesty. 'If *you* don't know then there's no hope for *me*. I've no clue how to read a man, to know what's happening inside his head… But I suppose you would. You must have grown used to knowing what your husband was thinking without being told, after being wed for all those years.'

The moment the words left her lips she wished she could snatch them back, her immediate regret burning brighter at Jane's bitter laugh.

'Oh, no. I'm not sure that's true.'

At once Frances sat forward, reaching for Jane's pale hand. 'I'm so sorry. I should never have spoken like that while you're still in mourning. It was inconsiderate of me to mention him without your permission. I won't do it again.'

Jane allowed Frances to take her hand but a frown creased her brow. 'I'm in mourning?'

'For your husband.'

'For my…?'

Her blue eyes narrowed briefly and then widened again in sudden understanding. 'Why, Thomas isn't *dead*. Not as far as I know, anyway.'

At Frances's look of obvious shock Jane shook her head. 'He took a ship to the Americas six months ago and I haven't heard from him since. I don't expect to either, considering he stole almost every penny of Jonah's savings while he was away at Waterloo and then left me and the children to fend for ourselves.'

Frances's lips parted but no words came out. She was only able to stare as Jane cocked her head curiously.

'Did Jonah tell you he was dead?'

'He said…'

Struggling to cast her mind back, Frances wondered how she'd managed to get things so wrong. Surely it was on her first visit to the cottage that Jonah had mentioned his brother-in-law. The only time they'd discussed Jane's pitiful situation. She'd been so sure what Jonah had meant but now doubt filled her, making her question what she'd once believed.

'Not in so many words. I could have sworn that it was implied…'

Jane gave another painful laugh that made Frances ache with sudden sympathy. 'I don't doubt it. As far as my brother is concerned my husband is no longer living, and if he ever catches up with him I fear he'd be the one to strike the final blow.'

She pulled her shawl tighter about her thin little body as if trying to protect herself from the cruelty she and her children had suffered. 'That's how we came to live here. When Thomas left with all our money we had to move to the cheapest place we could find. I begged Jonah not to leave the Army, but he knew I couldn't work or cope with the twins all alone, my health being what it is, and so he sacrificed his career to stay in England to help me. In truth I don't know what I would have done if he hadn't.'

Frances watched a fleeting glimpse of resignation cross Jane's white face. 'Once again I'm a burden on him, just as I have been since we were children. He told me this morning that his aim is to buy a better home for me, apparently before the month is out, but I can't see how he could afford such a thing…and frankly I shouldn't like to ask.'

A strange coldness began to grow in the very depths of Frances's stomach. It was small at first, like a patch of frost on a windowpane, but with stubborn perseverance it spread outwards, unwanted—but inescapable—suspicion stretching icy fingers further and further until it began to creep upwards towards her chest.

'Jonah has no money of his own with which to purchase one?' Frances endeavoured to keep her voice steady although the icicles forming inside were growing sharp. 'I don't need him to support me but I should be interested to know if his finances are as dire as you imply.'

'I'm afraid they are. If he was in earnest about finding another house he would have to find a great deal of capital from somewhere and very quickly indeed.'

Jane swallowed another dainty mouthful of tea but Frances's was left to cool in her hand. The chill suspicion stalking through her innards moved faster, well into her chest by now and beginning to squeeze her heart in its freezing grip as she combed through what Jane had just said.

His intention has always been to buy a new home for his family, but he has no money of his own. How, then, does he plan to raise such a sum?

Feeling as though a blizzard were tearing through her, Frances gazed down into her teacup, eyes fixed blankly on the pattern at the rim. Wary confusion gripped tighter as she tried to understand what she was being told, something below the surface niggling unpleasantly.

Surely Jonah didn't expect *her* to buy the property he couldn't afford himself? Barrow made money but not so much that purchasing another house would be easy. Such a large outlay would put immense strain on the farm's accounts. She'd have to sell a couple of fields to cover the shortfall, reducing the already neatly proportioned plot, and the money she'd saved over the years would be gone in the blink of an eye…

The ice in her chest reached higher and Frances choked on it, sudden dread stealing the breath from her lungs.

No. Surely he wouldn't...

Her money wasn't hers any longer, she realised with a sickening lurch. As her husband, Jonah had full control of everything she owned, and there was nothing she could do if he decided to take matters into his own hands.

Fighting back rising fear, Frances forced her lips to move. 'Where was it you said Jonah has gone?'

'To meet a Mr Reid, I believe he said.' Jane laid aside her empty cup and huddled deeper into her wrappings, although the next moment she frowned. 'Was it Reid...? No, no—*Reeves*, that was it.' She smiled, obviously pleased to have remembered, and Frances felt her heart stop. 'A Mr Reeves. Something to do with Barrow, I gathered, although he didn't say exactly what. I assumed you'd know about it...'

Frances sat very still.

The kitchen had dimmed somehow, all the colour drained from the world around her, and her head swam as blank horror and realisation roared up to ring in her ears.

He wouldn't. He wouldn't dare!

If Jonah had gone to meet Mr Reeves then it could be for only one reason and Frances's fingers clenched around the china in her hand so violently it could have shattered. Her mind felt splintered in exactly the same way, crammed with too many emotions and threatening to burst into fragments as she came face to face with the truth.

He's going to sell my farm.

An iron fist hit hard beneath her ribs, knocking her dizzy with a single merciless punch. Not content with that, it moved to her throat, gripping until Frances thought she might never breathe again and she sucked in a dry gasp, the air tasting sour on her tongue. Her worst nightmare, the very thing she'd sworn she'd never allow was happening at that very moment—and she couldn't stop it.

Out of the corner of her eye she could see Jane's expression turning slowly from placid to concerned but Frances couldn't manage to care, trapped in torment she couldn't escape. Jonah had tricked her into handing him the most precious thing she owned and she had nobody to blame but herself, both her home and her heart stolen by the one she'd hoped would treasure them.

Was this his intention from the very start? To lure me in, and then...?

She wanted to shy away from the terrible question but it pushed forward regardless, sparing not one ounce of mercy as Frances tried not to crumple in her chair. The desire to deny it was strong and she cast about desperately for any other explanation, any other way of making the truth kinder than this nightmare she'd stumbled into while wide awake.

But there wasn't one.

It had all been a lie, every word, every tiny show of consideration, the kindness with which he had knocked down her walls… Every last shred of respect and decency had been false, a cynical plot with the sole aim of winning her trust only to betray it. It was the farm he'd wanted all along, never her friendship or to help in her time of need, and Frances felt herself sway as a yawning chasm of despair opened up beneath her feet.

He's going to sell my farm. My farm, the only thing I have left in the whole world, and he's going to use the money to buy a house for his family. Which doesn't include me.

Her gut tied itself into an agonising knot as she looked reality in the eye, desperation raking her with its claws. Jane and the children were Jonah's sole concern and she would be cast out without a second thought now she'd outlived her usefulness, only ever a means to an end to a man looking to profit from her weakness. Once Barrow was gone she'd have nothing, no home and nowhere to belong, no way of escaping the relentless cruelty of the world that had pursued her since she'd been born and left alone with the knowledge that her uncle had been right.

She tried not to picture his face as she stared down at her lap, the thought of his disappointment shredding her already ragged soul. Uncle Robert had tried so hard to save her from herself and yet she'd been fooled just as easily as her mother, placing her trust in a man who would never deserve it. By some hideous twist of fate, both handsome wretches had shared the same cottage she sat in now, the place where two generations of Nettleford women had their hopes crushed, and she cursed her naivety at believing she would somehow be spared.

He was behaving strangely out of indifference, not love.

Dawning awareness mocked her pain, slicing her to ribbons without a care for how much it hurt.

I thought he was falling in love with me, but really he was already pushing me away.

She'd served her purpose. Now there was nothing for Jonah to gain by treating her well he'd dropped all pretence of caring, Barrow firmly in his hands and his future secure while hers lay in the gutter. He'd never valued her or meant a word he said and Frances thought she heard the crack as her battered heart split clean in two, the pieces lying in the dirt to be thrown away like a broken plate.

'Frances? Are you quite well?'

Her chest feeling as though it were filled with shards of glass, Frances forced herself to stand, Jane following her movements with worried eyes. Grief consumed her, both for the wreckage of her dreams and the knowledge of all she had lost, and she stumbled as she turned away.

'Perfectly. I've just remembered something I should be doing.'

A memory of Jonah standing in the doorway flashed forward and Frances screwed her eyes shut, desperate not to let him in. Her heart yearned for him, each beat a punishment she knew she deserved, but from among the ruins of her hopes a glint of pure crystalline fury began to rise like a phoenix from the ashes of her pain.

She loved him and probably always would, she admitted to herself with bitter resignation it was pointless to deny. No other man had ever scaled the walls she'd built around herself and now she would build them higher still, her feelings left to wither and die without anyone to sustain them—but even in the depths of her despair Frances saw Jonah's fatal mistake. He had forgotten who she was, had overlooked the steel that rejection and suffering had hammered into her unbending spine. There was no chance of a

Nettleford going down without a fight. Her future lay in tatters but that didn't mean she had to lie down and let him step over her. Sorrow and angry determination were a heady mix that drove Frances to the door.

'Please excuse me. I need to get back to Barrow right away.'

Jonah stared straight ahead, refusing to meet the eye of either man sitting opposite him across a wide and expensive desk. The lawyer had barely said a word but Mr Reeves had more than made up for that reserve, holding forth about the prosperity of his estate with self-congratulation that apparently knew no bounds. He'd hardly paused to draw breath and Jonah tried not to listen, although there was no escaping the continuous stream.

No wonder Frances detests him. Even if he wasn't after her farm, he's still everything I know she dislikes.

The thought of her made his stomach turn and Jonah bit down on his tongue to stop himself from dropping his head into his hands. The knowledge of what he was about to do was torturous enough without delaying the agony but it was still no relief when the lawyer expertly interrupted Mr Reeves's monologue, cutting in smoothly with the air of one who'd done so many times before.

'Are we to expect your wife, Lieutenant Grant?'

'No. She will not be joining us.'

A spasm whipped through his insides and Jonah was only just able to stop himself from wincing at the pain, almost sharp enough to make him double over. The memory of Frances as she'd been the final moment he'd seen her came to taunt him, with her lips still warm from his kiss and the sweetest look of confusion on her rosy face, and he wanted to cry out to think it was the very last time she would ever allow him the honour of touching her skin. As soon as she realised his betrayal she would withdraw from him for ever and everything they had made together would be lost, his love set adrift and nothing left for him to do but stand and watch it disappear.

Oblivious to Jonah's private agony, Mr Reeves leaned forward. 'Probably for the best. I understand from your letter that the sale of Barrow Farm will be something of a blow for her.'

Jonah nodded shortly. 'Yes. I'd like to have the whole thing over with as quickly as possible.'

'In that regard we want the same thing.'

The farmer smiled, satisfaction spreading across his ruddy face that Jonah itched to wipe away. 'I'm extremely glad you intervened. Frances—I beg your pardon—*Mrs Grant* has always had very decided ideas. Her uncle's fault entirely, but it's made her difficult to deal with over the years. Having a sensible husband to lead her is the best possible thing that could have happened for a woman like that.'

There was a hint of something in his tone that Jonah didn't like and he looked up sharply, noting with a kind of fierce satisfaction that the other man immediately hesitated.

'A woman like what?'

'I meant no offence,' Mr Reeves amended quickly. 'Robert Nettleford indulged her, that's all, encouraging the independence so ill-fitting for a young lady. Direction is what she needs, just like any woman, a strong hand to guide her, and now she's wed that's what you will provide.'

Jonah felt his lip curl but couldn't seem to stop it, contempt creeping into his usually impassive face. Mr Reeves's description of Frances was nothing like the truth. He made her sound like a flighty horse or disobedient dog, an undisciplined creature whose spirit he had to break, rather than a self-sufficient woman possessing more mettle than any man. It was her independence that had drawn him to her in the first place and the idea of anyone suggesting he try to stamp it out lit a flash of anger inside his heart.

'That isn't an accurate depiction of either my marriage or my wife.' He tried to keep his voice even but couldn't entirely prevent it from taking on a gravelly edge. 'Frances is her own person and there's nothing in her nature I would seek to change, even if I could.'

There was a momentary pause in which the lawyer gazed discreetly out of the window, leaving Mr Reeves to bear the full weight of Jonah's stony stare. His smile slipped a fraction but he pressed on, pursuing his argument with either courage or stupidity.

'But you've taken *some* steps. The decision to sell the farm was yours alone? You didn't feel the need to consult with her first?'

Jonah felt himself stiffen. As much as he wanted to deny the charge, he knew it was just, an accurate summary of his betrayal that made raw anguish well up in his chest. 'Out of necessity. Not because I think myself Frances's keeper in any way.'

'Well, I'm sure you're right.' Mr Reeves waved a magnanimous hand, evidently considering the matter closed. 'It hardly matters. As long as the contract is signed today, your motives are your own.'

The farmer turned to his lawyer, eyebrows raised. Clearly that was the cue for the agreement to be signed, as a collection of papers were slid across the desk to where Jonah sat, a handsome pen laid out on top of them.

He stared down at them, neatly printed words stark black against white. The prospect of this moment had been bad enough but now the contract was before him, tangible evidence of the treachery that would devastate Frances, Jonah couldn't seem to move. His arms were heavy and his head ached from the tension in his jaw, and the image of Frances's beautiful, beloved face circled inside his mind until he feared he was losing his wits.

She will hate me. I love her and yet I will cause such pain she'll curse the day I walked into her life—and I deserve nothing less, even her contempt too good for me when Frances learns what I've done.

'Shall we proceed?'

He could sense two pairs of waiting eyes fixed on him but he didn't lift his head, blind to everything but the papers spread out on the desk. As soon as he signed them his fate would be sealed, and so would Frances's, an innocent casualty in the battle to save his family from destruction. He could only pray Jane would indeed survive as a result of his actions. It was the only shred of consolation he could find among the misery dragging him down.

With his heart in pieces, he gathered himself

and, offering a silent, agonising apology to the precious memory of Frances's smiling face, he slowly picked up the pen.

Chapter Fourteen

Jonah walked Marchfield's main street with his head up, allowing the wind to buffet his blank face. It stung but he didn't try to duck away, every pinprick of pain exactly what he felt he was owed. He'd left the lawyer's office in a daze and his mind was shocked back into working by the cold, the reality of what he'd just done settling over his breastbone with the weight of an iron fist.

I did what I had to—and may heaven have mercy on me for it.

The usual curious glances came his way but Jonah didn't notice, nothing able to distract him from the heaviness in his chest. Consumed by his own thoughts, he was blind to everything around him and deaf to the bustle of the street, and it wasn't until he felt a hand on his arm that he paused his mechanical stride.

'We were calling you for ages! Didn't you hear us?'

Looking down, he saw Margaret clinging to his sleeve, Matthew following—as always—one step behind. They peered up at him with their usual innocent affection and Jonah's stomach churned to think how little he deserved it.

'What are you doing here? Why aren't you at home with your mother?'

'She sent us outside to play. We got tired of the garden so came looking for you.'

Margaret tweaked the button on his cuff, blessedly not seeming to notice the strain in his voice. She and her brother looked so young in their woolly scarves and hats and a wave of some protective instinct fought its way to the fore, momentarily elbowing aside the unhappiness fermenting in his innards.

Bending down, he gathered the children to him, looking into their pink little faces as passers-by stepped round them. 'You mustn't go roaming about wherever you choose. Go home now before your mother realises—you know she'll be cross if she looks out of the window and sees you've gone.'

Margaret looked mutinous. 'I don't think she will. She's too busy thinking about Aunt Frances to scold us.'

'Frances?' The sound of her name sent a static

shock through Jonah's nerves, looming so large in his head that to hear it out loud was a jolt. 'What do you mean?'

'She came to the cottage while you were away. We saw her leaving and I called out but she mustn't have heard me… She looked very upset, though, and Mama was worried. I don't know why.'

Jonah's roiling stomach tightened further, a vicious squeeze making him want to heave. The chaos running riot in his insides was already almost too much to bear but now it stepped up another notch, Margaret's unwitting revelation telling him more than she understood.

Jane must have told Frances who I went to meet.

He snatched a ragged breath, trying not to let the twins see the sudden despair that sent his heart plunging down into his boots.

Damn it—damn it a hundred times!

He'd needed time to think how to raise the subject with Frances, not have her told by anyone but himself. If he'd been the one to explain perhaps he could have found a way to appease her… But even as the thought crossed his spinning mind he knew it was impossible. There was no way anybody could have dressed up his plans to make them sound better and as he straightened up Jonah dreaded what reception would await him back at Barrow now that Frances had guessed the truth.

'Go home to your mother. Now.'

Margaret looked as though she was tempted to argue but one glimpse of her uncle's face clearly made her think the better of it. Instead she merely sighed and, taking her brother by the hand, the children wandered away, Jonah watching until they rounded the corner and turned safely onto the cottage's quiet street.

His own homecoming was certain to be far more dangerous, he thought bleakly as the two little figures disappeared. The walk back to Barrow was barely half a mile and it was all the time he had left to decide what to say at the other end, how to put into words everything that clamoured between his ears, all the while knowing Frances must hate him now with a bone-deep passion. A hundred miles wouldn't have been enough but there was nothing to be gained by delaying the inevitable, and with heavy steps Jonah turned for Barrow Farm.

By the time its gate came into view Jonah still had no idea where to begin. His mind raced and yet any explanation escaped him, every possibility too flimsy or mealy-mouthed to bear scrutiny. After his duplicity Frances deserved the stark truth. Anything less would be an insult to both her intelligence and pride. As he passed through the gateway he resolved he would never keep anything from her again…if she ever allowed him to speak a word in her direction, that was, her contempt for him without doubt now .

The empty yard bore no trace that anything was amiss but Jonah wasn't fooled. With rising foreboding he approached the farmhouse, grimly unsurprised to find the door firmly locked when he tried the handle. Clearly Frances was sending him a message. Her farm was her castle and she would fight for it until her last breath and, despite his anguish, Jonah felt that familiar spark of admiration. She was tenacious and he'd expect nothing else from her than defiance, never acting according to anyone's wishes but her own and so determined he had to shake his head.

Reeves didn't have the first idea of what he was talking about.

Jonah took a step backwards, craning his neck to look at the upstairs windows. There was no movement but he knew she had to be inside, listening to his footsteps as he paced across the cobbles and perhaps holding herself ready just in case he tried to break down the door.

I could no sooner tame Frances than I could teach a horse to speak—and why would I want to?

A man like Reeves would never understand, Jonah thought as he stood in the middle of the yard and wondered what to do. Frances was perfect just the way she was, suspicious and spiky and capable and kind, and every bit as worthy of respect as a born lady. Her beauty was so much more than skin-deep and the prospect of never again being granted the privilege of kissing her warm lips was like a living death, his existence hardly worth having if she slipped through his fingers, and Jonah heard his voice crack as he called out.

'Frances!'

There was no answer.

'Frances, please. I know you're in there.'

He waited, his heart in his mouth as his eyes skipped from one empty window to the next. Still there was no sign of her, however, and, gathering his resolve, he tried again.

'I know you're angry. You have every right to be. All I want is to speak to you. You deserve an explanation if nothing else.'

For a moment there was nothing. The hens ambled around his boots, pecking at minuscule pieces of grain, and the weathervane squeaked as it shuddered in the chilly breeze, but there was no movement from the house—until the bedroom window was flung open and Frances appeared, glaring down at him so coldly Jonah felt his blood turn to ice.

'You lying cowardly snake. I don't need anything from you, much less an *explanation*. I already know it all!'

Another man might have fallen back from the lash of her tongue, harsh as a whip crack and twice as sharp. Only Jonah's war-hardened courage saved him from doing the same and he didn't retreat from the fury he knew he had earned, although her barbs hit their target with merciless accuracy. Frances looked at him with the dangerous anger of a wounded animal but somehow the sight of her was still a blessing, the face he loved more than any other beautiful to him even when carved from ice, and with bleak determination he tried to memorise the final moment she might ever allow him into her presence.

'If I could just tell you—'

'No.' She cut him off at once, that one word like the blade of a knife between his ribs. 'I'll tell *you*. Any words out of your mouth will be more lies.'

Frances gripped the windowsill and Jonah saw how her chest rose and fell with heavy breaths, forcing herself to maintain some semblance of calm. She was keeping herself under tight control but it was clear the veneer was thin indeed, the rosy tint of her cheeks a tell-tale sign of her emotion.

'You are a lying, deceiving wretch. You intended from the very start to make me trust you, with the sole intention of securing Barrow, and then to go behind my back and sell it so you could buy a better place for your family. Is that true?'

Her voice was hard and Jonah hated the echo of pain not quite hidden by its savagery. She was in agony and it was his doing. The desire to take her in his arms was so strong it almost made him stumble, but he owed her the decency of meeting her eye.

'That isn't how it happened. I truly never had any such plans for Barrow when we married but I don't deny the idea of selling it came later.'

'You can't deny it because I know it's true. Jane as good as told me herself.'

The gulf of despair in Jonah's gut yawned wider. It cut him to the quick to see her so cold but she didn't pause, standing at her window and calling down to him as if commanding a siege.

'That's where you went this afternoon. To see Mr Reeves—and to sell my farm out from under me, without so much as a second thought for the cruelty of snatching everything I have, when I thought you were worthy of my trust. Did it make you laugh to think I'd fallen for your ruse? Did it amuse you to find I was so easily fooled by some kind words and a full woodpile?'

She paused to suck in a harsh breath and Jonah's throat ached to see something glitter on her eyelashes before she hastily rubbed it away. The sight took him straight back to the day they'd wed, when Frances had tried to hide her tears from him at her mother's and uncle's graves, and the rawness of it threatened to send his heart bursting through his chest. She had suffered so much already and yet she remained unbowed, taking everything life had thrown at her and still finding the strength to stand, and he wondered how anybody could look at her and not admire her courage.

He opened his mouth to reply but Frances held up a hand—one that shook but still managed to hold all the dignity of a queen.

'Let me tell you now, so there can be no confusion. I will not be selling Barrow and I will not be leaving this house.'

Her voice rang out across the yard, loud and crystal-clear as she looked him directly in the eye. 'And the only way that any greedy, patronising man will take my farm will be over my dead body.'

Frances lifted her chin, every inch of her rising to the challenge of protecting what she loved, and all Jonah could do was stare.

She was magnificent. With her face set and that fierce pride blazing she was like a soldier herself, perhaps afraid but determined not to let it show, and in that taut moment it felt to him that

she was the only woman in the world. Frances
might hate him for what he had done but for his
part he would love her for ever, a helpless slave
to the respect and adoration that had blossomed
like a flower where once he'd thought himself
an arid plain. If he was told his days were num-
bered he would want to spend every one at her
side—or as close as she would allow, willing to
walk in her shadow if that was the most grace
she'd bestow. If she let him stay he would dedi-
cate the rest of his life to trying to make up for
his mistakes and the yearning to tell her so was
overwhelming, words tumbling from his lips before he even knew they had moved.

'I didn't sign.'

His voice was hoarse and far too loud, trying
to make himself heard above the blood pounding
in his ears. It was the phrase that had repeated
itself in an incessant loop ever since he'd left
the lawyer's office and now the time had come
to speak it out loud, releasing it from the cap-
tivity of his mind and unable to control what
came next.

'I didn't sign the contract. Barrow Farm is
still yours and always will be.'

Frances's eyes narrowed to hostile chips of
ice. 'Another lie.'

'No.' Slowly Jonah shook his head, feeling his

pulse begin to climb. 'Everything I tell you from this moment on will be the truth.'

He saw her hesitate, suspicion lighting the tawny contours of her face. She didn't speak, only watching him with flat caution that was hardly better than a scowl, but she hadn't slammed the window shut and distantly Jonah supposed that was a victory in itself.

He closed his eyes, letting the tide of uncertainty and guilt that had followed him back from Marchfield wash over him again as he tried to order his thoughts. Jane's wan face swam before him, her frailty another dagger thrust, and he felt his heart pulled in different directions with the strain of trying to win two different wars, each threatening casualties he'd do anything to prevent.

'You're right that I intended to sell Barrow, but only very recently. As you are aware, Jane was—*is*—gravely ill and I needed money as quickly as possible to buy a comfortable house where she and the children would be safe. Prior to realising Jane would soon die if she wasn't moved, my initial intention was merely a convenient marriage to you, devoid of all the sentiment I thought so unnecessary and requiring nothing of me other than a physical presence. *That* much you already know.'

Frances's lips thinned as she listened to him

admit his guilt, although she didn't interrupt. Her hands were still tight on the windowsill, however, and even from a distance Jonah could see how her knuckles shone white beneath the skin.

'What *actually* happened I hadn't foreseen,' he continued levelly, surprised at his own composure despite the anarchy holding court inside. 'Far from maintaining a safe distance, I couldn't help but be drawn to you, your spirit stirring something in me that I hadn't known was there. Every time I spoke of your good qualities I meant every word. In fact, it was necessary to hold myself back, knowing you wouldn't welcome my regard. When circumstance forced me to sell your farm, placing me in a position I hadn't imagined, I felt for Jane's sake that I had to proceed…but with the contract placed in front of me I found I couldn't sign.'

Frances's brow creased in a wary frown. 'And why not?'

'I knew you would be devastated—and frankly that was more than I could bear.'

'You expect me to believe that? That you would give three straws for how I'd feel?'

'In a word, yes.'

He passed a hand over his face, hoping he could find the nerve to finish what he'd started. There was only one direction left to leap and he had no way of knowing what would await him on the other side, his respect for Frances the sole thing moving him forward. She deserved honesty and nothing less, and he was damned if he'd fall at the final hurdle when his whole life had led him to this point, even if he was doomed to failure afterwards.

'Something had happened that never featured in my plan. Something that made the idea of your pain impossible.'

'Which was?'

Jonah looked up at his wife, seeing the tension in every line of her countenance as she waited for his response. He'd have to lay himself bare if he wanted Frances to see his real feelings, offer himself up for her judgement with nowhere to hide. When it came to it, when everything else was stripped away and he had nothing left to lose, telling the truth suddenly seemed so easy, a guiding hand that would lead him back towards the light.

'Surely that's obvious.' He shrugged, unable to stop a hopeless half-smile as he submitted to his fate. 'I fell in love with you.'

Frances stepped back from the window, one hand on her heaving chest.

He didn't sell Barrow. And...he says he loves me.

Leaning against the bedroom wall, she stared

directly ahead, feeling the flutter of her heart like a caged bird. The mirror hanging opposite showed the blankness of her face, hardly knowing what to think in the light of Jonah's confession. Only a few hours earlier it would have been the most wonderful thing she ever could have heard, but now she felt winded by the rapid change. His unforgivable treachery when she'd believed he had sold the farm was still half true, even if he had abandoned his scheme—but surely even Jonah couldn't fake such an impassioned declaration of his feelings, putting into words the same sentiment Frances still carried, despite everything, in her heart.

A snatched glance out of the window showed he hadn't moved an inch, a tall lone figure that made her ache with the desire to touch. Still standing in the middle of the yard, he seemed to be waiting, only the scuffing of one boot against the cobbles betraying his unease, and Frances swallowed painfully. Anger and unhappiness still swirled inside her but bewilderment was slowly gaining on them, enveloping everything else until she could barely breathe.

'Frances? Are you still there?'

Jonah's voice sent a shiver through her and she flattened both hands against the wall, feeling its coolness beneath her palms.

Do I dare believe him?

Part of her wanted to stay there, safe in the locked fortress of her room where nobody could hurt her, but a much larger part drowned it out. The desire to run down and pitch headfirst into Jonah's arms rose unbidden and she struggled to wrestle it back, pride and uncertainty still refusing to set her free. She might love him but he had already fooled her once, and she was determined it wouldn't happen again, even if every fibre of her being longed to believe her wish had just been granted.

There was only one way to find out for sure, Frances thought resolutely. It would leave her vulnerable but she had to act, the frenzy in every sinew refusing to let her have any peace unless she moved. With one last glimpse of her reflection in the mirror—straight-shouldered, dignified and only a little afraid—she pushed herself away from the wall.

Her heart pounded as she wrestled with the front door's stiff bolt, giving herself no time to stop and consider the wisdom of her actions. There was always the danger that Jonah could storm the castle once the drawbridge was lowered, but something far deeper than rationality drove her on, encouraging her to ignore all caution and pull open the door. Until she jumped one way or the other she would be in limbo, her emotions insisted, unable to go forward or back—and in truth Jonah's presence called to her so temptingly it was almost impossible to resist. Her fingers were shaking as she reached for the handle and pushed it down.

The chill autumn air hit her full in the face, feeling refreshingly cool against cheeks that burned hotter still when Jonah turned to her and she saw naked relief kindle in his dark eyes.

They studied one another in silence, the very air between them charged with some unknown force as two fragile hearts wondered if they were about to be crushed by the other—and for one long, immeasurable moment neither could remember how to speak. All Frances could see was how the sunshine picked out bronze highlights in his chestnut hair and the quiet intensity of his gaze, fixed on her with adoration even her suspicious soul couldn't bring itself to doubt. He was only a handful of paces away and yet suddenly that was too far, and Frances had to dig her nails into the door frame to prevent herself from leaping down off the step and winding her arms around his neck.

'What will happen to Jane now?'

Jonah's straight brows furrowed as if he was pulling himself out of a daze. Perhaps he hadn't expected her to lead with that question but he answered regardless, his face so open and honest Frances felt herself weaken even more.

'I don't know. I'll have to think of something.'
A look of swift worry passed over his handsome
features, gripping Frances's gut in a vice, but he
wiped it away at once. 'But that needn't even so
much as cross your mind. I should never have
dragged you into my family's troubles in the
first place when I had no right to involve you.'

'Not without telling me, at least.'

A measure of frost still sparkled in Frances's
tone and she didn't try to prevent it. Jonah wasn't
yet out of the woods, even if the sight of him in
distress sent a skewer through her, and she had
to steel herself once more against the growing
temptation to throw off all restraint.

'Did it never occur to you that if you'd discussed things with me I might have had a solution?'

'I wanted to.'

Jonah spread his hands in a futile gesture and
Frances saw the fathomless shame in his face.
'As much as you might despise me, it can never
be half as much as I loathe myself. It was an un-
forgivably cruel thing I almost did and I'm sorry,
Frances, from the very bottom of my heart.'

He shifted slightly as if intending to take
a pace closer but caught himself just in time,
clearly not wanting to provoke her into retreating back inside. Instead he hesitated, so lost and
unhappy that it tore at Frances's insides, and she

couldn't help the incredulous shake of her head as he frowned down at his boots.

'But the whole thing was so *unnecessary*. All that unhappiness, all the worrying and fear… when surely the obvious answer all along was to have them move in here. With us.'

'Us?' Jonah's head came up at once, cautious hope lighting his solemn face. 'Is there still such a thing?'

'There might be.'

Frances felt her knees almost buckle at the longing in Jonah's voice, so earnest that she nearly faltered. 'I can't run the farm alone. We had a business agreement, if you recall.'

'Oh.' The light faded from his face like the sun disappearing behind a cloud but he tried manfully to hide it. 'Yes, of course.'

His gaze dropped back to his boots and Frances watched him trace a line through the straw scattered across the cobbles, wondering at the new-found power she had never known she possessed. How it had happened that Jonah now truly cared for her she didn't know…but she believed it, at last, the frank unhappiness in every line of his body enough proof for several lifetimes, and she felt her spirits begin to creep upwards as she took one step out of the doorway.

'There could be another reason I might possibly allow you to stay.'

Jonah glanced up, attempting to conceal the anguish the tightness of his jaw betrayed all too clearly. A brief frown crossed his face when Frances took another pace towards him, closing the gap between them with slow but steady steps, but he couldn't seem—or perhaps didn't dare—to read the intention written clear across her face.

'What would that be?'

Frances stopped an arm's length from where he stood. So close she could have placed a hand over where his heart must be aching with regret, she simply looked at him—the stern, proud man she had married thinking her feelings would never be returned. Somewhere deep inside he had found a spark to mirror the one that had lit the darkness of her lonely life, sending the emptiness of her future up in flames without even having to try. He had made a grave mistake in hurting her but he had claimed it, speaking honestly without trying to shy away, and Frances surrendered to the undeniable desire to be honest in turn.

'Because, heaven help me, I love you too.'

Once released the truth could never be snatched back and it hung in the air between them, the narrow gap separating husband and wife filled with secrets finally brought out into the light. For one terrible second Frances questioned if she should have kept her own counsel, as Jonah stared at her without reaction—but then her heart soared up to the sky as dawning wonder began to filter into his expression, slowly as if he hardly dared to believe.

'Do you mean that? After everything…?'

'I'm afraid so.'

She could hardly keep a smile from her lips as Jonah ran an unsteady hand through his hair, although she tried her hardest to look severe—something easier said than done when fireworks ricocheted beneath the bodice of her gown and her fingers itched to take hold of his lapels and pull him to her for a kiss. 'Not that it means you're forgiven. You have a lot of lost ground to recover before you've earned that.'

Jonah nodded. In the cocoa darkness of his eyes a new light was beginning to gleam, one that sent a shiver down every nerve in Frances's spine, and when he took the final step forward needed to bring them face to face she knew exactly what he had planned.

'I understand completely. That's a sensible precaution, considering my inexcusably bad judgement.'

He looked down at her, so close now that Frances could catch the unique scent of him that she loved so much, clean linen and warm skin, a combination more hopelessly enticing than anything else in the world. A lock of hair hanging loose from her untidy braid drifted in the breeze and slowly Jonah brought up a hand to capture it, tucking it back behind her ear so gently she felt herself wilt.

'If you're agreeable, perhaps I could start my repentance now?'

There was no real need for her to answer. Frances knew Jonah could see everything he needed to in her face, her feelings so plain that there was nothing to stop him from taking her in his arms.

They came around her and Frances fell willingly into their keeping, drawing close to Jonah and feeling the weight in her soul lighten as his lips sought hers. All the confusion, all the misery and grief, everything that had weighed her down was lifted from her shoulders by the protective circle of his arms and the soft movement of his mouth, her unhappiness disintegrating to float far away. She had no use for such things now Jonah was hers and she was his and the realisation that she didn't have to hold back any longer was like a shaft of sunlight slicing its way through a window left shuttered for far too many years.

She tightened her grip and felt the powerful muscles of his shoulders shudder at her touch, their lips still locked together and neither one willing to break the connection both had yearned after for so long. Jonah's hands on her waist were scalding and Frances gasped against his mouth, revelling in the strength of his unwavering hold. The farmyard around them carried on as it always had, the hens and wild birds going about their business as if nothing had changed, but as Frances and Jonah stood entwined both knew nothing would be the same again.

Still leaning unsteadily against Jonah's chest, Frances drew her head back a fraction so she could peep up into his face, noting with quiet satisfaction that he looked almost as dazed as she felt.

'You were indescribably stupid.'

'I won't try to argue with that.'

'But I suppose for the best possible reasons. I might even have done something similar myself if I thought it would have kept my uncle alive.'

It was the truth and for a moment Frances felt a sharp splinter of grief. Uncle Robert had done so much for her and it stung to think he would never see her happiness, which he had worked towards since the day she was born. He might not have approved of their unusual courtship, but he would have warmed to Jonah in the end, she was sure, and the fact the only two men she valued would never know each other lent a sober edge to her joy. Nobody should take their loved ones for granted and Frances swore to herself there and then that she would never let a day go by without telling Jonah how much he meant, each hour together a blessing she'd never expected to find.

Jonah's gaze swept over her upturned face, lingering for a moment on her lips to stir sparks low inside her. 'I still shouldn't have hidden my troubles from you.'

'No. No, you shouldn't. You'll have to work doubly hard to make up for that.'

'On the farm, you mean?'

'That's one place, certainly.' Frances raised a contemplative eyebrow, unable to stop herself from instinctively curving closer to Jonah's chest. 'Although perhaps you'd care to think of another…?'

He didn't need telling twice. With a smart salute any soldier would be proud of, Jonah obeyed his orders, gathering his wife into his arms as if she weighed nothing at all, and Frances's laugh echoed across the farmyard as he carried her over the threshold and towards the creaking wooden stairs.

Frances's toes were numb as she knocked the snow from her boots and opened the farmhouse's back door, both Gyp and the heat of the kitchen rushing forward to welcome her home. All the animals were tucked up snug in their barns and sties for the night and she felt a glow of happiness as Jonah rose from his place beside the fire, his face still pink from being recently out in the cold himself.

'All safe and sound?'

'Perfectly. Did you fix the top gate?'

'Without too much trouble.'

He came towards her and she smiled as his hand slipped around her waist, drawing her closer so he could cup the rosy curve of her cheek. It was easy to see what he wanted but Frances hesitated to obey the desire beginning to rise inside her at the intent look in his dark eyes.

'Where's Jane? And the children?'

'In the parlour. Last time I looked in they were playing charades, Jane demonstrating something very enthusiastically down on the carpet.' Jonah bent his head to gently nibble at her earlobe and Frances felt herself buckle, her breath hitching at the soft nip of his teeth. 'Her improvement since being here these past months has been miraculous. By the time spring comes I think we'll barely remember she was ever ill at all.'

Frances tried to nod but all her attention was bound up in the progress of Jonah's lips, now tracing an insistent path down towards her neck. Tilting her head back a little, she allowed him greater freedom to explore, although something hanging from the wooden beam above their heads caught the very corner of her eye.

'Mistletoe?' The little white berries were unmistakable. 'So that's your game, is it? Christmas isn't for another two weeks!'

She thought she heard Jonah laugh against her skin, his mouth chasing away the last traces of the December chill. 'It was growing in the paddock. Seemed a shame to waste the opportunity.'

He didn't sound the least bit repentant and Frances allowed him to hold her closer still, relishing the warmth of his body so firm against hers. The day had been long and cold but despite her exhaustion at the end of it she was perfectly content, safe in the knowledge that she no longer had to face each one alone. Her first Christmas without Uncle Robert would be difficult, she knew, but the new family she had found would help her to bear any sadness, Jane and the children bringing such life to the house and Jonah beside her every step of the way. Where once there had been nothing but pain, hope now shone like a candle set at a dark window to cast its light out into the night.

'I'm sure it did.' Frances tried to sound disapproving but failed completely, unable to resist the yearning that she no longer had to deny. 'I suppose, given that you went to all that trouble, I might as well play along.'

'You're too kind to me sometimes. Far more so than I deserve.'

Frances Nettleford had been an unhappy girl, scorned and unwanted and never expecting to be loved.

But Mrs Frances Grant was none of those things, and as she stretched up to kiss her smiling husband it was with true and hard-earned joy in her heart.

* * * * *

COMING SOON!

We really hope you enjoyed reading this book.
If you're looking for more romance, be sure to
head to the shops when new books are
available on

Thursday 18th August

To see which titles are coming soon, please visit

millsandboon.co.uk/nextmonth

MILLS & BOON

MILLS & BOON®

Coming next month

HOW TO WOO A WALLFLOWER
Virginia Heath

Hattie shook her head in exasperation. 'The last few weeks have been a never-ending maelstrom of nonsense. It is a relief to have an excuse to escape for the afternoon—although I have been deliberating whether or not I should walk to the hospital.'

Jasper wanted to ask if she was capable of a five-minute walk, but didn't, respecting her pride. 'As I have abandoned my own conveyance in favour of Shanks's pony, I would be delighted to escort you. That is if you do not fear what being seen with a scandalous reprobate like me will do to your reputation?'

She laughed and allowed him to help her out of her carriage. Because it felt appropriate given her injuries, he offered her his arm and pretended not to notice how heavily Hattie leaned on it. The first few steps were obviously difficult for her, but she covered her pain with breezy small talk about her dreaded debut, making his heart simultaneously bleed for all she had lost and swell with pride at her resilience and tenacity.

'You never know, you might enjoy it all once it starts.'

She blinked at him as if he were mad. 'It is difficult to feel enthused about taking up my place among the wallflowers.' Her expression was wistful. Accepting, and that bothered him.

'You shan't be a wallflower, Hattie.' The mere thought

was inconceivable. 'Your dance card will be so full I doubt there would be space for me to scratch my name on it. In fact, I shall insist you reserve me a waltz in advance.' An impertinent request which tumbled out before he could stop it.

'That is very decent of you to offer—even if it was done out of obligation—but I am afraid I shall have to politely decline.'

'It wasn't done out of obligation.' The truth, although he couldn't even explain to himself why. 'I would be honoured.'

Her smile this time did not touch her eyes. 'And yet still I must politely decline.'

The disappointment was instant. 'Because you *do* fear for your reputation after all or because you have already promised the waltz to someone else?' The flash of jealousy came out of nowhere, but he managed to cover it with a conspiratorial wink.

'Because I can't, Jasper.'

For the briefest moment, her light seemed to dull, before she banished it with a matter-of-fact shrug.

'I physically can't.'

Continue reading
HOW TO WOO A WALLFLOWER
Virginia Heath

Available next month
www.millsandboon.co.uk

Special thanks and acknowledgement are given to Virginia Heath for her contribution to the Society's Most Scandalous miniseries.

MILLS & BOON

THE HEART OF ROMANCE

A ROMANCE FOR EVERY READER

MODERN

Prepare to be swept off your feet by sophisticated, sexy and seductive heroes, in some of the world's most glamourous and romantic locations, where power and passion collide.

HISTORICAL

Escape with historical heroes from time gone by. Whether your passion is for wicked Regency Rakes, muscled Vikings or rugged Highlanders, awak the romance of the past.

MEDICAL

Set your pulse racing with dedicated, delectable doctors in the high-pressure world of medicine, where emotions run high and passion, comfort a love are the best medicine.

True Love

Celebrate true love with tender stories of heartfelt romance, from the rush of falling in love to the joy a new baby can bring, and a focus on the emotional heart of a relationship.

Desire

Indulge in secrets and scandal, intense drama and plenty of sizzling hot action with powerful and passionate heroes who have it all: wealth, status, good looks…everything but the right woman.

HEROES

Experience all the excitement of a gripping thriller, with an intense romance at its heart. Resourceful, true-to-life women and strong, fearless m face danger and desire - a killer combination!

To see which titles are coming soon, please visit

millsandboon.co.uk/nextmonth

JOIN US ON SOCIAL MEDIA!

Stay up to date with our latest releases, author news and gossip, special offers and discounts, and all the behind-the-scenes action from Mills & Boon...

 @millsandboon

 @millsandboonuk

 facebook.com/millsandboon

 @millsandboonuk

It might just be true love...

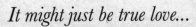

GET YOUR ROMANCE FIX!

Get the latest romance news, exclusive author interviews, story extracts and much more!